RAINFALL

ALISON RHYMES

To request permission, contact: alison@alisonrhymes.com

Editors: Zainab M. at the blue couch edits

Cover Design: Ben | Pilcrow

Cover Photo by: Ren Saliba

Formatting: Triumph Book Covers

A NOTE FROM ALISON RHYMES

Any trigger or content warnings for Rainfall, or any of my other titles, can be found on my website alisonrhymes.com

Kick them in the balls.
Punch them in their dumb faces.
Make them regret it.

PROLOGUE

I was ten when I met the love of my life.

As a hockey coach's daughter, it was inevitable that I'd lose my heart to a player. Though I doubt my dad expected it to happen during a summer hockey camp at such an early age. Had he, I probably wouldn't have been asked to tag along as often. It's not as though I even knew what was happening back then anyhow.

Besides, I've always loved the sport. My dad was blessed with daughters, and he encouraged our interest in his chosen profession.

My sister, Willa, played a few years of youth hockey, but it didn't last long and that wasn't ever the path I wanted to take. The sidelines are my favorite place. Catching the subtle nuances of each player, knowing their strengths and weaknesses, that's the part I love.

I might not have played the sport, but I'd been on the ice plenty, and the hero worship I always had for my dad had me soaking up every word he said like a sponge.

Dad played the game his whole life, as soon as he could toddle on both feet, my grandfather put him in a pair of skates and padded him with goalie equipment. He said dad had more horsepower at the age of three than a HEMI V8 engine and needed an outlet for it all. Personally, I think my grandfather fell in love with the sport too late in life to play himself, so he lived vicariously through my dad. Either way, Dad excelled at it and was drafted to an NHL team right out of college.

He left the league and started coaching junior hockey when I was six and Willa was four. He didn't quit the sport, though. Instead of playing for the NHL, he moved to coaching for the Wester Hockey League. Junior hockey always intrigued me. It wasn't the path my dad took; he played youth hockey and earned a college scholarship for it. A lot of boys don't do that and instead move to junior hockey at an earlier age, some as young as fifteen.

It's not easy. You often have to leave your family, and many will play until the age of twenty before they can pursue a full-time education. That was if they don't get picked up by a professional team, which wasn't guaranteed.

Grandpa felt like it would be putting life on hold in hopes of the pros, if my dad went to play junior hockey rather than college hockey. Anyone who hoped to play a professional sport took a certain amount of risk, but I always looked at WHL players as edgy rebels because of my grandfather's take on things.

Because if my dad hadn't been drafted at the end of his college career, at least he already had the education and a degree to fall back on.

Growing up with a dad that coached a WHL team meant an endless stream of teenage boys around all year long. But it was the summers I remember best. Dad coached a hockey camp at the University of North Dakota and brought the family with him most years when Willa and I were on summer vacation from school.

That was where I first saw Cillian Wylder. He stood out for all the wrong reasons. Dad always started with skating drills; Cillian wasn't the best. Not the worst, either, but the middle of the pack wasn't where any elite player wanted to be and that was firmly where he was. His speed on a straight away was fine, good even, but he'd lose it all with every turn and then needed to play catch up to the leaders.

I wrote him off as just another helmet head with dreams that would never come to fruition. That was most of the boys Dad worked with honestly. Except the following day when he switched them over to drills that included a stick and puck. Cillian's puck handling was exceptional. Not only could he shoot from the center of his stick, but from the heel and toe as well. All with a high degree of accuracy. It's not a common trait in seasoned players and certainly not something seen regularly at peewee levels.

I couldn't take my eyes off him while he had the puck. Looking back, I recognized it was the first time I'd ever been fascinated by anyone other than my dad or the random celebrity that me and all my friends had a crush over.

Hanging out by the tunnel to the locker rooms wasn't something I ever did, instead keeping my interaction with the players to a minimum. My dad and hockey were the reason I was there, not to meet a new batch of stinky boys that would be gone in two weeks' time anyhow.

That day was different.

That day, I moved down to the ice so the boy with so much potential couldn't help but hear me.

"Lunge into your turns more. You'll move with more power and won't fall behind as easily."

"Me?" he asked, removing his helmet as he paused to look me over the same way I did him. Sweat soaked his light hair, dripping and running down his face. It didn't take away from his gleaming blue eyes that pierced me so directly I didn't think my feet could have moved from that spot even if I had tried.

"Yes. Bend your knee more, it will make a difference."

"Who are you?" He blinks at me a few times as if he hadn't noticed me at all until I spoke. Maybe he hadn't. But I was one of only a few spectators allowed in to watch and since I didn't take much time to brush my hair back then, it was a mass of messy curls making me even harder to miss.

"That's coach's daughter, dude," another boy said, bumping Cillian as he moved past into the tunnel.

"I have a name, *dude*," I said with an exaggerated eye roll. I idolized my dad, but I hated when someone wrapped my entire identity around him. When I turned back to Cillian, he was smiling.

"What is it?"

"What?" I asked, confused.

"Your name?" he asked, beaming.

"Isla Cole."

"Thanks for the tip, Isla Cole. I'll work on it."

Work on it, he did. By the end of camp that year, he could almost keep up with faster skaters. The following summer, he was faster than most. After the first day, he pulled his helmet off and searched for me in the stands to wave at me. I reciprocated and moved down to the ice.

"Better?"

"Much," I confirmed. "Did you get a skating coach or something?"

"No, we can't afford that. I hung out at the rink when the figure skaters were getting coached," he said. "You can learn a lot if you listen and watch."

"That's smart. Figure skaters are great with edge manipulation and body position. Dad sometimes has some come in to teach his players a thing or two."

"Maybe one day I'll be lucky enough to play for him."

"Keep up the hard work, and you'll play where you want," my dad chimed in, stepping up behind Cillian.

"Yes, sir."

"Now leave my daughter alone."

Cillian flushed, and I chuckled. Dad liked to come across as a hard ass, but he was a big cinnamon roll.

"Yes, sir," Cillian repeated, then took off.

Conversations with him were similar the following few years. Brief and revolved around his improving skills. He wanted my approval, I supposed. Though I didn't understand why.

I didn't go with Dad to the camp when I was fifteen, opting instead to take a trip with my grandparents and Willa to San Diego. The beach sounded better than Grand Forks, North Dakota, for my summer before high school. That meant I didn't see how much Cillian Wylder had improved. It must have been great though, because the following year, he moved to Seattle to play center on my dad's WHL team.

Cillian scored two goals in that first game with the Timberwolves. After, he looked for me while I waited outside the locker room for my dad.

"Am I good enough for you to go on a date with me Isla Cole?"

"You know you've never even told me your name, right?"

"Cillian Wylder, but I think you already know that," he answered, eyes sparkling at me. He'd been a cute boy, but he was past that now. At sixteen, he was getting handsome, chiseled and defined in ways guys were when they spent all their free time working out, instead of partying in the woods with cheap beer and cheaper joints.

"Do you have a death wish, Wylder?"

"No, I asked your dad first."

"So, you're either brave or stupid. What did he tell you?"

"He said, and I quote," he said, using his fingers to emphasize the word, "'You can fucking try but she'll probably eat you alive for having the audacity to ask me before you ask her.'"

"He's not wrong." Dad always knew me well, but he also taught me well. "Ask me again after your next game, and we'll see if your playing can earn a shot with me or not."

"Deal." He extended his hand out for me to shake. I grasped it with a smirk and a shake of my head.

The motherfucker scored a hat trick the following game.

"Dinner tomorrow?" he asked after the game.

"Why me?" We had been acquainted in a strange way for six years, but all added up, our conversations never lasted more than an hour tops. He knew nothing about me other than who my dad was, which made me suspicious of his intentions.

"Why not you?"

"Answer the question, Wylder. Or it's a no for me."

"You were the first one, other than my mother, who saw potential in me," he said, his thumb nervously pulling at his bottom lip. "Yes or no, Isla Cole?"

The words were enough, but the anxious gesture was what tossed me over the edge I'd been teetering on. I was just a normal girl, nothing particularly special or outstanding, yet I made this beautiful, talented boy's confidence waver.

Such small things wreaked havoc on a young girl's confidence and heart.

I said yes and the following night he took me to the cheapest burger joint in town. It impressed me because he didn't care how different we were. It didn't matter to him that I had money, and he didn't; he wasn't trying to impress me in ways that didn't count.

Instead, he leaned on his charming personality and our mutual love of hockey.

I met the love of my life at ten, though I didn't love him until we were sixteen.

Willa once asked me if I'd known then how my life would take shape, if I'd have still agreed to that first date with Cillian Wylder.

"Yes," I'd answered her with a confident nod. Despite it all, yes.

1

ISLA

THREE YEARS LATER

"How does it feel to be the second all around pick in the NHL draft, Wylder?"

"It doesn't even rank compared to being inside you, Isla," he grunts as he thrusts into me. It's been a long, long two days with the draft but we're finally back home in Seattle. Regardless of how exhausted we are, he couldn't wait to get me undressed as soon as we walked through the door of our condo.

Cillian has always been insatiable since we first lost our virginity to each other at sixteen. It didn't happen right away; we'd been dating for months before the subject even came up. Neither of us felt rushed or pressured about it. But once we did take it that far, it opened a floodgate on his libido.

And mine.

Cillian isn't a selfish lover, nothing like what I expected after hearing other girls talk about sex with their boyfriends. Never once has my boyfriend finished before me. Hell, he practically makes a game out of seeing how many orgasms he can give me before his own. Competitive even with himself.

We're in his favorite position; him propped up against my headboard, my knees on either side of his hips while he pumps them up into me. When he really needs the connection with me, this is how we start. Cillian says he likes to watch my face, but I know he also likes the easy access to my pussy and breasts. Regardless, this is how he makes love to me. As opposed to post game sex which is more just adrenaline rush fucking. Not that I don't love that, too.

"You're so beautiful, Isla. I don't tell you enough," he says, one hand cupping my cheek as the other weighs my breast.

"You tell me all the time." I laugh, and he doubles his thrusts. "Oh god."

"Don't argue with me." He lifts me off his dick. "Get up here," he says, beckoning me with his chin as he guides my core to his mouth after scooting his body down into a lying position.

When I picked out this bed, I didn't consider how often I'd appreciate this upholstered headboard being both comfortable for cushioning my head banging against it as Cillian rails me, and for times like now when I can grip it as I ride his mouth.

Cillian moans at his first taste of me, his tongue dipping in when his fingers spread me apart. My hips sway with a slow rhythm at first, picking up pace the more enthusiastic he gets. Gripping my ass cheek in one hand, he pushes the fingers of his other into my pussy, all while his mouth focuses on my clit. In seconds, I'm exploding on a scream, eyes blurring at the edges.

"Fuck, I love how you taste," he says, still lapping up my release.

"You tell me that all the time, too."

"Reminders of how perfect you are never hurt," he tells me, once again maneuvering me into the position he wants me.

"Spread wider for me, Isla," Cillian commands, bringing me out of my orgasm brain fog. I make room for him between my legs, and he wastes no time slamming his hard cock back inside me. "Give me that mouth."

I arch my neck up to mold my lips against his, and he grips the back of my neck with his large hand to remove any discomfort. Holding me, he kisses me deeply until he's fully spent inside me.

Pulling my legs up over his hips, I lock my ankles around his lower back and my arms around his shoulders.

"I'm proud of you, Cill."

"Wouldn't be here without your advice," he mumbles into my neck, making me laugh.

"I just gave you a simple pointer at the age of ten. You did all the work."

"You gave me simple pointers every summer and I took each one as a mission. Don't sell it short."

"Whatever, Superstar." I press a kiss to the top of his head that rests on my chest.

"It's going to suck being so far away every season."

"We'll figure it out," I promise. His contract is for three years. I have two more years of school here in Seattle.

"I'll be making real money now. It will be nice not to have to rely on you for so much and be able to take care of you."

"You know that's never been an issue."

"It's an issue for me."

"I get that."

He rolls us so we're on our sides, face-to-face.

"I love you," he tells me, brushing the hair off my face.

"I love you, too."

I'm not perfect, though he makes me feel like I am. But maybe that's because we're perfect for each other. Cillian is very tolerant of my fiery temper and impatience; in return, I'm accepting of how his schedule rarely can prioritize me. He works hard and when he gets a break, sometimes he needs to entertain himself with things that allow him to decompress. If that means he needs a couple of hours playing *Modern Warfare* or whatever, I don't complain. I'm perfectly capable of entertaining myself on the other side of the couch. I love video games anyway, so we often play one together.

In the three years we've been together, we haven't had many hard times or arguments. Speed bumps, sure, but nothing that we haven't gotten past with anything more than a thoughtful conversation. He shows me the same type of care and support that my family does, and I do the same for him.

"We're going to be okay." The words are meant to reassure me, but I think he's trying to convince himself. And for the first time, I'm nervous about it all.

The months pass too quickly, and before we know it, the day of Cillian's departure is upon us. My anxiety has been at an all-time high these last two days while helping him make last-minute arrangements and pack his belongings. Though, I've tried very hard to hide it from him, I know he's picked up on some of it.

We've been so connected at the hip since we were sixteen that it's going to be a huge adjustment, not to mention that I'll miss him like crazy. Everything since draft day has been a whirlwind. Cillian has dealt with so much press and paperwork, on top of the logistics of moving across the country. Luckily, one of the guys on the team, Torsten, is someone he knows from youth camps and has offered to let him room with him. It's made everything easier, since Cill only had to worry about clothes and gear instead of apartment and furniture shopping.

It makes me feel better knowing he won't be completely alone either.

"You'll be there for the first game?"

"Quit asking, you know I will be. I wouldn't miss it for anything." I press another kiss to his lips.

"I'm going to miss you," he tells me between kisses.

"The way you've been stripping me naked every chance you get kind of clued me in to that."

"Two months is a long time; I'm just stocking up."

"Orgasms? You're stocking up orgasms?"

"No, brat. I'm stocking up on you."

"Time will fly, Cill. You'll be busy with practices, and I'll get a jump on all my classes. Before you know it, you'll be scoring your first goal in your NHL game and then fucking me blind afterward."

He pulls me closer, wrapping his arms more tightly around me. So much shorter than him, I have to tip my chin up on his chest to maintain eye contact. Cill has grown to six-foot-two, three quarters of a ruler taller than me.

"We'll video call every night," he says almost like it's a question.

"Hey." I squirm my arms under his so I can reach to cup his cheeks. "I'm never going to not be there for you. If you need me, call, and I'll answer. Night or day."

We're both fully aware that Cillian is closer to me than anyone in his life. Including his mother. They love each other, unconditionally, of course. But he grew up so much on his own until he moved here, and we started dating. It's made us very dependent on one another. For all the parts I hate about him moving away, maybe it's good for us in ways too.

Maybe this will make us stronger as both people and a couple.

"Who's going to hang out with you when there's a thunderstorm?"

"In two years, we'll probably only have two at most." I'm a storm chaser at heart, completely fascinated by them. While we get plenty of windstorms here, thunder and lightning are fairly rare. I love them when they do occur. "I'll call you if there is one and you can still hang out with me."

"Not the same," he mumbles, kissing my forehead for punctuation.

"No, not at all. But it's temporary and this is a huge accomplishment. Live it, Cillian. I'm not going anywhere."

"It's good advice, son," my dad says, walking up behind Cillian. He has come with me to drop him at the airport, but he kept his distance while we said our final goodbyes. "Take it to heart. Enjoy every moment you get in the league; it doesn't last forever."

"Am I supposed to be this nervous?"

"Yes, Cillian." Dad laughs. "I'd be seriously worried if you weren't. You're going to kill it, kid."

"Yes, Coach."

"Get a move on, or you're going to miss your flight," Dad tells him, patting his shoulder and stepping away.

"I love you, Isla Cole," he says, dropping his forehead to mine.

"I love you, too, Cillian Wylder-future Hall of Famer." He laughs, but I shut that down by sealing our mouths together with a kiss full of love, pride, and promise. "I'm so proud of you."

"Be good," he says, wetness shining in his eyes that I know matches mine.

"You know it."

I don't take my eyes off him until his large build and messy blond hair are out of sight. He turns back once, sending me a reassuring smile at the last second before disappearing. Then my dad's arm lands on my shoulder, giving me a comforting side hug.

"You ready to go home, Isla?"

"Yeah, Daddy," I say through the tears.

"The two of you will be okay," he says when we're back in the car.

"How do you know?" I ask, turning down the radio that plays as the ignition starts. I want to believe what he's telling me, but I can't help being frightened of our distance. Or of his new life that won't include much of me. Insecure isn't a word I think anyone would use to describe me… before now, anyway.

"This is how," he says, unlocking his phone and pulling up an app. "This was your seventeenth birthday. It's the day I decided to stop hating the kid for dating you."

He's pulled up a folder labeled Isla. The first picture is Cillian and me sitting at the table of the restaurant we went to with my family on that birthday. I'm blowing out candles on a ridiculously elaborate cake, but Cillian's sight is focused on me. Full of the same love and pride I feel for him every day. As I flip through, there are so many more pictures just like the first one; me doing something and him watching me.

"He loves you the way men love a woman they've been with forever. I'm not saying it's going to be easy, you're both young and life is throwing some major changes your way. But in the end, I think you're going to be okay. Love like that doesn't just go away."

"We've never spent any lengthy time apart, it's scary when I let myself think about it. I've been so excited for him, but now that it's happening, I keep thinking he's going to see that he doesn't need me?"

"Love isn't about needing each other. You want each other, which is much more powerful and profound. Hockey is a hard life; you know that because you've grown up in it. And you've seen how it can work."

I've never seen my mom worried or stressed when Dad was away, be it for a short trip or an extended one. They have always had an unwavering faith in one another. He has never given any sign that he's been anything but true to her, and he's always so happy to get home after a trip to see 'his ladies'.

The same can be said for Cillian. Never in our three years together have I had doubts that he's been with anyone else when he's away. I don't doubt him now either, only the situation. *The time.*

If we're as strong as I think we are, and we're meant to be, then this is just a stepping stone. One of what will surely be many in our long lives together.

If we can survive the next couple of years, we can survive anything.

2

ISLA

Cillian left Seattle in an August heatwave in order to get settled in Boston before the training camp started. As I step off my flight at Logan airport the excitement of seeing him settles on me along with the chill of the October fall air. One I know will disappear as soon as I see him because of the heat we've always shared.

ME:

Deplaning now.

CILL:

Waiting for you in baggage.

His reply warms me some, liking that he's already here waiting for me. We've mostly kept the promise of video chatting daily, only missing random days here or there when our schedules are too full to align. He's incredibly busy with training, practice, press, and promo. The team even asked him to start an Instagram page because he never had social media before, so that has taken up some extra time, even though I know he's been getting help from the team. It all adds up, and some days, the only time he has to connect with me is a few minutes before he crashes at the end of the day.

I hate it, but I also know it's new and it will calm down and get easier. The schedule is temporary; we are not.

I've reminded myself of that so many times over the past few months. It all seems so silly though when I turn the last corner and he comes into sight.

Cillian's eyes scan over all the other wayward passengers, thumb playing with his bottom lip the way he always does when emotions take over him. The thrumming stops as soon as he spots me and his shoulders drop in a sigh of relief, as if he didn't believe me when I told him I was here.

Strangers pass between us, occasionally blocking my view of him as I weave through on my way to him, until I finally stop only inches away. I take in his form that seems impossibly bigger; he's bulked up and it's evident beneath his joggers and form-fitting dark tee.

"Hey, Isla Cole," he says, his sky-colored eyes bouncing quickly between mine.

"Hey, Wylder."

"Come here."

Without hesitation, I jump, knowing he'll catch me in his strong grasp, his hands instantly cupping my ass to hold me in place as I wind my legs around his hips. Wrapping my arms around his shoulders, I dig one hand into the thick hair, pulling his face up so our lips can land on each other. His tongue plunges into my mouth as I breathe him in, the familiar scent that eases every tense knot in my body.

"I've missed you," I tell him as soon as he lets me up for air.

"You have no idea," he mumbles back, but I do. Even on my busiest days, the ache of his absence was a dull pain my heart never forgot.

"Well, I'm here for two nights. Let's not waste time in a dirty airport."

He laughs, pressing a few more kisses to my lips before lowering me back to my feet. He fills me in on his day-to-day routine on the way to his house, then peppers me with questions about my course schedule.

"How's the family?"

"They're good. Mom's taken up knitting, making scarves for all the guys on the team. Willa's wreaking havoc as a high school senior."

"Probably leaving a trail of broken boys in her wake," he teases.

"You know it."

He holds my hand the entire ride. I raise our entwined fingers, studying all the new marks his skin wears. I've been witness to his bumps and bruises for so long, I feel like I have to chart new maps of him. I can't wait to strip him down and do just that.

"Take me to bed or lose me forever," I tell him as he piggybacks me through his front door.

"Fuck, Cole, you don't even have to fucking ask. Bed was going to be my first stop."

"Oh, I'm so sorry," a light voice says from around the corner. A blonde woman comes into sight a moment later. "Tor let me in before he left. I thought I'd be done before you got back from the airport."

"Hey, Trina. What's going on?" Cillian asks her as I drop from his back.

"I brought by some dinner. I thought it would be nice if you didn't have to worry about that."

"That's great, thanks," Cillian responds, while I try to figure out who this person even is. "Isla, this is Trina, one of the team photographers. Trina, this is Isla."

"Hi," she exclaims, her eyes bright and cheeks a bit flushed. "It's so nice to meet you. Cill speaks of you all the time!"

"It's nice to meet you, too." *Woman I have never heard of before this very moment.* I offer a hand, and she shakes it with the same bubbly enthusiasm her words hold.

"Okay, okay, I'll get out of your way now. But the fridge is stocked!" She gives Cillian a hug, and I get a quick wave as she hurries out the door.

"The fuck?"

"Yeah, she's on the, uh, exuberant side," Cillian says.

"I don't like that she was so comfortable in your space."

"Ah," he says softly, fingers coming to smooth out my furrowed brow. "You jealous?"

"Fuck yes, I am, Cillian. I've never been in your home, but she has." With strained effort, I keep my hurt out of my voice. It's not his fault that I'm feeling so uncharacteristically insecure. And the last thing I want to do with my short time here is fight with the man I love. My temper has other plans though. "I ever walk into your house again to another woman; I'm cutting appendages off, Wylder. Now take me to bed, damnit."

"You don't want a tour of the place?"

"Later. After."

"Yeah? You need my dick that bad, Isla?"

"About as badly as you need me, Wylder. Unless you've been getting that from your little cheerleader photographer," I counter, letting more of my jealousy heard.

"No." He snorts. "But my hand probably has new callouses. I haven't beat off this much since I was thirteen."

Cillian grasps my hand and pulls me to his room. We don't resurface for hours. Not until I have spent all the time I needed studying his body, and he mine, both of us refusing to reclothe until we feel reacquainted physically.

Sweaty and spent, we stumble over each other on the way to the kitchen.

Trina seemed so at ease in the space. I could probably write that off to Torsten, who has been on the team for a few years now, but should I? Is she here often because of my boyfriend's roommate or because of my boyfriend? They must be close enough that she knew when I was flying in.

Cill hasn't given me any sign to worry, and I need to have faith in that before I self-sabotage our relationship. Shaking off my weird mood, I pull out the artfully crafted charcuterie board with a laugh. The woman obviously underestimated how many calories hockey players burn every day, especially after a three-hour bout of sexual activities.

"You need more than this," I tell Cillian. "Do you have pasta?"

"You don't have to cook, Isla. I can order something."

"Let me take care of you," I argue. "I've missed it."

"I've missed *you*," he says, swatting me lightly on the ass as he moves past me to pull items out of a pantry on the other side of the kitchen. He lets me make the pasta for him, standing behind me the entire time, his arms wrapped around me while I work.

The position doesn't change much while we eat, me sitting on his lap at an oversized dining table that I imagine doesn't get used often.

"I have to be at the arena early tomorrow, but you can come too. They said someone will show you around before the game, if you want. Mom will be flying in late; she'll meet you there."

"I'd like that," I tell him. "It will be nice to see Erin. I'm glad she's able to make the trip. Dad was sorry he couldn't make it, too." Cillian's grandmother's health hasn't been the best recently. Erin was able to find a friend to keep watch over her so she could fly from Omaha for the game. She's heading back shortly after the game. It's the best she could manage, but I know Cillian appreciates it.

"I'd love for him to be here, but I get it. He's got a team to work with and his own game coming up," Cillian says, popping another piece of cheese in his mouth.

"Mhm, but mom says she and Willa will come along when we can all make it for a weekend game."

"Hopefully sooner rather than later," he says, chin resting on my shoulder and giving it a slight nip.

"Hopefully."

"You ready to spread those pretty thighs for me again, Isla?" he whispers in my ear, sending a shiver down my spine and a thrill through my core.

"Always, Superstar."

The following day, I keep to the background, watching Cillian go through his gameday routine. It hasn't changed much over the years, and I enjoy the familiarity of it. Whatever nerves he had when he flew to Boston have disappeared. He's as ready for his first game as a professional as I've ever seen him as he checks that his duffle has everything packed in it just the way he wants. We stuffed it last night, but this gameday ritual is always performed, regardless of how much care he took previously. Cillian doesn't like to show up at any arena unprepared or without his comfort items, like his headphones so he can listen to his carefully curated pre-game playlist.

"All good?" I ask when he finally zips it up and stands.

"All good," he confirms.

"You're going to kill it today, Wylder."

He looks at me, blinks a few times, maybe dazed by it all. Afterall, he's realizing his lifelong dream tonight.

"Yeah, I fucking am." He beams proudly.

"Yeah, you fucking are," I agree on a laugh that he ends with a searing kiss.

The arena is a hive of workers, busy prepping for the first game of the season. I'm allowed to walk Cillian to the locker room, and from there, I'm escorted around by Cindy, a woman around my mother's age who's been working the arena for over a decade. I'm getting special treatment because of my name, my dad, more than being Cillian Wylder's girlfriend. But I won't complain since the tour gives me something to occupy my time before Erin gets here and the game starts.

"Mr. Sterns offered access to this suite for you and Cillian's mother," Cindy says, opening a door to a fully equipped suite, complete with food, beverages, a private bathroom, and seating above the rest of the arena. Sterns is the general manager and an acquaintance of my dad—again, the team showing deference to my last name. "Of course, there are also seats down below, if you'd prefer to be closer to the ice."

"I would. It's where I'm most comfortable."

"Makes sense," she says, leading the way back out of the suite. "I imagine it's where you grew up."

"I spent my fair share of time there."

"I can bring Miss Wylder to you when she arrives."

"Thank you, Cindy. That would be wonderful."

I take my seat along the boards, the player's bench only a section away from perhaps the best seats I've ever had. I'm certain Dad called in favors for this one, but I enjoy the placement as I take everything in. The excited chatter of young fans taking their seats or vying for a spot along the glass in the hopes of gaining the attention of the players with their homemade signs. There isn't a lot of this that I remember from Dad playing in the NHL, I was so young and once Willa came along it was harder for my mom to take us both to games like this. But the atmosphere, as a whole, runs through my veins, this world is in my blood. Sharing it with Cillian now only makes it more special.

Warmups start with blaring music and cheers from the crowd. Cillian spots me on his first lap, sending me a chin nod and a half smile.

Focused on the game the way he is, I'm surprised he even spotted me. Only a few minutes later, Erin arrives.

"Hi," I greet her, giving her a warm hug. She's about my size and I always wonder how she birthed a practical giant. "It's so good to see you."

"You too, sweetheart," she says emotionally. She gave up a lot of time with her son for him to achieve this. It could have easily gone a different direction and maybe then she'd regret some of the decisions she made. Cillian doesn't have much family. He was conceived from a one-night stand at a music festival. His mom never got the guy's last name, so when she found out she was pregnant, there was no way to contact the man. She's a single mom and an only child whose father died when she was in her teens. When Cillian came to the Timberwolves, he moved in with a host family because his mom couldn't afford to relocate, nor did she want to leave her own mom alone. It sounds harsh, but it's quite common for WHL kids.

For the past year, he's lived with me. Dad bought a condo close to the University of Washington campus for me to live in while I'm at school, studying marketing. Willa's goal is UW, too, so she'll live here if she's accepted. It will be nice to have company the year after next with Cillian across the country, playing in Boston.

"Can you believe this is happening?"

"Absolutely."

"Of course." She laughs.

"Are you hungry? There's food up in the suite, or I can go grab you something?"

"No, no. I don't think my nerves could handle anything right now. I'm so excited for him." As she says the words, Cillian skates back around. When he sees her, he slows, placing a gloved hand over his heart as he does. Erin lets a few tears fall but hurriedly swipes them away. I grasp her fingers in mine and hold them through the rest of warmups.

Trina shows up, introducing herself to my boyfriend's mother before she proceeds to repeatedly get in our way while she takes photos of the players. It adds to my annoyance and wariness of her, but she has a job to do, so I do my best to let it go.

Besides, it's not as if I can start a rink side brawl with the woman right before Cillian's first game. No matter how much I'd like to put the blonde in her place.

"She's something," Erin whispers to me conspiratorially after Trina moves on. Her response to Trina only confirms that I wasn't imagining her intent to be a nuisance. "How's school?"

"Good. I have a busier schedule than I'd like, but my professors are great."

"That's a plus, sweetheart. And how are you doing with the distance?"

"Well, that part sucks," I tell her, dropping my head on her shoulder. "I miss him every day, but it's overshadowed by how proud of him I am."

"You've always had an unwavering confidence in my boy. He's never had a bigger supporter."

"That's not true, he's always had you."

Erin quiets and I sit with her in silence. I know she wishes their lives could have been different. Cill's profession changes a lot for all of us.

Being a rookie, it's impressive enough that the team has him on the starting roster. It shows a huge amount of confidence. He proves he's worthy of the spot when he scores the first goal of the night. Cillian tends to get attitude on the ice, but tonight his game is clean. No penalties, no sin bin. The team goes on to win and Erin's in tears by the end, so happy for her son.

Letting the crowd die down, we stay seated and wait for the three stars to be announced. It's a hockey tradition for three outstanding players to be acknowledged after the game. Cillian is one and it brings on a fresh round of Erin's tears of pride. This time, I join her, shedding a few of my own as he skates off the ice, waving to the dwindling crowd.

We're on cloud nine until we get to the family room, where we're to meet up with Cillian. As he comes into sight, so does Trina, who throws her arms around him in a big hug. It would be friendly, except the touch lingers, and not only hers.

My step falters, and Erin's hand grasps mine.

She sees it too.

Me losing him, she sees that.

Trina fades from existence and all his attention turns to me and his mother. He's all smiles and excitement, hugs and kisses. It's hard to believe that I have any reason to worry or to be jealous when he dotes on us as we grab a bite to eat before taking Erin back to the airport.

I all but forget there is a new woman trying to work her way into his life when he fucks me stupid for hours, worshiping my body like I'm his lord and savior. Cillian ignores everything but me until he takes me, too, to the airport the following day.

The entire flight home, I talk myself out of the idea that Trina is, or ever will be, anything more than just his coworker.

3

ISLA

"Are you seeing what I'm seeing?" Willa asks, her iced coffee nearly tumbling over as she slams it down on the table.

"Yes," I say, trying my best not to let tears fall. My emotions have been out of control since my last visit to Cillian. It didn't go well. I've visited him three times now. During each trip, my anxiousness has spiraled to a new high. Trina not only still has a weird attitude with me, but she's become an almost permanent fixture in Cillian's life. He chalks it up to her being buddies with Torsten, but I didn't buy that the first time he said it. I sure as fuck don't believe it now.

Regardless of my protests about how much time she spends at their apartment, nothing has changed. I hear her in the background when I'm talking to Cillian on the phone, she shows up unannounced when I'm there, and she makes a point to show how much she knows about my boyfriend whenever she can.

The proof is in the picture I'm stretching out on my phone to get a better look at. Cillian has been filling his Instagram with shots of him on and off the ice. Mostly the ones that aren't game related are of his training. This one is him shirtless in the gym, sweatpants riding low enough that you get a full view of his happy trial and a hint of more. But also, being as experienced with his dick as I am, I can see he's half hard.

To further my distress, Trina's reflection is visible in the mirror as she takes the shot of him.

She's barely dressed herself, only wearing tiny workout shorts and an even tinier sports bra.

He's commando, showing too much of himself, and has the beginnings of a hard-on… *for her.*

I want to die. No, I want to murder them both, then I want to die.

"Are you going to call him on it?"

"Yes."

"If you don't, I will. I'll fly my ass out there and find a big knife—"

"I'll handle it," I interrupt Willa's plan of murder. I leave her in the kitchen and retreat to my room.

Cillian doesn't answer the first time I call. Knowing his schedule, he should have down time right now. My nerves ratchet up, but so does my anger. He doesn't get to avoid this and damn him for even trying. Because I'm feeling very unhinged right now, I watch the phone on my clock and wait exactly three minutes before calling again.

"Hey," he answers as if it's any other phone call on any other day.

"Are you trying to avoid me?"

"No, Isla. Of course not."

"Is she there with you?"

"Who?"

"You know who! The blonde that had you in such a tizzy at the gym that I can see your fucking semi on a tiny Insta photo."

"It wasn't like that," he starts. "I'm trying to build up a fanbase is all; it's good for the team and might help them want to keep me around."

"Why are you lying to me, Cill." My voice breaks. I can't keep it under control. I've loved him so much for too long now. "I *know* what I see. Just don't lie to me."

We've had three great years without trust issues, without petty arguments, or even any major conflict. It seems incredible, considering our age and lifestyle now that I think about it. But it's true; we've been supportive and honest. I don't want that to change now, though I know it already has. He's been distant this past week and I'm simply not stupid enough to think Trina isn't a big part of the reason why.

He goes deathly quiet for a few long moments. I know it's coming, his admission. The truth, finally, that all isn't well and fine between us anymore.

"It's been hard, Isla. Being away from you, it's been hard."

"For me, too, Cillian. But be honest with me. Because what has been hard for me is not being able to see you every day, not being able to be at every game to support you in person the way I want to. Not being able to tend to your bruised body after a tough game," I ramble. "It's not tough for me to ignore the guys in my face every day at school. It's not tough for me *not* to grow close to them because I miss being close to you. It's certainly not hard for me to *not* be turned on by them."

"Fuck, Isla. I hate everything about this. I mean, except for playing, everything else about me here and you there is shit," he says with no small amount of fear in his own voice. "I don't want you to be worrying."

"Well, I am. I can't help that, especially not when you post stuff like that. If you're putting that in the open, what's happening behind the scenes?"

"Nothing has happened," he says with conviction.

"Yet?"

"I'm not seeking out other women. I hope you know that. I love you and I want to be with you," he says, but it's not an answer to my question. Not really.

He hasn't said nothing will happen. He hasn't said he's not attracted to Trina. He's said so much, but none of it has been the words I need to hear him say.

"That doesn't mean there isn't a willing woman consistently putting herself in front of you though, does it? Loving me and wanting me doesn't stop you from being aroused by her," I tell him, completely defeated by this entire conversation. I knew when I called him this was coming, but love makes us stupidly hopeful. "You're attracted to her, aren't you?"

"I don't want to hurt you, Isla," he admits after another quiet moment. "But I don't want to lie either."

"Too late," I say with a sob. "Where do we go from here?"

"Nothing has to change," he demands. "I don't intend for anything to happen with Trina or anyone else. Yes, sometimes, my body reacts, but that's because my dick is an asshole, Isla. I'm not giving up on us, so please don't give up on me."

"How am I supposed to keep fighting for us when you throw that kind of thing in my face, Cillian? How? It kills me to see you hard for her! But I'm supposed to just accept it as what? Fucking biology?"

"Nothing has happened, okay? I haven't done anything, and neither has she. I'll be more careful about what I post."

"But you won't be more careful about what you do? Or, who you do it with? Jesus, Cillian. How much time do you spend with her anyway?"

Again, he grows quiet, giving me my answer.

"I'll set some boundaries there," he finally says.

"I don't trust her."

"Then trust me."

I'm trying. My stomach is in more knots now than it was before this conversation. For days afterward, an ominous feeling shadows me. As if the ghost of my future is trying to warn me that my relationship is already over, and I should just succumb now. Give in to the inevitable and start my grieving process so I can move on.

My stubbornness won't allow that. I'll hang on until the bitter end. If he wants to end this, he's going to have to do it. Whether with words or actions, it's his call. I'm not the one walking away until I no longer have a choice.

Willa doesn't agree with my attitude. She's always adored Cillian, but she's not keen on giving him the benefit of the doubt right now. I can't blame her, her anger with him comes from a place of love. We're fiercely protective of one another. Nightly, she reminds me that she's ready and willing to fly to Boston to 'cut a bitch'.

Part of her attitude is fear. I'm not handling the stress very well. The following days, I am restless, and my appetite is all but non-existent. If I can't get a handle on it soon, Willa threatened to tell Dad and he'd sic our mom on me like a bulldog. I won't get a moment's peace.

Willa has even warned that she'll take my phone away from me just so I'll stop scrutinizing every post that Cillian, Trina, and even Torsten post. I obsess over them all to glean some sort of information that says either, yes you can trust him. Or no, no you most certainly cannot.

I'm losing my grip on reality fast. Though I can see that, I can't seem to stop myself from letting it happen. My brain is bombarded with intrusive thoughts all day, my nights filled with nightmares. It's like watching a movie of my own life play out in front of me. One where I become the stupid girl hung up on a guy that's already moved on.

Except, he says he hasn't.

Days go by with nothing new happening. And yet my stress level hasn't subsided. No matter how often I tell myself everything is okay, I can't shake the feeling that it isn't. My obsession has morphed into depression. I barely leave the house for anything other than class.

When knocking sounds on my front door, I blink as the intrusion brings me back to my reality. Which consists of me staring at the television for so long that I don't even know what I'm watching anymore. It's definitely not what I put on, but I've been so in my own head I hadn't even noticed that one movie stopped and another started.

Fucking snap out of it, Cole.

The banging doesn't stop.

"Calm down," I say.

"Go pee on these," Willa says, shoving a bag in my hands. "On *all* of them."

"What?"

"Pee. On the sticks, Isla. Now."

Eight packages of pregnancy tests? The fuck!

"Not possible." Except a weight as heavy as a bowling ball settles in my gut.

"You don't know that."

"I do, actually. I'm on birth control and am religious about it."

"Do you know how many women get pregnant every year while on birth control?"

"No," I answer, pulling out one of the boxes.

"Somewhere between two and eight percent. That's a lot of damned women. Now, go pee!"

"How am I supposed to supply this much urine? You're unhinged."

"I don't know! Pee in a cup and we'll drop from there, I guess? I don't know, just do it!"

"Fine!"

"You'd probably have plenty of piss if you were eating and drinking like a living human instead of the creepy-ass zombie you've been the past few weeks," she grumbles as she follows me first to the kitchen to find a cup and then to the bathroom.

"It's just stress, I'll get through it."

"What if it's not just stress though, Isla?"

What if I'm pregnant? At nineteen, with a man who lives thousands of miles away, while I'm in the middle of getting a college degree. Yeah, what if?

"I'm not going to be that statistic. There's no way. Right?"

"You could very well be that statistic. In case you haven't noticed, you're a fucking mess."

"That's stress!"

"Stress over a dude, Isla. That's not who you are. You've never taken shit from anyone, but you're letting him destroy you. It makes sense that something inside of you is stealing your backbone to grow their own."

Well, fuck.

When she puts it so bluntly, I can't help but take the idea into serious consideration. I've never been great at keeping track of periods, mostly because I've always felt secure in my birth control. Grabbing my right breast, I weigh it in my hand.

Does it feel heavier? *Maybe.*

It is a little tender, but hormones do that at times anyway. There hasn't been any weight gain, the opposite really. Food hasn't settled well as of late.

All I can do now is pee in the cup and wait.

"You need to call him."

"I know."

"You should do it now."

"I know."

"I'll stay the night here tonight."

"I know," I tell Willa while I stare at the line of tests. All positive.

It's a strange feeling to have your entire purview shrink down to one, or multiple in this case, plastic stick. Every turn I thought my life would take is now in question. Every goal is in jeopardy, or at the least delayed. My priorities that have always been neatly organized start to shuffle and shift.

How will Cillian react?

My finger shakes violently as I press call on his contact. Willa grasps my free hand in hers, squeezing it to offer support. It doesn't help. Of course, there's no answer. A pattern that has been growing and growing since he left for Boston. I end the call and pull up our text thread.

ME:

Call me. It's important.

"No answer?"

"No," I say, dialing again and getting no response.

"Call Tor, maybe he knows where he is," Willa suggests when fifteen minutes has passed and still Cillian hasn't called.

Tor answers after a few rings, but he doesn't say hello. The other end of the call is garbled mumbling and rustling for a few seconds.

"Dude, you need to break up with her," Tor says.

"I don't want to do that. I love her, man," Cillian answers him. I put my phone on speaker and set it on the coffee table in front of me, allowing my sister to hear the conversation as well.

"You say that, but that hasn't stopped you from hanging out with Trina. Is she coming over again tonight?"

"I don't know, probably."

"How have you not fucked her yet?"

"Dude, it's been so hard. After you crashed last night, we stayed up to finish the movie. She dropped her head in my lap, rubbing her face along my dick. It was all I could do to not pop it out and shove it in her mouth."

My stomach rolls as they laugh.

"She'd have loved that, the way she's always throwing herself at you. Have you kissed her?"

"Twice, but I stopped it and told her it was a mistake. Because it—"

Willa grabs my phone and ends the call.

"Fuck him, Isla! Seriously, fuck him."

"I knew, you know? I knew there was more than what he was telling me. I knew and I still chose to give him the chance. What an asshole!"

"Finally." Willa sighs.

"Finally what?"

"Finally, my sister is back. Not the pathetic creature who's been in your place for weeks."

"He's fucking cheating on me!"

"I know!"

"And I'm fucking pregnant," I yell, but it ends on a wail. As mad as I am, the tears win over. At least now I know what I can blame that all on. Cillian Wylder and his fucking super sperm.

"I know," she consoles, wrapping her arms around me as anger, grief, and general anxiety wash over me. "What are you going to do?"

Mom always taught us to take life as it comes. Nothing is predictable, and rarely, things go as planned. Cillian and I have talked about marriage and family vaguely. We never let the conversations get too deep because we're still so young. Childhood dreams change as you grow, and we were not naïve to that.

Whether I stay pregnant or not, one thing I'm feeling very sure of is that I don't want him in my life *right now*. Maybe that's rash, maybe it's more hormonal reaction.

At this moment, though, I need to be thinking about me and this potential baby, not what—or *who*—Cillian is doing.

ME:

The next time she rubs her face on your dick, shove it in. I'm not standing in your way.

Tell Torsten thanks for the heads up.

Fuck you.

Then, I block the only guy I've ever loved, in every way I can think of and on every app I have. It doesn't take too long before Willa's phone starts blowing up.

"You can answer if you want, but I'm not talking to him and you can't tell him about this," I tell her, pointing to all the pregnancy tests that I can't bring myself to throw away just yet. "Not until I figure out what to do."

"As if I would," she says in disgust. She's ignored all the calls and texts, but I can tell by the finger tapping on her thigh that she's itching to answer.

"Go ahead," I tell her when her phone starts to ring again.

"What," she demands into it. "No, you cannot talk to her because you're a lying asshole and she sees that now." Willa pauses to let him speak, but it's brief. "You fucking kissed Trina the twat! Twice…Yes, she heard that…Oh, cut the bullshit, Cillian! You told Isla you were going to set boundaries and you obviously haven't. Unless the boundary is your sweatpants…"

Her tirade continues, and funnily, as I listen to it, I feel a little bit better about my current position. It's not something I would have wished for or chosen, by any means. But with a family like I have, I'm going to be okay and so is any child I may choose to bring into my life.

If it's a boy, I'll teach him to be a better man than his father.

If it's a girl, I'll teach her to be as fiercely loyal as my little seventeen-year-old sister is as she wins a verbal argument with an NHL player twice her size.

"I will not tell her that. I hope she never unblocks you! She needs a man, not some boy who can't even manage a few months without sex on demand. Is that all she was to you? A convenient body?"

Damn. That one hurts because it's all too easy to believe. Cillian has spectacularly failed the first test we've had in our relationship. It's telling as to how much I really mean to him. While plenty of girls throw themselves at WHL players, I was the most convenient, being the coach's daughter and all.

"I do *not* know that. Because you've been living your life and gaslighting my sister every time she brings it up. All while she's here, faithfully pining away for you!"

Maybe it's finally knowing what has been going on that has brought me out of my stupor. Hearing him admit it, even if not to me, or maybe it's shock, because for the first time in weeks, I'm not feeling much of anything now. Just a metric shit ton of muted emotions all vying for attention as Willa stomps around my living room, yelling into her phone.

"Ooh, I'm so mad at you right now! If I ever see you again, I'm punching you in the eye. Even if I have to get a ladder to do it!"

Fuck, I love my sister.

"Tell him I need a little time," I whisper to her. There's still a huge conversation we need to have, obviously. Right now, I'm in no shape to be remotely rational though.

"She says to give her some time. She'll call you when she's able to stand your stupid voice."

———

Turns out it only takes a few hours for me to succumb to the pressure of telling Cillian what lies ahead of us. Or, potentially, anyway. I've made no final decisions, it's something I would like to do with him. Despite the late hour on the opposite coastline, I take a chance that he's left his ringer on in the hopes I'd call. Opting for video, because I think this is a face-to-face conversation, I hit his contact.

He answers, but it takes a second for the video to pull up. The camera bounces around a few times before focusing on Cillian's profile on the bed.

"I've missed this," he slurs.

I nod, because we haven't been video calling as much lately. "But we need to talk, Cill. Something has happened."

"She's never going to talk to me again," he mumbles. "This feels so good."

What?

Is he talking about Trina? Does this mean he broke off their *friendship* finally?

"Cillian, can you focus? This is important."

"It is. It's the most important time in my life and she's not even here for it," he says, and I know now he means me. I'm not there for him the way I've always been. He's also never asked me to be, not once did he ask me to move with him to Boston.

I would have gone.

"Cillian, can you look at me?" He hasn't looked at the phone once, still only giving me his profile while he's focused on something else in the room. Someone? *Oh god.*

"No. If I look at her, she'll look sad, and I'll feel sorry."

"You're not sorry, you've wanted this as much as I have," another voice purrs in the background and I tremble. With hurt, with anger. He didn't even wait a fucking day.

"Are you kidding me? It's been hours and you already have her in your bed?" His phone shifts, panning down his naked body to where Trina is perched between his legs, one hand on the phone, the other on his dick. "I'm fucking pregnant, you assholes."

There's a gasp from the other side of the call and then it ends. Someone hung up on me. Dread washes over me with my tears.

Every goal, every dream I've had slips away. Pregnant, no boyfriend, and a completely uncertain future.

I cry myself to sleep, gripping my phone, hoping that he'll call back and ask for an explanation of what I just told him.

Morning comes; his call doesn't.

So, I block him again and start building my new life, shaky brick by shaky brick.

4

ISLA

FIVE YEARS LATER

D ad called for a mandatory family dinner tonight, something he only does whenever there is important information he wants to share with all of us at once.

"What do you think this is about?" Willa asks as we walk up to the front door of our parents' house. The weather is nice today, clear and sunny. Mom will probably have dinner set up on the back deck that overlooks Puget Sound. Works for me, since it gives Sadie the yard to run around in. She enjoys chasing Mom's poodle, Curly.

"The draft," I answer, knowing in my gut I'm right. Two years ago, the NHL approved Seattle for an expansion team. Dad was hired to coach. The team, Seattle Blades, is about to make its official picks from all the other teams in the league.

Every team in the league has two options on protecting a certain number of their players from being drafted by the Blades. Neither option allows for them to protect more than eleven players. The Blades have to pick one unprotected player from every other team.

"Oh fuck, Cillian?" she asks, wide-eyed. I shrug. It's an assumption that the Seattle Blades will draft him, but my gut says it's the truth.

"Grams! I'm here," Sadie yells as soon as we get the door open.

"Where?" my mom asks, looking all around at her own eye level.

"Here!" Sadie jumps up and down, causing Curly to bark excitedly.

"Oh! There you are." She feigns astonishment, picking my daughter up in her arms. "We're on the deck."

"Hello to you too, Mother," Willa snarks.

"Hello, daughters," Mom says with exaggeration. Following her through the house and out the French doors that lead to the deck and yard, we find Dad on the grill.

"Pops!"

"Sadie," he hollers back at her, taking her from my mother's arms so he can hug her and blow a raspberry on her neck. It sends her into a fit of giggles and again Curly barks. It's my dad's cue to release the toddler so the dog can have his turn with my daughter.

My daughter Cillian has never met. That he's never cared to meet. There has been no contact between us since that video call. Though I tried a few times to work up the courage, I never got far.

"Hey kiddo," Dad greets Willa with a hug before giving me one. He's tense, further confirming the information I know is coming. Pressure builds in my sinuses and temples. It doesn't matter how certain I've been that this day would eventually come; I'm still terrified of it. For many reasons.

"How is work, Willa?" Mom asks as we all sit at the patio table that's already set and full of food.

"Fine. Nothing very exciting has happened. I'm still waiting for my dream man to walk through the doors and sweep me off my feet." She's taken a summer job at the local gay bar. Her chances of meeting a straight man there are slim, but she holds out hope that some spectacular specimen will walk in and steal her heart away. It's crap, and we both know it. Willa uses her sham dream as a way to keep pining after her current crush.

"You're too young for that bullshit," Dad admonishes her, and my mom hits him for his language. Sadie is immune to it, though. She hears it all regularly enough but has yet to be the one to repeat any of it. Thankfully. "Give me another decade before you try to marry yourself off."

Willa playfully sticks her tongue out at him.

Dad gives Mom a pointed look that makes my stomach churn. She engages Sadie in conversation while dishing and cutting up a plate of food for her.

I've always had my dad's temper. Mom is calm, cool, and collected. Willa takes after her, not me though. Mom always said it was something to do with my star sign; quick to rain hellfire on a direct offence though if someone makes an honest mistake, like bringing me the wrong order when we eat out, I never make a fuss. That's her area of expertise though, and not something I learned because it didn't have anything to do with ice or pucks.

Maybe they think I'm about to lose my shit at the news.

"I already know what you're going to say," I start. "Boston didn't protect him because his contract is coming up and based on how well he's played, he deserves more money than they likely want to pay when they already have several great players to pay. Seattle would be stupid not to have drafted him."

"They would have been," he agrees, but the tight muscles in his neck say he's still not happy about it.

"It's fine, Dad. We all knew something like this would happen sooner or later." The words ring hollow, even to myself. They're true, but there is no certainty in my voice. I'm not ready, even though I have always known it would happen. Some days, I even hoped for it. Some days, I even thought about calling him and asking him to come home.

"We didn't know we'd both have to work with him."

"Yeah," I agree with him. Not only will my dad be Cillian's coach, but I've been hired as part of the Fan Development team. I won't have the same contact with him as my dad, but we'll still run into each other regularly enough. "I'm surprised we've gone this long without bumping into him."

Maybe he hates me as much as I've hated him these past years. They haven't been easy years. I've had plenty of support from my family. Willa is the best auntie, and my mom has taken on the main role for childcare while I was at both school and work. Willa still lives with us, which means Sadie and I share a bedroom, but we've made that work. So far, anyway. She's getting too old now though, so we've been floating the idea of trying to find a larger space. Except, that requires more help from our father and neither of us wants that. He does enough for us as it is.

Of course, I could have pressed for child support from Cillian. The extra money would go a long way. Only, I never could muster the courage to have that conversation with him. And I'd have to tell him all the reasons why I didn't force some involvement from him.

There's no real way around that now. Even if we don't see each other right away, it's only a matter of time. Sadie loves going to Papa's games. Hockey is in her blood and we're a close family. Of course, word would eventually get around that Cillian Wylder and the coach's daughter have a love child.

Love. She was conceived in love; I refuse to believe otherwise. Despite how it all fell apart.

"I'll support whatever you decide to do, kiddo."

"What options are there?" Willa looks much like Dad does, tight jawed and fighting back her anger on my behalf. I love them for it, but this is my battle. Or mess to clean up, depending on how you look at it.

"None, really," I say before starting to nibble nervously on my bottom lip.

"We'll be here for the fallout," Dad says, reaching over to pat my shoulder in support.

"Maybe it won't be too dramatic," Mom suggests. "He was horrible there at the end, but we all loved him once."

We did. A small part of me still loves him. But that part is a stupid romantic that doesn't know what's good for her. It's difficult to love Sadie as much as I do and not love Cillian for giving her to me. Whatever he feels about me or her, I'm grateful for our surprise. My daughter is the greatest thing in my life; all the best parts of him. Determined, strong, passionate. Let's just hope she gets her loyalty from me.

"There's no way to know until we know, you know?" Willa teases, easing some of the tension.

"Is it Saturday?" Sadie asks.

"Yes, munchkin," I answer.

"Yes!" Sadie throws her arms in the air in excitement. Mom keeps her overnight most Saturday nights. She likes her grandma time, and it allows me a night to 'be a kid'. Often on my childfree nights, I can be found at home with Willa, her best friend, Kit, and a box of pizza.

That's not to say I haven't dated or had sex since giving birth to Sadie. I'm relatively active on a few apps, and I'm not above the occasional one-night stand. The man I was in love with may have broken my heart and left me pregnant, but I sure as hell haven't been silently pining after him all these years.

I even tried a boyfriend for a short period of time. It only lasted a few months; he's a nice guy and another hockey player. It was casual since he played for Vancouver's farm team just across the Canadian border. Eventually, Tyson was called up to play for the league, and I ended things before my life could repeat itself. No more seriously dating NHL players for me.

Maybe when Sadie is older, when she's more self-sufficient, I could try going for a serious relationship. *Maybe*. It's not my priority anyway. She is, then family, then career. A man ranks damn low on my list right now.

Especially with Cillian coming back to town.

"Do we know when he'll be here," I ask.

"He's flying in for the announcement. He'll be here on Tuesday," Dad says.

Fuck.

"Are they drafting anyone else I know?"

"We both know I can't tell you that. I'm already risking my contract, but this was information you needed to have."

"I appreciate it."

"I'd risk it all for my girls."

Someday, I hope Sadie and I find someone who feels the same.

"Fuck. That. Man." Kit tries hard to enunciate each word with a sense of righteous indignation, but we're all drunk so it isn't working out too well.

"I did. A whole bunch of times." I sigh before taking another shot of vodka.

"Did he look as good back then as he does now?" She rolls over onto her stomach, propping her chin so she can see me better.

"That question is a girl code foul," Willa shouts from the kitchen where she's scrounging for junk food.

"I know," Kit yells back. "But for real, did he?"

"No, the stupid asshole has only gotten better looking. While I gained baby weight and stretch marks, he's probably in the best shape of his life —Ouch!" A Tootsie Roll hits me in the head. Willa stands at the edge of the room, pissed off.

"Shut the fuck up, Isla. You grew a whole-ass human and still look beautiful."

"You make it sound like I planted her in a plot of dirt. Or am I the dirt in this scenario?"

"He's the dirt, you're the sun," Kit says.

"You're drunk." I laugh. "Where the fuck did you find a Tootsie Roll?"

"There was a half empty bag of candy in the back of the pantry, must be left over from Halloween." Willa shrugs, dropping the candy stash on the floor between us.

"Are there mint patties?" I dig through it, looking for the telltale silver wrapping.

"Gross," Willa groans.

"Your face is gross," I tease, and we laugh.

"Who's this?" Kit holds her phone so close to my face, I have to adjust my eyes to focus on the picture. "She's the only woman in multiple pictures."

"That's Trina." The blonde woman brings on a wave of nausea from memories of my past fragile mental state mixed with the booze.

"The one he cheated with?"

I nod, so I don't have to admit it with words. Cillian's social media was a huge point of contention between us, because of Trina. Because it clued me in to what was happening when I wasn't around. While I still follow his career, I quit following his personal life a long, long time ago. For all I know, they're still an item.

"She's not even that pretty," Kit says. It's a lie; of course she's pretty. But I love Kit for saying it.

"It's hard to resist a woman throwing herself at you when your girlfriend is across the country, I guess."

"He kept posts up with you in them too. Shit, you look so young," she muses. "How do you think he's going to react to Sadie?"

"I don't know," I answer Kit. "She's so damned loveable. I can't imagine anyone not wanting to be part of her life once they've met her. But it's been five years, so maybe he'll just be indifferent."

"Assuming he remembers you telling him," Willa says. It's something we've discussed more than once. The possibility that Cillian was more out of it than I thought. Or more than I wanted to admit to myself.

"If that's the case, he'll be shocked and furious. It would explain some things, anyway."

"Why?"

"If he knew, I can't imagine he'd have hidden it from Erin. She's going to hate me, too."

"Is that Cillian's mom?"

"Yes. I think she would have found a way to get ahold of me, if she knew."

"Didn't you block her, too?"

"Not at first. Not until after shit got bad."

"You were in a shitty situation. She has to understand," Kit says. Willa stays quiet though. She sees the joy Sadie brings my parents; she knows what I've deprived Erin of. I've always felt guilty that I haven't allowed her the knowledge of her granddaughter. "I can't imagine she'll hate you. Who could?"

"It's like you don't know me at all."

"I know all the parts that matter," she says. "Are you nervous?"

"Fuck yes."

"About how he's going to react to Sadie or to you?" Willa knows what my answer will be but poses the question regardless.

"Both. You can get mad at me all you want, but it doesn't change the fact that I'm not the perfect size four I was back then. While I don't want his cheating ass back, I'd still like to be appealing."

I'm in good shape. I've worked hard to drop most of the weight I gained while pregnant. Especially this past year, with the help of Zander. He's a defenseman for the Timberwolves and as soon as Dad brought him around the first time, we hit it off. He's a great friend, my best. Though, he's four years younger than me. He's mature for his age, more responsible than most guys I know. And he adores my kid.

Zander comes from a large family, spending time with me-knowing that it will almost always include Sadie-didn't phase him at all.

If the man was straight, he'd be a dream boyfriend. There was never interest in that department, not even before I knew he liked sex with both men and women, but mostly men. It wasn't something he came forward with right away. The hockey world isn't the most accepting, unfortunately. Zan took a few months before trusting me with it, and even then, he only dropped small hints until I finally confronted him with it in a cautious way. It was important that he felt safe with me.

"You want to see that fire in his eyes just so you can be the one to extinguish it," Kit says.

"That part," I say, pointing to our friend, then continuing to dig through the candy bag for anything that looks appetizing.

"What if he does want you back?" Willa hedges.

"Fuck. That. Man," Kit repeats.

"That part," I say with conviction. "Fuck Cillian Wylder, and not in the good way."

Tuesday comes before I'm ready.

"I think we're ready for tomorrow. What about you?" Katherine asks. She's my new coworker, and so far, seems laid-back. Her sense of humor is great, too, so I'm hopeful we'll make a good team.

"I agree. Jimmy seems pleased with what we've come up with."

"He does, and he strikes me as the type to be direct about not being happy with something."

"You caught that, too?" I ask with a smile.

"Yeah. Don't get me wrong, he's nice. But I think he won't hesitate to speak his mind." Katherine is around my age, fresh out of college and eager for the opportunity we've been given. She's bubbly, blonde curls bounce around her when she speaks animatedly about an idea. Her rosy cheeks and big blue eyes radiate kindness. I already love her a little.

Jimmy, on the other hand, is tall, always looks impeccably put together and screams all business. Opposites sometimes make the best coworkers though, so I'm not worried. About that, anyway. I do worry that folks will think I'm only here because my daddy landed me the job. Nepotism isn't a game our family would play though. I earned the position fair and square. That doesn't mean I won't have to prove myself, likely I'll have to work harder than the rest of my team until they see how talented and capable I am.

"I agree, but I'm good with direct. I prefer that to people holding back and the job suffering for it."

"For sure," Katherine agrees when a knock sounds on the shared office door. The space isn't very big, especially for us to be sharing, but I don't know how much time we'll be spending here. Mostly, we'll be at the Iceplex, youth camps, community outreach programs, and the arena.

"Hey, ladies," Greta calls from the doorway. She's the executive secretary to the General Manager, older than us by a couple of decades, but sweet and gives off big 'team mom' vibes. "I'm showing the guys around before they meet with the coach. This is Gavin Vaughn and Cillian Wylder. Fellas, meet our fan development team, Isla and Katherine."

Cillian is looking down at his phone until Greta says my name, and that's all it takes… four little letters to gain his full attention. His face snaps up to mine and a thousand emotions flash through his eyes. I imagine they mirror my own. He takes a big step toward me, and a cold shiver shoots down my spine.

It's been years. It could be years more and I still wouldn't have been ready to see him again. Or to feel the bitter sting of lost love and the burn of hurtful hatred.

"Isla," he breathes on a smile, wide and bright.

What the fuck are you so happy about?

"Wylder," I say, erasing all evidence of the feelings coursing under my skin. The pounding in my chest is so violent, I fear Cillian will hear it if he gets close.

"Oh, of course you both must already know each other from the Timberwolves days," Greta says, laughing in the soft, tinkling way that she does.

"It's nice to meet you, Vaughn. Welcome to the team," I politely greet the other man. Vaughn is older than us, more seasoned in the sport. His smile is polite and kind, but his vision bounces between me and my ex-boyfriend as if he's figuring us both.

Surely, the tension, or whatever this is, between us is as thick as an autumn morning fog.

"Great to meet you, too," Vaughn says with some humor before exchanging pleasantries with Katherine.

"No welcome for me?" Cillian's voice carries a playfulness that once made me excited. Now, I know he's probably used that same tone to bed who knows how many women.

I glare up at him, ready to deliver a scathing reply, but his eyes remind me of Sadie, and I falter.

Damn you, Cill.

"Let's not pretend we're friendly." His smile dims. I wish I felt good about it, but I can't seem to feel much except the horror that I will have to talk about the daughter he seems oblivious to. *Soon.*

Because surely this isn't the reaction I'd be getting from him if he knew about Sadie and just wanted nothing to do with us. Right? There are no tight muscles, no gazes being avoided. By him, anyway. The man in front of me looks like someone who has missed me and is happy to see me.

What the fuck.

"We were once. Maybe we could try again," he says. It sounds so sincere, but this is the same man that ripped my heart out and didn't look back.

It would be rude and unprofessional to tell him to get bent, but if he ever knew me at all, he'll catch on by the scathing look I send his way. Instead of getting the reaction I hope for, he beams.

"I'll find you," he says confidently. "After I meet Coach, I'll find you."

An ominous promise if I've ever heard one.

5
CILLIAN

Obviously, Isla still hates me.

Vaughn is called in to speak with Coach before me. While I wait for my turn, I search the internet for anything on Isla I can find. She must still have me blocked on social media, because I can't see anything there. Same with Willa.

There is a ping regarding her graduation from the University of Washington. However, the dates don't align. When she started there, she had enough credits to graduate in three years. Seems it took her four anyway.

After that, she took a job at a Seattle based women's football team. That's all I can find. Her digital footprint is nearly nonexistent. Well, what I can see of it anyway.

It was a shock when Greta introduced us. Sure, I expected to see her soon enough, since I'll be playing for her dad again. But I hadn't even considered she'd be here today. Nor did I consider her mere presence to bring me such a guttural reaction. Seeing her made the yearning that has been dormant for so long now sit up with renewed attention.

Isla's more beautiful now than I remember. Her body womanly, her look less casual with her dark hair pulled back neatly and dressed in something other than yoga pants, which was always her go-to. And she carried herself with a stoicism I don't remember from before. Or maybe it's aloofness. Whatever it was, it was hot as Hades.

Just looking at her sent my body into a bloody inferno. It always did; that was never a problem. Distance was.

And my utter stupidity.

Isla was always stubborn as hell. It's doubtful that's changed, so the chance of her forgiving me is slim as shit.

Coach is going to be a problem too, I'm sure. No way that man doesn't hate me as much as his daughter does.

I get it. Hell, I deserve it. Fucking over Isla was never something I wanted to do. She probably wouldn't believe me now, but I did love her. In hindsight, there are so many things I'd change from the time I was drafted to the time Isla dropped my dumb ass. The problem is that even the things I would change wouldn't eliminate the distractions I had. They sure as fuck wouldn't change the fact that I was a horny dickhead who had the world at my feet and no experience with how to handle that.

My first step would not have been moving in with Tor. He's not a bad guy, but if ever there was a man determined to never commit, it's him. There were always people at our apartment. Women and booze aren't easy to ignore when you're a nineteen-year-old kid who just landed in the pros.

Then there's Trina.

The office door opens, and Vaughn walks out.

"Your turn, player," he says with a nod.

He and I are acquainted, but I wouldn't say we're friends. The way he eyed up my ex-girlfriend earlier tells me we won't be easy buddies right away. He read more between me and Isla than I care for him to know. Our past isn't fodder for the guys she's going to have to work with.

Stashing my cell in my pocket, I give my fingers a quick wiggle to clear the nerves. Coach Cole is the closest thing I ever had to a father figure. His opinion has meant more to me than even he probably knows. When he took notice of me as a scabby kneed kid with only a spark of potential, it made my world.

How did I repay that? I broke his daughter's heart.

He's going to have words about that, for sure.

I knock and wait for the gruff voice on the other side. He takes his time. Because of course he does.

"Enter."

"Hey, Coach," I say, stepping through.

"Close the door," he commands and waits for me to follow instructions. He's standing just inside, not sitting at his desk across the room like I had expected. It's a big office with floor-to-ceiling windows covering one wall. The sunlight brings a false sense of brightness into the room that's heavy with his dark ire. "I'm going to say something that has nothing to do with the team first. It's off the record, you understand?"

He's an impressive man, standing an inch or so taller than me. He still has that goalie build from his professional days. When I was very young, he terrified me. Each time I got on the ice at camp, I expected the worst. Most of the coaches I played for in peewee were gruff, abrasive, brutish types. Coach Cole is different. He's reserved. Quiet until his fuse blows, which doesn't happen often, but when it does... well, like I said. It's impressive.

I never gave him a reason to unleash that temper on me when I played for him. And when I started dating Isla, I got to know him well enough to understand him. He cares about his players at a level I've never seen in another coach. Not even in Boston. I learned not to be afraid of him.

Today, I am.

"Yes, Coach."

The fist that hits my jaw surprises me, though I don't know why. It shouldn't, all things considered. Besides, we're hockey players. This is how we resolve shit. With anyone else, I'd instinctively throw one back.

But I deserve this. So, I take it like the man I wasn't the last time I saw him. Coach may be a couple decades older than me, that doesn't mean he can't throw a punch with the best of them. It staggers me back against the door, and I barely catch myself before falling to the ground.

"After we dropped you off at the airport, I promised her you two were going to be okay. That's for making me a liar to my daughter," he says, then lands another hit about an inch higher. "That's for hurting her. You do it again and I'll fucking bury you. Understand me, kid?"

"Understood," I tell him, flexing my jaw to make sure nothing is broken. "For what it's worth, I'm sorry."

"It's not worth shit, and I'm not the one who needs to hear it. You have a long road before I even consider trusting a damn thing you say. Personally or professionally."

The fucking thing about it is, I would have apologized every day for the past five years to Isla. If only she'd given me the chance. She made it clear that contact with me wasn't wanted. Willa blocked me everywhere too.

I'll ignore all the excuses I've told myself for why I didn't get in touch with Coach through the Timberwolves, or why I didn't just show up here and force her to talk to me. I'm good at that.

Coach can hate me all he wants for what I did; it still won't be with the same intensity I hate myself for how I behaved and how I hurt Isla. That girl supported me in every way, even financially. In return, I fucked her over at the first opportunity.

"Yes, Coach."

"Are you going to have a problem playing for me?"

"No, sir."

"I don't fucking like you, kid. That said, I'm going to do my best to keep it professional with you. I'll probably fail here and there, but you're going to take that the way you just did. Got it?"

"Yes, Coach." *Fuck me.*

"Sit," he says, finally moving to his desk. "You haven't been playing to your full potential. I know what you can do, and though you did well in Boston, you should have been their top scorer. Instead, you were barely third this past season. Why?"

Blunt to a fault, I always did appreciate that about him.

"The first season was hard on me. I was distracted by all the changes; the ones you know about and the ones maybe you don't. My grandmother died not too long ago. I moved my mom out there, that helped in some ways and not in others." I spill my truths to him because this isn't a man who accepts anything less. "I was a mess from the start, and even though I tried to battle back, I never could get my footing. In Boston or with the team. Physically, I'm great. Mentally, I haven't felt good in a long time."

"I remember my first season in The Show. It's an adjustment. But what makes coming here any different?"

"I'm home," I return just as bluntly. "Seattle is the only place that's ever felt like that. I'm focused on my game and my fitness. I dreamed of this before they even announced the expansion. This is where I'm supposed to be, and I'll do whatever it takes to be a success for this team."

"You think there are less distractions here than you had in Boston?" His eyebrow raises in clear skepticism.

"You mean, Isla?" He narrows his gaze. Something tells me he means more than his daughter, but I don't know what else he could be thinking about. "I ran into her earlier. She still hates me. Rightfully so. I'll be working to earn her friendship back, but Isla was never a distraction."

She was my motivation. She was the best support I had. Until I fucked up.

"Life throws shit your way, kid," he says after a drawn-out pause. The moniker chaps me. He called me Wylder as a kid, that turned to son after I'd been dating Isla for a while and had earned his respect. Now, I'm 'kid'. "It's not going to be any different here. You've got the rest of the summer to figure shit out. I want your head in the game come season open."

"Yes, Coach."

"Now, let's talk about why you've been slow as shit on the ice lately."

For the next twenty minutes, he hounds me on everything he thinks I've been doing wrong. By the time we're finishing up our chat, I feel properly scolded for not working as hard as I could have. Also, I feel more confident in what I said about knowing this is where I'm supposed to play. Because even though he dealt me a ration of shit, it means he's paid attention to me while I was in Boston.

It gives me hope and fuels my desire to make him proud of me again.

"How's Erin?" he asks, standing to lead me out of his office.

"Great, really. She's retiring out here. We're meeting with a real estate agent this afternoon to try and find her a little place where she can have a garden. She'll need some hobbies," I tell him. She's worked at least one job, usually two, my whole life. On top of taking care of my grandmother before she died and hauling me around to various hockey games and practices. She more than deserves a chance at a quiet life and I'm happy to be able to provide it for her. Even if she's going to be bored out of her mind at first, she's not good at being idle.

"That's hmm... that's good," he says, faltering, before he heaves a sigh. "Tell her not to be too hard on Isla."

"Why would she be?"

"We're done. Get the fuck out of my office, kid."

With that, he shuts his door in my face. I head back to Isla's office but the other woman, Katherine, tells me she's left for the day to go pick up someone named Sadie. I'm not sure how I'm going to track her down outside of these office walls, but I'll find a way. Isla can't escape me. Not again.

There's little chance I'll get a second shot with her, but I'm going to try to make things as right as I can. I owe her that. I owe Coach that. And the team, too. She's part of the organization, both professionally and personally through her dad. Her hating me will take a toll if I don't find some way to ease her hatred.

For the rest of the day, I focus on my mom. The agent found a few options for us to look at and Mom fell in love with a small two-bedroom cottage on half an acre in Issaquah. Not too far from Seattle but far enough away to that it still feels private and cozy. The best part is there is already a garden bed in the backyard. She cried when I told the agent to make a full price cash offer.

The place couldn't be more perfect for her. It's painted a bright yellow with dark green shutters and a sky-blue door. Eclectic and whimsical, a lot like she is. It needs some work, a new roof and flooring to start, but that's what she wanted. It's the first house she's ever owned, and she wants to make it hers.

After that, we viewed a few condos in the city for me. All of them were fine, none of them stood out. I'm not picky, it's just a place to store my shit and crash at the end of the day. Yet I'm not ready to throw down a million plus on a mortgage for a place that doesn't feel like home.

Hockey players make decent money, me included, but we're not at NFL salary levels. My first contract with Boston was five and a half million for three years. My second contract bumped me up to four million for two years. The new contract with the Seattle Blades is even better. It's very good money, but it's not the kind of money that lasts me a lifetime if I'm not smart about it. I can't afford to splurge on a penthouse with three-sixty views of Seattle, or a prime Medina home where I'd bump elbows with the ultra-wealthy.

"Maybe find a few to look at a little farther north," I suggest to my agent, Peter. "Our practice facility in Northgate. Just nothing east of I5."

"I'll work up a list. Are you opposed to untraditional? I have a client ready to list on Eastlake. It's at the high end of your budget, but ones like this don't come up too often."

"Email me whatever you have. We'll narrow down showings from there," I answer.

"Great, I'll email you a list shortly and set up viewings for the morning."

———

"How is she," my mother asks at dinner later in the evening. We're staying at a hotel for a handful of days, then we'll head back to Boston to pack up and head out this way. I left the travel arrangements to her and as I should have known, she's picked a more frugal location than I would have. She doesn't love me spending money on her, it was a battle to convince her to let me buy a house for her. Easing her into being comfortable with my salary is a long road.

Even though I would love a steak right now, I opted to grab burgers from Dick's, a local legend around here. One of many things I've missed about this city.

"I can't say," I answer, not pretending that I don't know who she's talking about. "She still hates me, that much was clear. She's more beautiful than I remember." I drop my napkin to the table, luckily done with most of my meal as my stomach tightens.

"Being a beautiful woman was never an issue for her, inside and out."

"No," I agree. My mom loved Isla, too. When I told her we broke up, she wasn't only upset with me for how it all happened. She was sad that she'd lost someone she'd considered a friend and something like a daughter. The one person who, for three years, was always by her side at my games. Isla was a loss for us both. "Her issue was me. Still is, apparently."

"How are you going to fix that? She's part of the same organization, Cill. She needs to feel safe in her position. At least comfortable enough around you to be able to do her job," she says, then finishes her bottle of water. "Besides the fact that it will weigh on you if you don't make things right."

"If you know a way for me to make it right, I'm all ears. But I do intend to talk to her. I tried to find her after I met with Coach, but she'd left already."

"And how was your talk with Robert?"

"It went about as how you'd expect. He punched me. Twice."

"Cillian," she gasps. "He didn't!"

"He did, and it's fine. I deserved it, even if it's a bruise to my ego. And maybe my cheek." I turn my head to the side and point at the spot his fist landed. Mom scowls but shakes her head. "Well, at least there's that."

"How are you two going to work together?"

"It's going to be okay. I still respect him, maybe even more after today. He fought for her. Which is more than I did." Though I wanted to, so fucking badly. Youth and ego stopped me.

"She didn't give you much choice there," my mom says, but I know she doesn't disagree with anything Isla did.

"I didn't give her much choice, either."

"Mmm, decisions of a broken heart," she muses.

"Yeah." I let out a long sigh. "Where do I even start with her?"

"With the truth, Cillian. That's where you lost your way before, don't repeat the mistake."

She heads off to her room after that. Leaving me to replay every detail of today and all the big life moments that have led me here. Fuck, if Isla doesn't play a starring role in all of it. I've gone years without so much a mention of her name. Today, hearing it and then seeing her, brought back so much. Not only the good times, but the guilt and pain too.

My situation with Trina wasn't what I intended, and I would change so much if I could go back. When I left for Boston, I was as confident as

Isla was in our relationship. I'd never once had a wandering eye; Isla was my world. Besides hockey, anyway. It quickly became apparent that my world up to that point had been incredibly small.

Now, all I can do is move forward. And hope that Isla gives me a second shot at being a person in her life. Even if not in her bed.

I'd be a dirty liar if I said I didn't hope for that. Isla always made me want her merely by existing. A few short minutes with her today was a bleak reminder of what I had and lost. Her smile is like a ray of sunshine, but it was her spicy temper that I always loved most. She feels with her whole heart, rational or not, it's just who she is. I never considered that as a flaw, I loved her temper. Until she broke shit off with me, then it terrified me.

Like I've done so many times before, I type her name into a search engine on my phone in the hopes of learning some new tidbit about her life that she couldn't bar me from. I sit straight up in the bed I've been lounging on when a link for a social media profile pops up. Clicking it takes me to her profile, which is mostly private. But not as locked down as it was the last time I tried.

Scrolling through it, I learn two things. One, it seems Isla has unblocked me. For the moment, anyway. Two, someone named Kat Hendricks has tagged both Isla and Willa in a recent picture. Though the furnishings have changed, the room is unmistakable as the condo I shared with Isla. Which means, I know exactly where to find her.

6

CILLIAN

The following morning, Isla's profile is locked up tight once again. I can guess she was as curious about my current life as I am about hers. She probably only unblocked me for enough time to snoop and I got lucky with my timing.

I got enough though.

I'm smiling like a fucking fool when I meet my mother for breakfast before another long day of house hunting.

"Peter is on his way to pick us up. The offer was accepted, you'll be a homeowner in about thirty days," I tell her when I sit down, dropping my plate of questionable hotel buffet food down on the table.

"Oh my," she says. "Are you sure about this?"

It's at least the twentieth time she's asked me.

"You know I am. This career is unexpected; I could get hurt any day or get traded and have to move again at the drop of dime. I want you to settle in a place where you can be happy. You can build a life here and not worry about things, which means in turn I won't worry about you. Regardless of where I end up."

It's a little like beating a dead horse at this point, but I remind myself that Erin Wylder has never taken a handout a day in her life. She's the hardest working woman I've ever known, and this is a huge adjustment for her.

"If you're sure," she says, quietly letting her words fade.

"I am very sure. Quit fighting me on it. You loved the place, and I can afford to get it for you."

"Buying it makes it harder for you to get a place for yourself though. Imagine where you could live if you put that money toward it?"

"Have I ever struck you as a guy to live in a fancy high-rise penthouse?"

We're eating the free breakfast at a three star, at best, hotel. Fancy, we are not.

"No. But you could be, if you wanted."

"I don't want that. I *want* you to have a home."

"Fine," she concedes. "Finish your food so we can go find you a home, too."

Hours later, I've made an offer on a place for myself. Peter was right; it's more than I'd initially wanted to spend. But it's unique and I love it, so I caved and made a very good offer. Now we wait to see if it's accepted by the seller. Being that they're also Peter's client, I imagine he would have told me if he thought it wouldn't be, though.

Hopefully, by the time my mom and I return from our last trip to Boston, we'll both have new places to lay our heads. She's tired after another day of running around, so I leave her at the hotel to rest while I tackle my next big Seattle obstacle.

Isla Saint Cole.

It's nearly seven when I reach her building. I try to ignore the sharp pain in my heart as memories of better days flood my head. That proves too difficult. I'll never not feel guilty for how I let things fall apart with her.

The building within walking distance of the UW campus is locked down tight. The only way in is by punching in a code or buzzing up to a unit for them to let you in. I can't buzz Isla; she'd never open the door to someone she isn't 'friendly' with.

Taking a stab at the code I used to use to gain entry, I type in the five digits and smile when the doors sound with the familiar click. Stepping through, my smile fades. Because for the five years Isla so eagerly blocked me from her life, I could have merely flown out here and knocked on her door.

It's something I contemplated many times. On more than a few occasions I had the flights pulled up and ready to purchase. And for various reasons, I talked myself out of it. She said to give her time. I did, days then weeks that turned into months. I regularly tried to text, call, or see if I was unblocked. I never was and so I gave her more time and as those months turned into years my shame grew. Along with some indignation that she never gave me a chance to talk it out. I don't blame her for that, not directly anyway. It added to the fester, though, and that rotting part of me couldn't commit to seeking her out on her own doorstep. Not to mention how my preoccupation with Isla those first few weeks consumed me to the point of affecting my career. The assistant coaches even had to sit me down and lay into me. Basically, I was told to get myself together or I was going to the farm for 'development'. I couldn't let that happen and it was one more reason I never came back to force the conversation with her.

But there are no wounds preventing me today. Tonight, I start the hard work of rebuilding some sort of relationship with the most important girl of my childhood. With the daughter of the man I respect most in the world. With the only woman I ever loved, even though I didn't love her right.

The route to the elevator and up four stories is familiar. Nothing about the building itself has changed. An old, converted soldier's home that was originally built in the twenties; it's full of untold stories and unseen ghosts.

I have changed, though. I'm sure Isla has as well. All I can hope is that she gives me a shot at getting to know the new her.

Nerves stop me at her door. Maybe the universe is sending me a sign that I shouldn't be doing this. Or maybe it's saying to take it seriously because I only have one shot at getting this right, at getting Isla's smile back in my life.

That smile that lights up a room, it makes her freckles more pronounced as if her happiness alone makes the sun shine on her. Fuck, I miss it more than I realized.

I knock because I no longer have the choice. I need to see her. *Now.*

Willa answers the door. She takes after Marney, their mother. Where Isla has darker attributes like Coach, Willa is more on the fair side. They both have their mother's amber eyes, though. Another way they differ is that Isla was always a little powder keg ready to explode, Willa takes more time to ignite. Typically, anyway.

Right now... not so much. I see her fingers clench tightly into a fist, but not before I can dodge it. What can I say? I expected discourse, not violence at first sight. Willa lands her shot right to my left eye.

"Fuck, Willa. Damnit, that hurt," I tell her, holding my eye that wells with water.

"What did I fucking tell you, Cillian? I keep my promises, unlike you."

"Yeah, I get it, but when the fuck did you learn how to hit?"

"When it became evident I needed to protect my sister from assholes," she snipes back.

"Truce?" I ask, holding my hands up in surrender. "I come in peace."

"Fuck you. Go away."

"Is she here?"

"No."

"I can hear her talking to someone."

"No, you can't," she rebuts, hands going to her waist as if daring me to call her bluff.

"Listen, Willa, I'm trying to make some amends here. If she really doesn't want to talk to me, I'll walk away. But can you at least ask her? Please?"

Her eyes narrow as she contemplates her next move, and I'm sure she's going to tell me to go away, when she surprises me yet again.

"Wait," she says, closing the door hard in my face.

I pace the hallway in front of their door for the several minutes I wait. I sense her before she opens it, some intuition telling me she's just on the other side. She's probably composing herself, trying for some calming breaths before she invites the enemy in. I bet her heart races as fast as mine right now, with the anticipation of the unknown. Maybe she hopes for the same things I do.

More likely, she hopes I'll disappear. That's not happening, though.

In my dreams, she opens the door with a welcoming smile. One that says she's glad to see me after so long and that the stupid mistakes of our past are long forgotten. They don't call them dreams for nothing.

In reality, she opens the door, wearing a turned down mouth and troubled eyes. Isla isn't excited that I'm here; she looks more terrified than anything else.

"Hey."

"You can't just show up here," she says with trembling lips as she wedges herself in the doorway, only opening it far enough to stand in.

"What choice did you give me? We should talk. You know we should."

"I... I know. But this isn't the place." She pauses to wipe a tear. Her body rattles as she fidgets from foot to foot. I've never seen her even slightly anxious like this. Never.

"Hey," I say, taking a step closer but holding my hands out to my side. "I'm only here to talk. I promise, I don't want to fight but I'll let you lay into me all you want, if that's what you want. Just tell me what you need, Isla."

"We do need to. Talk, I mean. We do need to talk. But..."

"Sadie, no," Willa says from behind Isla. A set of tiny little fingers creeps around the side of the door and starts to pull.

"I want Mommy to do it."

"In a minute, Sadie," Isla says, tears now streaming down her face.

"You have a kid?" I'm... well, shocked really. Stunned, as a million questions fly at me at once. The one most clear is who did she have a baby with?

The door opens a little further and a face appears at Isla's hip. Sadie is the spitting image of her mother, right down to the freckled nose that scrunches up when she's deep in thought.

"I know you," she says.

"Do you?" I squat down to get closer to her level. "Did you see me on television?"

"I don't think so," she says as she taps a finger to the tip of her chin. "Oh! Oh! Oh!"

She disappears behind the door again, and I train my eyes back to Isla who is now covering her face as she sobs.

"Well, fuck," Willa says. "You should probably bring this

conversation inside now." She holds the door open for me, but Isla doesn't move an inch. I don't know what the hell is happening, though I know I don't like Isla being such a mess. I wrap an arm around her and pull her inside with me. As soon as the door shuts behind us, she steps away and resumes wiping the silent streams along her cheeks.

"What's going on, Isla?" She doesn't answer and tiny footsteps come running our way.

"You're him," Sadie says in awe, her eyes big as she holds up a framed picture. It's me from the year I played for her dad, and we won the Memorial Cup.

"I am," I say, again squatting down to look the girl in the eye.

"I thought you knew," Isla says, but Sadie interrupts.

"You're my daddy," she whispers.

Holy shit.

My initial reaction is to tell her no. No, I am most certainly not your daddy, kid. Because of course I'm not. Why would she even think that? Isla wouldn't lie to her, but since I haven't been with her in almost five years now…

"How old are you, Sadie?"

"I thought you knew," Isla says again through hiccupping cries.

Fuck no, I didn't.

I can't concentrate on that now though, because this little human is staring at me like I'm a fairy princess come to life or something. She's grasping my photo to her chest. I get the feeling this isn't the first time she's done it.

Sadie holds up her hand, first dropping two fingers and yeah… three would mean I'm not her dad. But then she corrects herself and only leaves her thumb down in her palm.

"Four."

I drop to my ass on the cold, hard floor. Stunned, once again. I feel the truth of it all as it mixes with other things. Anger because Isla didn't tell me. Guilt because of the reasons she wouldn't have. Longing for so many things I must have missed.

Sadie matches my position, sitting on the floor in front of me. She scoots close enough for her bare toes to touch my shoes. I take in every detail of her. Pale complexion like her auntie, silver-blue eyes like her dad, but a wide bright smile that is all her mother.

I don't know how this happened, or why I wasn't told, but looking at this little sprite in front of me; it's clear as day she belongs to me and Isla.

"Why is your hair wet?" The absent-minded question pops out while I study her small features.

"I just had a bath," she says with a crooked smile that I feel in my chest. I have a daughter and somehow, I make her smile. Fuck me, if that's not the most amazing feeling in the entire damned world. "I'm Sadie."

"It's fantastic to meet you, Sadie." My voice breaks, sending Isla into another fit of sobs. Sadie looks up at her with concern.

"It's gonna be okay, Mommy. I think he's nice."

Isla kneels next to her daughter. *Our* daughter. She smooths Sadie's hair back and kisses her on the forehead. "It is going to be okay, baby. I promise."

"You are nice, right," she asks me as Isla moves further inside. She sits with Willa, wrapping their arms around each other not too far away and not out of sight. Both train their eyes on the interactions between me and my daughter.

My daughter. I repeat it a few more times in my mind but it's still wildly unbelievable.

"I am, Sadie. I'm very nice."

"And you play hockey," she says with a nod of her head. "But somewhere far away."

"I do play hockey, but I play here now. In Seattle for the Blades. Have you heard of them?"

"With Pops! They're my favorite team," she says, dramatically throwing her head back.

"Mine too." I laugh. "Even though they're brand new."

"Yeah, they're still the best though. Cuz Pops bosses them." She yawns and rubs her eye.

"You tired, kiddo?"

"Yeah." She sighs. "Will you read me my story?"

"Um," I hedge, looking to Isla for guidance here. Her nervousness is evident, but I plead with my eyes. I don't want to say no to the first thing my daughter asks of me.

"I'll come with," Isla says cautiously.

"Sure, Sadie, I'd like that."

She bounces back up to her feet, leaving the photo of me discarded on the floor. She reaches a hand down to me, and I smile at the girl no bigger than a Tater Tot offering to help me up off the floor. I accept her help and laugh when she grunts and throws her whole body into trying to pull me up.

She doesn't let go of my hand as she leads the way to the bedroom I used to share with her mother. Everything about the room is different now, even the bed, that's been replaced by two smaller ones. One queen, one twin in the corner that is obviously designated as Sadie's space. Twinkling lights hang over the bed that's laden with stuffed animals.

Sadie merely pushes them around until she's found her happy spot in the middle of them and points to a book sitting on a small, but very bright pink, nightstand.

Two pages into *Stellaluna* and Sadie's eyes are barely staying open.

"Maybe that's enough for tonight, kiddo. What do you think?"

"I know that's right," she says sleepily. "Will you still be here tomorrow though?"

"Maybe not here, here. But I'll be around from now on. I promise."

She smiles and lets her eyelids close. As badly as I want to go talk to Isla, I don't leave. Instead, I watch my daughter fall into a soft snore.

My daughter. *Mine.*

She's perfect, too. Of course, she is, with a mom like Isla and an auntie like Willa.

"Hey," Isla calls from the doorway in a hushed whisper. I look up and she motions for me to follow her. I do but only after I pull a blanket over Sadie and watch her snuggle into it.

I find Isla in the kitchen pouring two glasses of bourbon.

"What the fuck, Isla?"

"Don't you start with me, Wylder," she says, shoving a glass into my chest. "I fucking told you. And then everything... you don't know shit about anything."

"You're damn right I don't, because you *didn't* tell me." I drain my glass. How am I expected to keep my cool in this situation? I have a four-year-old daughter that I had no idea existed. "How did she know I was her dad?"

"She's always known. I didn't hide it from her. I'm not a liar." I don't miss her accusation. I didn't ever lie to Isla, not directly anyway. I omitted and I evaded, for sure. But if I lied, it was to myself, not her.

"It's equivalent to a lie not to tell me though, don't you think?"

"I did tell you! And had you ever asked for more information, I would have given it to you," she says, her eyes alight with rage. "If you don't believe me, ask your girlfriend. I'm sure your dick in her mouth didn't impair her hearing."

"I don't even know what the fuck you're talking about! You should have told me as soon as you knew." I let my own anger be heard, and in return, she slaps me. It's the same cheek that's taken several punches now. "Damn it, Isla. Is your whole family going to hit me this week?"

"I did! I called you as soon as I knew and you didn't answer, you *ignored* my calls. At the most crucial time in my life, when I needed you most, you didn't answer," she says, her eyes shine but no more tears fall. "I called Torsten to ask if he knew where you were."

Fuck me. Fuck. Me.

That call changed everything. Torsten had hounded me for weeks to decide; either cut Trina's attention off completely or break it off with Isla. He knew I was struggling. Instead of letting me teeter for longer, he took the opportunity to make the decision for me. We argued over that, but eventually, I forgave him. After all, all he did was answer a call. I'm the one that did all the harm.

More than I knew, apparently.

"I'm sorry that I didn't answer, but that doesn't excuse five years of keeping her from me." There's no excuse for what she's done.

"The first apology I get and it's for not picking up the phone," she says. She can try to hide the hurt behind her indignation, but I hear it anyway. As if I can hear her heart breaking, but that can't be right because that happened a long time ago now.

As angry and hurt I am right now, and it's a lot, I can't help that I hurt a little for her too. I dig my hands into her hair, one at each of her temples, bringing my face closer to hers.

"That's why I came here tonight, Isla. To apologize, to try and make some sense of it all."

"Your apologies are years too late, Cillian." She blinks rapidly, fighting so hard to keep the sadness away and to hold on to her hate of me. I hate her too at this moment, but that doesn't stop the connection we've always shared. The undeniable yet invisible thing that has been between us since we were children. It's still there and I know she feels it the same as I do.

"What is my daughter's full name?" I rub my thumbs back and forth along her hairline, trying to keep her on the calmer side.

"Sadie Nadine Cole."

Nadine was my grandmother's name. But Cole is all wrong. I want to fuck her over and fuck her stupid at the same time for that.

"Why doesn't she have her own bedroom," I ask, and she blinks a few times before answering.

"Willa moved in as soon as she finished high school. I was having... it was hard. Being a mom, trying to finish college. We've been talking about a bigger place, but it hasn't been a priority just yet."

"I made an offer on a house today; she'll have a room there."

"The fuck she will," she snaps, pulling away from my touch.

"She's my daughter too, Isla. You can't keep her away from me anymore."

"I won't, but that doesn't mean she gets to stay with you."

"Yes, it does."

"No, it doesn't. You can't be trusted, Wylder. You couldn't be trusted to care for me when I was an adult. I sure as hell can't trust you with her. Even if you had any idea of how to take care of a toddler."

"I'll learn," I say confidently.

"Maybe," she says with a heavy shrug. "But I'm not taking chances with my daughter."

"*Our* daughter. And neither will I. We can reasonably work something out or I'll lawyer up and fight you tooth and nail, Cole."

"I fucking hate you," she spits, her tears making another appearance.

"I hate you, too," I tell her, stepping back into her space, pinning her with her back against the countertop. She takes a few heavy breaths, the rise and fall of her breasts grazing my chest. *You're just as affected as I am,*

Isla, you can't fucking hide from me. Her face lifts to mine and those trembling lips of hers grab my attention. So, I take them. Consequences be damned, I've missed this too much. I've missed *her* too much. Hating her doesn't stop my wanting her, as fucked as that is.

Wherever we end up after all of this, at least I'll have tasted her one last time. Savoring the slide of her tongue against mine and the slight hum she releases as her body relaxes in my arms. It's only a brief few seconds before she pushes me away and punches me in the *same damned cheek*. If it wasn't bruised before, it sure as hell will be now.

"This isn't over, Isla," I bite out before leaving.

7

ISLA

"**I**s he coming back?"

"Of course, baby. But I don't know when. He's super busy with the new team and moving back from Boston."

"He didn't say when?" Sadie pouts, and I feel badly that our argument last night ended with Cillian walking out the door with no clear plan ahead. It was irresponsible of me when I know what meeting him means to Sadie.

She keeps his picture in her room, and though it's not often she asks questions about him, she has been known to. I've never lied to her about him, and thankfully, she's never asked directly why he wasn't around. But she cherishes his picture, as if knowing she has a hockey playing father out in the world is enough to keep her happy.

It will all be different now.

"No, Sadie, he didn't. You know we'll see him tomorrow though; he'll be at the Blades draft announcement."

"Oh yeah! With Pops."

"It's an exciting day, yeah?"

"I know that's right," she says and sprints off to her room. I'm not sure where she picked up the saying, but she says it all the time right now. Her habits change like the weather though, in a few days she'll be on to something new.

My phone chimes on the kitchen counter. I've avoided the room altogether today, since every time I step into it, I reminisce about Cillian invading my space with his stupidly big body. It makes my blood boil how he threatened me with lawyers. He's angry, I understand why, but I'm not handing Sadie over to him when they met for a whole five-ass minutes.

He's fucking delusional if he thinks that. He's also delusional thinking he can kiss me that way. I know where he's been, and that knowledge induces vomit to stir in my system.

TY:

Hey, Freckles. I'm headed your way.

ME:

You coming to visit?

TY:

Yeah, promo shit. Be there for the weekend.
Dinner Saturday?

ME:

Yes. Please and thank you.

TY:

Pick you up at seven. Maybe brunch on Sunday
so I can see Squirt?

ME:

That would be great. Thanks, Ty.

Tyson and I aren't in a relationship anymore, but our break was amicable. He's one of the very few people that know of my situation with Cillian. Not that it was something I was upfront about. There's always been a weird sense of betrayal that niggles at the back of my skull when the subject of Sadie's father comes up.

Even though he betrayed me first, it felt wrong to talk about it all with people who know Cillian, when he and I never had a proper conversation about it. Ty's been around long enough, in one way or another, to remember the days that Cillian and I were together. He put the pieces together himself and never asked me to clarify. Though I eventually did tell him why I broke things off with Cillian.

Since he knows my past, he understood that I feared a repeat when he was called up to the NHL. Still, he never fails to get a hold of me when he's in town. Dinner, and sometimes sex, is something we do as often as we can. No strings. No drama. No expectations.

We have a wonderful friends-with-benefits arrangement. On top of that, he likes Sadie. If you don't put my child first, you don't get to be a part of my life.

"Hey, Sadie," I call to her from our bedroom door. She's taken each of her stuffed animals off the bed and is meticulously placing them back in new order. "Ty will be here this weekend. Do you want to have breakfast with him on Sunday?"

"After Gram's night?" she asks, and I nod. "Yes, please."

She pokes her tongue out of the corner of her mouth, contemplating where she placed her purple panda. Sadie must not approve of the placement, because she snatches it back up and drops it to the floor, replacing it with a giraffe. This is a pattern for her, and I've come to recognize that she does it when she's trying to process something.

"Do you want to talk about anything?"

"No, thank you."

"Okay, you let me know if you change your mind."

"Okay, Mommy."

Okay, then.

I don't push her, opting to let her mull on it for a while. Though I'll be keeping a closer watch just to be sure she's not overwhelmed. Or dangerously so, anyway. This situation with Cill is going to be consuming. No way around that. This will be hard on us all. I only hope Cillian will be reasonable. I can lawyer up just as easily as him; my parents would happily help me pay for that.

Except, I don't want it to come to that. I don't want my panic attacks to return, and most importantly, I don't want to put my daughter through a big custody battle. It wouldn't be good for any of us, or even the team.

"Zan will be here soon," I remind her as I leave the room.

"With pizza!"

"Yes, ma'am," I confirm just as a knock on the door sounds. Only when I open it, it's not Zan.

"Let me in."

"Ask nicely, geez."

"Let me and my mother in so she can meet her granddaughter. Please." *Ah fuck.* Sure enough, when Cillian moves to the side, Erin comes into the picture.

"Is it an okay time, sweetheart? We would have called but… well, you know," she says with a soft smile.

Right. Neither of them has the ability to call me. I didn't want to block Erin, but I didn't want Cillian using her to get ahold of me. It's the thing I'm most ashamed of, when I allow myself some honesty.

"Can you give me a second to let her know?"

"Of course, Isla," she says even though Cillian huffs.

"Thank you." I ignore him, leaving the door open for them while I retreat back to the bedroom. "Sadie, someone is here to meet you."

"My dad," she asks with excitement.

"He's here, too. But it's his mom that wants to meet you for the first time. She's your other grandma. Do you want to see them?"

Sadie nods and grabs onto my hand. She's being shy and clingy, hiding her face behind my back as we walk down the hall to the living room. It's not unusual for her. Though she isn't an overly cautious kid with strangers, she does stick close to me or a family member when she's overstimulated. I rub my fingers over hers, letting her know it's all okay.

Cillian is sitting on the floor when we get to the living area; Erin is on the couch beside him, her eyes shining but happy.

"Hey, Sadie," Cill says, flashing her a big smile.

"Hi," she says back, sucking her bottom lip in.

"How are you today?"

"Okay." She rubs her cheek along my arm but takes a step closer to him.

"Good," he tells her, caressing her cheek. "You look nice."

"Thanks!" The smile she sends back shows her dimple, the same one her father has. She dressed herself today, which she does most days. I don't much care if she's a color clashing mess, as long as she loves what she's got on. Today, it's pink and purple striped tights under yellow overall shorts and a baby blue tee.

The compliment is enough to get her to release her hold of me and go stand as close to Cillian as she can. She keeps side-eyeing Erin, who is wringing her hands in her lap, probably in effort to not grab the child up and smother her.

"This is my mom," Cillian tells Sadie with a head nod toward Erin.

"My other grams," Sadie confirms. "Hi."

"Hi, sweetheart," Erin says, and a tear finally falls.

"Are you sad?"

"No, sweety. I'm very, very happy to meet you."

"I know that's right," she says, and I can't help the laugh that bursts out of me at the catchphrase she has apparently learned from somewhere.

"I'm going to make some cookies. I'll be in the kitchen if you need me. Okay?"

"Okay, Mommy."

My retreat is two-fold. Yes, I'd planned on making cookies for Zander. Also, I'm still adjusting to Cillian being around. There wasn't enough time to prepare myself for it. Even if he is going to be a regular fixture in our lives, that doesn't mean I can't keep some boundaries with him.

It's the best thing for all, since I figure we're going to be at each other's throats for the foreseeable future. The asshole may have come by to apologize last night, but he still hasn't. He's had years to do it; I wasn't that hard to find, had he really tried.

He chose to discard me and then didn't explain his reasons either. I'm not a saint, despite my middle name, but I wouldn't have done that to him. I'd never intentionally make someone feel like they didn't matter. Like they were temporary. A throwaway. Especially not someone I said I loved.

Cillian couldn't have loved me. Not in the way that I loved him. It's an acknowledgment that always breaks my heart all over again.

"Do you need any help?" Erin walks in as I'm dropping the last glob of dough onto the baking sheet.

68

"No, thanks. I'm just finishing up." I slide the tray into the oven and set the timer, before turning to her. "I'm sorry I cut you off. There were reasons." Emotions clog my throat, and her face falls.

"Sweetheart," she says with a sigh, wrapping me in her arms. "I was a single mother, too. I know how hard it can be. I'm not mad at you. I'm sad you had your reasons and I only hope one day you trust me enough to tell me them."

Erin doesn't let me go until my heart rate slows back down. Maybe it's her motherly intuition that lets her know when I'm ready to speak again, but something lets her know when it's time.

"Sadie is perfect."

"Well, I tend to agree," I say. "But I'm probably biased."

"I don't think that's it," she says with a wink. "Cill bought me a house in Issaquah. I hope you'll let me get to know you both better since I'll be here for good now."

"Of course, Erin. I've wanted that, truly I did. It was just complicated, and I didn't handle it well."

"No judgment, Isla. Let's just move forward. Okay?"

"Thank you," I tell her, feeling weepy all over again. I don't deserve her understanding, but I appreciate it. "I was so worried you'd hate me."

"Oh. Never, darling girl," she says, giving me one more hug. "Regardless of what's happened, you've given me the greatest gift. I'm going to focus on that, and you and my son can work out the rest."

"Where is my favorite ankle biter," Zan asks, walking through the front door, balancing two pizza boxes in one hand.

"Here I am," Sadie yells, bounding around the corner.

"Wow, am I glad to see you. The pizza place put pineapple on one pizza, so you're going to have to eat that one. It's too gross for me." He rubs her head in greeting.

"I'll eat all of it!"

"Sorry, didn't know you had company," Zander says when he sees me standing next to Erin. At only nineteen, he is still in his bulk-up stage, but he's made big strides there and is large for players his age. While he's been trying to gain mass, I've been trying to lose it.

Zander is also a total heartthrob. He's got those typical all-American looks you'd expect from a wholesome Midwestern born-and-bred athlete. Though, wholesome is a stretch.

"Oh, we were unexpected. I'm Erin Wylder," she says, reaching a hand out for him to shake.

"Alexander Fane," he tells her, grasping her hand in his as he gives me a pointed side-eye.

"Nice to meet you, Alex. I'm Cill." He enters the kitchen behind Zan. He never introduces himself as Cill. At least, he never did when I knew him. Maybe he's changed his habits, or maybe, probably, he's trying to be an intimidating asshole.

"How about y'all take this to the dining room," I suggest, grabbing a stack of plates and handing them to Erin to carry. As suspected, Cillian stays behind while the others leave. "Don't be rude to my guest."

"How was I rude?"

"By just being you, I guess."

"Why is he here," he asks after a hefty eye roll.

"He's a friend and he often comes over for dinner."

"And more?"

"Hardly your business." I scoff.

"Everything that happens in the house my daughter lives in is my business," he says in a low voice as he stalks dangerously closer to me.

"If you think for one fucking second that I bring dangerous or problematic people around my daughter, you never knew me at all," I whisper-shout, hoping we can't be heard by the others chattering in the next room. "Is that what you're insinuating? That I'm the one with shit judgment in others?"

His ruffled brow softens a minute when my blow lands. He's the one that jumped into a 'friendship' with a woman determined to break us up and he wants to tell me who I have a right to invite into my home. Or even my bed.

Fuck you, Cillian.

"Listen, I'm having a hard time here, Isla. It's not easy to come to terms with the idea that I have a four-year-old daughter. And it stings like hell to see that she already has relationships with other men in your life."

"She knows the people that I'm close with, get over it."

His silver eyes bounce over my face for a few long moments, weighing how heated my temper is. This habit of his hasn't changed, evidently.

"Is she coming to the draft announcement tomorrow?" he finally says, completely changing the subject.

"Yes."

"We need to talk about arrangements. Does Saturday work for you?"

"No. I have a date Saturday night."

"Sunday, then," he grits out.

"Later in the day, maybe. Sadie and I are having brunch with my date."

"Is your *date* staying the night?"

"Maybe." I shrug.

"Hell no, he is not," Cillian says so slowly, standing chest to chest with me so I'm left with no choice but to crane my neck up to keep eye contact. "You are not fucking someone a few feet away from my daughter."

"Did you always think this poorly of me? Because, wow…" I push him away and step aside. "Sadie stays with my mom on Saturday nights. It's their special day."

Seriously, this guy. I get I'm being difficult but what kind of person does he think I am?

"I didn't think poorly of you until I walked in here the other night and was faced with my Child Surprise," he taunts.

"Oh, bullshit. You didn't think much of me when you were trying *so hard* not to shove your dick inside your *friend*."

He blanches and drags his hand down his face. I guess maybe he forgot I heard him say that.

"Now isn't the time to get into that."

"Never would be great with me. We can just keep on ignoring it, you're good at that," I snark.

"Can you make time after your mom takes Sadie but before your date?" He says the last word like it tastes bad in his mouth. Comical, since I'm sure he's been out with more women in our time apart than I could have even imagined having time for.

"Be here at four, leave promptly at six so I have time to get all sexy for him," I say, and he glares at me with so much disdain. I love that he hates the idea of me giving attention to another man. Being touched by another man. Fucking another man. "I'm hoping to get lucky."

It's only a small amount of the discomfort I've felt since he started hanging out with Trina.

"Let's go eat dinner with our daughter and your *friend*. We'll discuss the rest later. But you need to unblock me so I can contact you like responsible co-parents."

"Ooh yes, sir." I leave him in the kitchen in favor of a chicken bacon ranch slice of pizza with a toddler that has red sauce smeared all over her cheeks.

Dinner is awkward but amicable, neither of us willing to make waves with an audience. By the end of the meal, Sadie is comfortable enough with both Cillian and Erin that she's crawling from lap to lap and hand feeding them pieces of pineapple.

Watching her with Cillian stomps my battered heart even more. After I'd decided to keep my pregnancy, I started researching everything I could about being pregnant and having a newborn. My social media algorithms hardly showed me anything that wasn't baby related.

My first ever panic attack happened because of those algorithms. A video came up of a father sleeping face-to-face with his infant child and she was suckling on the tip of his nose in her sleep. I was so emotional over it that I decided that it was time to call Cillian and discuss me being four months pregnant. I'd planned on doing it before my due date anyway. Whether he wanted to talk about it or not, we had shit to work out.

My nerves were like livewires, so I started by unblocking him on Instagram. I was going to scroll through the past couple months of his life while I tried to compose myself. Except, many of his pictures had Trina in them and it was clear to me that their relationship was no longer just friendly. Whatever happened after that video call had progressed, because she draped herself all over him on camera and he didn't seem to have any problem posting such things for the world to see. Even knowing I could see them, after our fallout, hadn't dissuaded him.

The stroll through images of his life didn't make me miss him, as I'd thought they would. They made me feel insignificant, so alone, and unlovable. And if I was unlovable, how could I bring a baby into that life? How was I going to raise a child in love and keep her from knowing that her father wanted nothing to do with her? That he'd rather spend his life with a conniving woman instead of us. The thoughts spiraled.

I ended up in the emergency room that night, having no idea what was happening to me. I thought I was having heart failure and that fear only made things worse.

I wish I could say things got better from there, but they didn't. They got far worse.

"Breathe, babe," Zander whispers in my ear as he stands. It brings me back to the present, and to Cillian piercing me curiously. "I'll help you clear this up."

"Th-thanks," I stammer as I grab empty plates and follow Zander into the kitchen.

"You good?"

"Yeah, just a trip down memory lane."

"That been happening a lot?"

"No, surprisingly. The last few days have been crazy."

"Can I make it a little crazier? But in a good way."

"Always," I answer. There isn't much I'd deny him, but especially not my confidence.

"They're talking about making me captain," he says, almost shyly.

"That's not crazy, that's amazing," I say, stepping into his arms so I can hug him while I rest my chin on his chest. "You deserve it, you work harder than anyone else on the team."

"Thank you." Zander presses a kiss to the tip of my nose at the same time Cillian walks in.

"Is this who you're going out with Saturday?"

"You have a date Saturday night?" Zander, like the best friend he is, just smiles.

"I do. Ty will be in town."

"Ooh, you have *that* kind of date. Be safe, have fun," he says, then presses another kiss, this time, one on my lips.

"Jesus Christ," Cillian mumbles. "How many guys are you dating?"

"As many as I can," I answer, turning my head to look at him but not leaving the comfort of Zander's arms.

"Seems responsible," he mumbles.

Zander tenses around me, ready to blow his top before I have a chance to retort. He knows my history well enough to know that suggesting I'm a shit parent stings like hell. I wasn't always great at it, but I strive to be every day.

"Isla is the best mother I've ever known, if that's what you're fucking implying, Wylder. As for responsibility, you're one to talk. You couldn't even manage breaking off one relationship before you started up another. You watch what you say to her around me." Zander moves to stand toe to toe with my ex-boyfriend, both of their chests puffing up with stupid male ego.

Fucking hockey players.

Cillian sizes my friend up, the smug grin on his face saying he knows he could take Zan if it came to that. Not that I'd let it. Zander is tougher than he looks but Cillian has both height and bulk on him. Still, I love that my friend stands up for me the way he does.

It's more than I can say for certain others.

"It's getting late, time for you to say goodnight to Sadie," I say to Cillian, leaving little room for argument as I brush past him to find my daughter and Erin.

They're arm in arm on the sofa; Sadie has pulled out the baby book my mother insisted I keep and is showing her grandmother all the photos.

"If Grams is Grams, what do I call you?"

"Should we come up with a name for me so it's not so confusing," Erin asks her.

"Yes, please."

"How about Nana? That's what I called my grandmother when I was your age."

"Okay, Nana," Sadie answers easily. "What do I call you?"

Cillian stops abruptly next to me when she asks him the question. Me, well, I start to tremble. Thankfully, Zan's hand gently soothes my lower back. I've been telling myself for days that this, and so many other crucial moments, would be coming sooner rather than later. Nothing really prepares you for moments that could easily break your daughter's heart. If Cillian doesn't handle this right, I'm starting by cutting off his balls, then moving to gouging his eyes out with a rust covered spoon.

"I think that's up to you, kiddo," he answers.

"Mommy calls Pops daddy, so maybe that." Her eyes are wide and worried, bringing all my fears to the forefront. Because if Cillian can't commit to being her father, it will shatter her tiny soul.

Then I'll be left with no other option than to chop his dick off and force feed it to him in retribution.

"That's the best thing I've heard in a very long time, Sadie. I love it."

I guess I won't be serving life in prison, after all.

8

CILLIAN

ME:

Are you on your way?

ISLA:

This was just a test to see if I unblocked you.

S *he's infuriating.*

ME:

I'd like my daughter with me today. I'm just checking to see if you'll be here soon.

ISLA:

We'd get there sooner if you'd stop texting me. I'm about to drive.

"She's infuriating," I groan aloud.

"You used to love that about her," Mom says with a small eye roll and a sweet smile. I did love that about Isla. Her snark and no-bullshit attitude used to turn me on like nothing else. Now, I want to choke it out of her.

"How can you be so easygoing about all of this? She hid your granddaughter for four years."

"I don't judge what I don't understand, Cillian. Isla said she had her reasons. Something else you used to love about her was her strength. It was admirable, but even I can see her flame has dimmed. She's changed and I'll save my opinion on that until I know all the reasons why."

"That's probably just her guilt," I grumble, unwilling to consider anything else. At this point, I can't. I'm still too angry.

Looking into my daughter's eyes for the first time, knowing who she was, *changed me*. When she said she wanted to call me daddy last night... I swear I grew a whole extra heart inside my chest that's reserved for her and only her.

"A heavy weight to carry. Something you know quite well," she says. My mother has never been shy about reminding me of how I fucked up. It's her way of keeping me grounded in reality; she's determined to never bloat my ego.

"It's not on the same scale though, is it? I kissed another woman; she hid my child from me for years," I protest.

"No, Cillian, it's not on the same scale. But don't downplay what you did. It was more than a kiss. Or two," she says, raising her eyebrow at me. "You fostered an emotional connection with another woman that blurred the line between friendship and something more. And you were so terrible at hiding it, that poor girl saw it all unraveling in front of her. You've both messed up. I love you, but I'm not going to lie to you for your own sense of righteous indignation."

"I can't just stop being mad about this, Mom, regardless of the part I played," I argue. "I can't get those years back."

"I'm not asking you not to be mad. Though maybe if you cut her some slack, she'll do the same. For the sake of my beautiful grandchild, you two need to find a way to coexist and that's likely going to mean you both eat some damn crow."

She leaves me with a pat on the shoulder and a mountain to climb. I'm no more ready to forgive Isla than she is, but she's had years to digest what I've only had days to do. My mom is right about Sadie; she's my priority and I do need to do what is right for her. Which isn't being in a constant battle with her mother.

Today's expansion draft announcement is being held on an old-ass boat. Being on the shores of Lake Union wasn't enough, I guess, so we'll be cruising the lake for the two-hour program. We're all still milling about in the parking lot waiting for the rest of the team staff and press to arrive. My mother talks to Isla's mom, who I haven't had the guts to go say hello to yet. My cheek is still healing, after all. But the view lets me see Isla when she pulls in. She still drives the same Honda sedan she's driven since she was sixteen. The car I'm bringing from Boston is worth about ten of her cars. I swallow down the lump in my throat as I walk over to help her unload Sadie.

Did she ever consider telling me about our daughter and asking me to provide child support?

Isla has always had an enormous amount of pride. Her family has money, of course, but she hated the idea of Coach paying her way in life or even getting her extravagant gifts. I never knew her to be materialistic or to covet the latest brand name anything.

Coach had to really put his foot down when he convinced her to move into the condo he'd bought near campus. And even then, she worked a part-time job after classes to pay the utilities and buy her own groceries, though he'd offered to do both.

With money from me, she'd have been able to afford a new car and a place to live where Sadie could have her own room.

I open the back door when Isla shuts off the engine.

"Hi, Daddy," my sweet girl says with the same timid look she gave me when she offered to start calling me that. I beam at her, and it washes away the apprehension between her dark brows.

"Hey, baby girl. How are you?" I fumble with the buckle of her car seat, and she places her small hands over mine to show me how to do it, making me laugh lightly. "Thanks."

"You're welcome," she says, easily. "I'm good. Mommy says we can have sketti for dinner."

"Oh yeah? Spaghetti is one of my favorites."

"Mine too," she confirms, as I hoist her out of the car.

"I think she has your pallet," Isla says behind me. It might be the first thing she's said to me unprompted. A small win, but a win nonetheless.

"You probably like grilled cheese too, huh?"

"Yes! But only if it's super gooey."

"I think you're right," I say, turning to Isla. Her eyes are rimmed in bright pink, a telltale sign she spent time crying recently and it hasn't had a chance to fade from what was likely an angry red. A safe bet it was because of me, even though I left her last night without signs of tears. I palm her cheek with the hand that isn't wrapped around Sadie. "You okay?"

She flinches, either from my touch or the softness in my tone. Evidently, it's easy to both hate her and care about her at the same time. If she showed signs of the same, I'd believe we could find some amicable place between her hate and mine.

"Why don't you go say hello to your grandmothers, Sadie. We'll be right behind you," I tell my daughter, placing her on her feet. "Isla?"

"It's not easy for me, either. Okay? This is hard." Her lip trembles, and my mother's words rush back. "You being back brings up a lot of... raw memories."

Isla was always the toughest, most confident girl I knew. Nothing ruffled her nerves. Her ire, sure, but not her nerves.

One time, we were maybe seventeen, we were hanging out with a bunch of the guys from the team and three of them broke into a fight. Isla, knowing her dad would kill them all, jumped in the middle of it and broke it up. A spitfire of five-foot-four and barely over a hundred pounds against three bulky hockey players, and she handled it like it was an ordinary occurrence that she dealt with daily. That's how she handled everything, head-on and straight forward.

It's how she dealt with me when I began getting closer to Trina, too. Isla routinely called me out on it, and I evaded the truth.

The woman standing in front of me now is not the same one I knew back then. Her spine is straight, chin lifted in defiance as her rose-colored lips pull taut. But the frayed edges show, the wear and tear of years that maybe haven't been so kind to her... I see them. I feel the pressure of them weighing me down as if I'm moving through quicksand.

Wrapping her up in my arms, her back to my chest, I look to where our daughter stands surrounded by family.

"You hate me, and I've never been so mad at anyone in my life as I am with you. But that curly-haired beauty over there is more important than that," I whisper into her ear through hair that smells like fresh rain and comfort. "We're going to have some knockdown, drag out fights, Isla. I think that's inevitable. But we're going to get through this. For her and for our family."

"I don't trust you."

"Fucking mutual, Isla. But we'll change that." If not fully, at least where Sadie is concerned, I'll prove myself. I'm making the promise to the only woman I've ever given a shit about, but also to the people watching us right now. Our mothers, who look on with concern, and Coach who looks like he's seconds away from marching over and keeping his promise of burying me six feet deep. "I'm not going to be a shitty father, Isla. I learned from the best man I know. Sadie comes first."

Her chest hitches at my words, knowing I'm talking about her dad. I pull her tighter, and after a long sigh, she finally relaxes with a nod.

"No tears today. This is a big day for us all, let's enjoy it. Set it all aside, we'll start wrestling in the mud tomorrow." With a final squeeze, I let her loose and lead her over to where everyone waits. If I can play nice, she fucking can, too. For a single day, anyway.

Vaughn and the few other guys that came in for this are grouped just past where our families stand. There is something important I need to do before I can go chat them up, though.

"Hi, Marney," I greet Isla's mother.

"Cillian." She turns toward me, presenting her back to the rest of the group.

"It's your turn to take a swing."

"Well, I'm sure you remember that's not quite my style," she says pleasantly. It's hard to read her right now. This could be feigned politeness for the crowd, or maybe she feels sorry for me. Marney is wholly unreadable with all her class and grace. "I was sorry to hear about your grandmother."

"What," Isla gasps.

"Thank you, Marney," I say to the older woman before addressing the younger. "Gran died a little over a year ago."

"I didn't know," she says, voice rattling over the words.

"I know, I couldn't… It doesn't matter. Not today, Isla."

"Cill…"

"Not today," I repeat before finding my new teammates. "Sadie, you want to meet some more of the Blades?"

"Yes!"

I introduce her as my daughter. Vaughn is the only one who shows any sign of surprise. Oliver Lehtinen, Axel Wallin, and Hugo Blom don't show any indication that me having a daughter is a shocking surprise. Sadie shakes hands with them all, very officially, before she runs back over to her grandmothers.

Hugo is a seasoned goalie who has played in The Show, an old term for the NHL, for a few years longer than I have. He's tall, but agile and lean. Outside of his pads, he's an unassuming guy. Suit him up and he's a dragon defending the treasure trove in his cave. The Blades were lucky to get him.

Axel and Oliver are both wingers. Axel has played pro for three years, he hasn't always been given the advantage of ice time, but when he has the chance-he's a sniper with his shot. Oliver is an all-around solid player. And a borderline goon, which will make him a fan favorite.

"She's cute," Oliver says with a nod who is giggling loudly with her mother. Pride like I've never known fills me up. Stupid really, I had such a small part in who or what she is as a tiny person. It's more powerful than what I experienced being drafted or playing my first NHL game, though.

"The cutest," I confirm.

"Her mom, too," Axel adds. Every muscle in my body tenses. She's not mine, but she sure as fuck isn't for any of these guys either. "You two together?"

"Not anymore. But watch it, Coach will have choice words if you make a move on one of his daughters."

"Speaking from experience?" Vaughn eyes me with that same knowing he had the other day. His brain is probably working overtime putting puzzle pieces together.

"Something like that." I laugh, trying to brush away the conversation. Our messy personal lives are none of his business. I may very well become friends with these men; I hope that's the case anyway. But we aren't there yet.

"Everyone ready," Coach asks as he steps up behind me. He flashes a smile to each of the others and a glare my way. I just smirk.

"Yes, sir," Oli says.

"Let's board this tin can," Axel jokes, heading toward the ramp to load.

I hold back and wait for my mother to catch up so we can follow my daughter aboard. We follow her closely, watching the youthful exuberance she has for everything. The way she marvels over all the newness of being on an old ferry boat is almost infectious. She leaves no surface uninspected or untouched.

After about twenty minutes, once the boat is on the part of the lake the press team wants, the program starts. First up is our General Manager, Jonathon Markel. He's a legend in the hockey world. Not only did he have a long and lustrous career as one of the best centers in the game, but he raised three sons who all played professionally as well. One of them has a son with the same phenomenal potential too. They're a motherfucking dynasty.

He mostly speaks about the long struggle it was to get a team in this city. It always struck me as strange that they didn't have one. Seattle and Vancouver practically bleed all over one another, and the youth and league hockey scene here is very well established. Every third person you meet here will have played as a kid, has a kid who plays, or is currently playing in some men's league. Seattle has always been a 'hockey town'. We're only making it legitimate.

Coach is next, he's never been wordy unless he's pissed off, so he keeps his speech short. It's a lot of gratitude to the city and the fans. Then Jonathan comes back up to start introducing the players.

Hugo is called up, handed a jersey, and asked to say a few words. My turn is coming but Sadie is still next to me, leaning her small body against my thigh.

"Do you want to go up there with me?" I whisper. Her eyes widen, and she shakes her head vehemently, making me laugh. I hand her my cell phone so the bulk of it won't show in my pocket on the camera. "Can you take this over to your mom and grandma for me?"

She nods and moves over to where the crowd is seated so she can climb up on Isla's lap. My ex-girlfriend makes eye contact with me. *Again.* We've been dancing this dance all day. She's struggling to keep her eyes off me, and it's impossible for me to look anywhere but at her. It's a happy day, Isla is all smiles. That same wide grin that used to pump life into my veins. Somehow, even through my disdain, it still pumps blood to certain parts.

At least she hasn't been glaring at me all damn day. A few times I've caught her with a look of longing. Or that's what I want to believe it is. As if maybe, there is a part of her that misses what we were the same way I do. An ember in her heart that still holds on to the heat of what we could have been. What we *should* have been.

Wishful thinking on my part, I'm sure. Why am I wishing for it anyway? She's a damned liar, she's betrayed me horrifically. Except I want, no... I need an amiable relationship with her. For Sadie. If that means fanning that tiny flame, I'm not above it.

Jesus, we're fucked up. Hot and cold, love and hate.

Blinking away from her eyes that are far too kind right now, I pay attention to Jonathon as he calls me front and center.

"Welcome back to Seattle, Cillian," he says, extending his hand out to me.

"Thank you."

"How does it feel?"

"It feels like coming home." I face the camera crew, but I speak to Isla and Sadie. "Seattle has always been a special place for me. It's where my family is, where I want my daughter to be raised, and I couldn't be happier to be back."

Isla's shock is apparent. She must not have expected me to claim Sadie so openly and publicly, but it feels right. More right than so much else in my life that the words flow right out. If I knew more about my daughter, I could talk about her for hours. She'd be my favorite subject.

Of course, that isn't what Jonathon asks me about. Instead, he peppers me with a few game-related questions and I answer all of them the way I'm trained to do. Isla doesn't break eye contact with me until I'm walking off the small makeshift stage. She flinches and looks down in her lap. So I don't miss when her features melt from the awe she wore only a few seconds ago to the haunted mask she's had since I arrived back into her life.

I don't know what happened, but I get the feeling any progress we made today just jumped over the side of this boat and into the deep, dark waters of Lake Union.

9

ISLA

"It's not four." I open the door for Cillian at three-thirty. The least the guy could do is follow instructions.

"You know I'm a perpetual early bird."

"I don't know you at all."

"Do we have to start this on that note?" Cillian asks. He sounds as tired as I feel.

"It's going to get ugly, but no, we don't need to start ugly." I lead him to the living room and curl my legs under me as I sit on the far end of the couch.

"I want to get to know Sadie," he says, taking his own seat on the other end. "I want shared custody."

"That's something we should take slow," I say. My voice shakes the slightest bit. My biggest fear for years has been that he'd waltz back into our lives and try to take her from me.

"I don't want slow, Isla. I want every spare moment until I know everything there is to know about my daughter. That's fair of me to ask." His fist clenches atop his knee.

"Fair? Nothing about us is fair. Fair would have been you not falling for another woman as soon as you left Seattle."

"It wasn't as soon as I left. And I didn't fall for her," he argues, standing back up to pace the patch of carpet in front of me. "Fair would have been you telling me I was going to have a child as soon as you knew."

"I did," I grit out. "But you were too wrapped up in *her* to spare me the time."

"I'm pretty sure I'd fucking remember that, Isla," he says, rubbing a hand down his face. "Let's take a step back. I can apologize until my death bed, and you still wouldn't forgive me. But this is about Sadie and what's best for her. Can we focus on that? On her?"

"What exactly are you asking for?"

"Equal time. We'll need to work around my schedule, of course, but Mom would love time with her, too. She could take her on my nights if I'm out of town."

"Equal?" He's kidding. He *must* be kidding.

"Yeah. Three nights every other week. Four on the other weeks."

"You're joking," I say, shakily. "If she keeps her nights with my mom, which she loves, that will leave me with just two nights every other week."

For as hard as I fight it, the panic starts to rise. My vision blurs and it gets increasingly harder to breathe. He doesn't get to take her away from me. She's my life, my heart. My whole reason for being. He doesn't get to take her away and raise her with fucking Trina.

He doesn't get to teach her to be a horrible person who is duplicitous and without loyalty. She's a good girl and she's staying that way.

They can't have her.

They don't get to have her.

"Isla."

"You don't get to take her," I squeak out between labored breathing. "Trina doesn't get to take her away from me, too."

"Isla."

"I won't let it… I won't let it happen, again."

"Isla! Fucking breathe. Right now!" His hands grip my head and hold it mere inches from his. "Breathe."

I hiccup and gasp into the horrified expression he wears as he looks on helplessly. His fingers rub my temples back and forth. Focusing on the small movements, comforting, despite who the fingers belong to.

"Breathe with me," he says. I concentrate on the rise and fall of my chest, matching the rhythm to the pace of his thumbs. "What's happening?"

"Panic attack," I rasp.

"Since when do you have those?"

"You're not taking her away from me," I say, a little stronger now. A little less manic. Completely ignoring his question and letting my rage take over my fear.

"I'm not trying to take her away from you. I'm trying to share her."

"Like you wanted me to share you with Trina? Where it was all weighted to your favor and I was left with scraps? Like that?"

Cillian curses while rising back to his feet, then moves to the far side of the room.

"Fuck, Isla. I'm sorry. How many times do you want me to say it?"

"Considering that's the first time you've ever said it, try it a few more times and we'll see if it's enough!" I rise, too. Unable to stay seated now that my temper is in full swing.

"What?"

"What part didn't you understand?"

"All of it," he roars. "I don't understand anything, Isla."

"Welcome to the fucking club, Cillian. I haven't understood anything for years!"

His large frame, so much bigger than mine, barrels around the room like an angry bear. I can't help the hazy awe. Cillian's presence is larger than life, naturally exuding a sense of strength and dominance. Dad and I used to talk about how teammates naturally took his lead even though he was oblivious to it. Cockiness was never in his wheelhouse; he was even a little doubtful of himself. Always second-guessing his talent and skill. It worked for him though, because it made him strive to be better.

He's different these days. Now, I think he knows exactly how talented he is and how much power he holds. Me challenging him the way I do sends him into a tizzy.

It's fun to watch, the way his temples crease and his forearms tense. I could keep attendance for hours. Which is probably a really, really bad sign for him. Because this Cillian, the one running a rut in my carpet, gives me joy.

I like his suffering all too much.

"We're not going to get anywhere with Sadie until we rehash the past, are we?"

"The past where you were a cheating asshole who ditched your pregnant girlfriend? Probably not."

"You broke up with me," he accuses, pointing a finger at me.

"As if you left me other options! You were snuggled up with her every spare moment, getting hard and taking pictures of it as if you were a Magic Mike dancer instead of an NHL player. Not to mention answering calls while she had your dick in her hand," I roll my eyes and stomp to the other side of the room.

"Isla, I don't know what the hell you're talking about." He sighs.

"How are you in so much denial?"

"I made stupid decisions," he snaps. "Don't you think I know that? It was harder than I expected. The pressure, the distance. Then there was this nice woman paying me more attention than I knew what to do with, and who understood everything I was going through because she'd seen it with other players before. I fucked up. I know I fucked up, but I was stupid and nineteen."

"So was I," I rage. "I was nineteen. Confused and alone, watching the guy I loved fall in love with another woman. Nineteen and pregnant. Nineteen and having to figure out how much of my life was going to change, how much was even under my control. Nineteen and growing a whole human inside me while I was so thoroughly heartbroken. Nineteen and having emotions I couldn't understand. Nineteen and being hospitalized because my emotional state was so messy, I stressed my body to the limit and ended up in pre-term labor. *Nineteen* and thinking I was going to lose my baby because I couldn't understand why a man who loved me threw me away like I was nothing but trash!"

"Isla."

"And now you're back and making demands as if I'm just going to hand over the life that I fought so hard for to you and your goddamned girlfriend? Not in this lifetime, Cillian," I say, holding my hands up to stop him from getting any closer. "You wrecked me. You let her wreck me and it will only be over my dead, cold body that I let you do that same thing to my daughter."

Cillian stares as awestruck as I was only moments ago.

"I don't even know where to start," he finally says, much calmer than either of us has been since he walked into my house.

"The floor is yours," I offer, then move to the kitchen to pour myself a healthy dose of pinot noir. I hold up the bottle to him, but he shakes his head.

"She's not my girlfriend. Trina was never that," he starts.

"Please spare me the details," I groan out.

"No details, I promise. Just a quick clarification before we get to the more important things," he says, trailing me to sit beside me on the sofa. He's closer this time, and I don't like it. In fact, I despise the way it makes me feel. "When did you have to go to the hospital?"

"Far too early."

"How early, Isla?" He leans toward me, pressing his stupid newfound bossiness on me, making me more uncomfortable.

"I was only four months pregnant the first time I ended up in the emergency room. I was closer to six months along when I went into preterm labor."

"What does that even mean, Isla?"

"It means that she tried to come too soon. They gave me an injection of something," I say, waving a hand. I can't remember what it was called because it was too much to pay attention to when I was as worried as I was. "Kept me overnight to make sure I didn't continue to dilate, then sent me home with a long list of instructions. I had contractions every day from then on, but in the end, Sadie waited until a week after her due date to finally show up."

"When was that?"

Right, he doesn't even know his daughter's birthday.

"April 2nd." My voice is quiet, with maybe a little shame seeping in. This is not the way I wanted to raise a child. Sometimes life deals you a tricky hand and you make a choice that's best at the time, but then it snowballs. Growing into a larger problem that quickly feels insurmountable. The news of Sadie's birth is a discussion we should have had ages ago. I know that. He knows that, too.

"And she was healthy? She *is* healthy?" His concern is another knife in my side.

"She's perfect, Cillian. She's never had anything more than a head cold."

"And you?"

"Me?"

"You, Isla. Were you okay?"

No. No, I was far from okay. But I am now.

"I'm not your concern."

"That's a lie."

"It's not," I argue. "I wasn't a concern after you left for Boston, and I haven't been since."

"Another lie." Cillian lifts my wine glass, placing it on the coffee table so he can turn me to face him. "I loved you. Even after I went to Boston, I loved you. It was agony, Isla. Every day without you was."

"You don't know agony, Cillian. Agony is the bone-deep knowledge of the truth but hearing the lies day after day. It's seeing the evidence right in front of you and being helpless to do anything about it. Misery is having regular reminders that you weren't the choice."

"What reminders? Sadie?"

"No," I balk. "Sadie is nothing but love. She doesn't remind me of you. The reminders come from the same place they always have."

"What do you mean?"

"I mean, Trina."

"What does she have to do with anything? I betrayed you, and you betrayed me."

"Yes, you betrayed me. Just like she wanted you to. And she made sure I knew," I say.

"Trina is… a subject. But she didn't cause this. I did."

"You're still a liar. Or you're plain stupid. Which is it? Because there is no way that woman had the information she did without your involvement."

"What are you even talking about?"

Huh.

He's actually confused. Which means he has no idea what she's been up to.

"Stupid it is, then," I say, shrugging. "She's been sending me shit for years. Mostly now, it's only on special occasions, like my birthday or the anniversary of our first date. Dates she could have only gotten from you."

"What? Why?"

"Why?" I laugh. "Ask her, Cillian. You've been with her longer than you were with me. Do you honestly not know her by now?"

"I'm not with her," he argues, clamping his thumb and pointer finger on my chin to turn my face to him. "I've never been in a relationship with Trina."

The laugh bursts out of me spontaneously and uncontrolled.

"Label it whatever you want, but I won't be playing into your fantasy. You know I saw what she texted you yesterday, right?"

When Sadie eventually left his side so he could get in front of the cameras and press, she'd placed his cell phone into my hand. Within minutes of him mentioning his daughter on live television, a notification popped up on the screen. Since the idiot doesn't have privacy settings, it was right there for me to see.

TRINA:

She had a baby and didn't tell you? What a cunt!
I can't wait to meet your daughter!

She followed it up with several kissy face emojis. It ruined the rest of my day for me, then it ruined my night because I was so mad at myself for letting her get to me. *Again.*

"She shouldn't have called you that. It was out of line and completely uncalled for," he says, contritely.

"Tell *her* that, not me. And under no circumstances does she ever get to meet Sadie. That's one rule I will never bend on."

"I will tell her," he agrees with ease. "If I ever even talk to her again."

"It's that easy?"

"Yes, it is, Isla. Trina is in Boston, and I've already told you we aren't in a relationship. She's just a friend."

"You can stop lying now. I already think so poorly of you that the truth won't make a difference there. In fact, I might find it admirable," I snark. Cillian grins, wide and bright. Even his eyes are smiling at me. "What's funny?"

"Not funny. Refreshing," he says. "I've missed how honest and blunt you always were. Besides my mom and Coach, you're the only other person I could count on to not constantly blow smoke up my ass."

"I'll happily list all your misgivings any time you need to hear them," I tell him, and his smile grows impossibly larger.

"What kind of bullshit has Trina sent you? And how does she even know your birthday or when our anniversary was?"

"Ask her."

"I'm asking you."

"Why, don't you trust her to tell you the truth?"

"I do. But she isn't here. You are, and you're the one I want to talk to."

"Ask her," I repeat. For one, they aren't things I particularly want to rehash. Also, I don't think she'll tell him the truth. If he even decides to ask her. Call it a test of sorts, but I want to see if he confronts her and what she says. "She was there when I told you I was pregnant, you may as well keep her in the loop now."

"What the fuck are you even talking about? You never told me," he says adamantly.

"I did! I video called you hours after that call to Torsten and you were in bed with her."

"Bullshit! Who's the liar now, Isla?"

"It's the fucking truth. I thought maybe you were tired or something because it was late, and you weren't making much sense, but it was because you were talking to her, not me. And she ate it up and made sure I saw her and what she was doing to you."

"I didn't fuck around with Trina the night you broke up with me," he says, his brow furrowing as if he's trying hard to recall something.

"You sure about that? Because I know what I saw, and I'll remember it clearly until the day I fucking die!"

"Okay, calm down. We're not getting anywhere here," he says. He gnaws on his bottom lip with his thumb for a moment, eyes bouncing between mine. Cillian's trying to suss out the truth, or remember things he's forgotten, but the pieces aren't lining up for him. "I won't push you about Sadie just yet, if you can promise to try to accommodate me. Let me get to know her, Isla. Let me be a real daddy to her."

Fuck, if that doesn't just hit me straight in the uterus.

It's what I've always wanted for Sadie. Cillian in her life and making her the priority she deserves to be. He seems genuine in his desire, even though my heart is screaming at me that we can't trust this giant looking at us with a strange mix of longing and determination that still borders on anger.

Letting him spend time with her isn't a big hurdle here. Trust is, and my lack of faith in him to be responsible with her body and soul.

"She doesn't get to meet any of the string of women you will probably have in your life."

"Done," he says, again so easily it causes me to throw him a side-eye.

"We'll work up to her spending nights with you, because you have no idea how to care for a toddler."

He makes a vaguely agreeable noise after a long minute of narrowing his gaze on me. "But I won't wait too long on that. Once I get settled in my new place, I'll get her room set up and you'll help me learn what I need to know."

"Oh, will I?" I bite back. Not because I won't help, of course I will, for Sadie's sake. But because he's being so arrogantly domineering.

"You will," he says, leaving no argument. "There is a lot I want to fight with you about, but not that. Not her or my time with her. I won't push you if you won't push me."

"Fine." I sigh. "I'll try. It's hard though, when I hate you so much."

"The feeling is completely fucking mutual, Cole," he says, the corners of his mouth tipping up in amusement. "Speaking of last names…"

"I know what you're going to say," I tell him, holding my hand up. "Prove you're in this for real. Prove you aren't going to break her little heart, and then we'll discuss her becoming a Wylder."

"I'm never going to break her heart, Isla." He squeezes my hand.

"You said that about me once, Cillian."

10

CILLIAN

I f I could go the rest of my life without hearing the hurt in Isla's voice, it would be enough to say I lived a good life. Forget the NHL, the Memorial Cup, the possibility of the Stanley Cup at some future date. None of those personal accomplishments would compare to living out a life without the reminder of how I betrayed her.

Regardless of where we are now, or of how she's hurt me and my relationship with my daughter; the Isla Cole I was dating at nineteen did not deserve what I did to her.

She's still that young woman to me. I still love that person. There's still the urge to haul her over my shoulder, drop her onto her bed, and sink so far into her that she'll never be able to rid herself of me. I'll never stop wanting to poke at her until she bites back because I know how that works her up. I remember how her body responds when it's on that adrenaline rush she gets every time her temper is flared.

I recall how hard she comes, and I want to take her there again. And again.

My reaction to her is bone-deep, it always has been. Isla was the first girl to give me a boner. She was my sexual awakening. That's not to say I haven't learned a lot since being with her, I have, and I would love to show her. Even if only so I could take it all back.

So she can know I'm the best she'd ever have and then know she can never have me again. As much as I want to fuck her brains out, I equally want her to miss me the way I've missed her. To yearn for me the way I've yearned for the tiniest fucking scrap of her attention.

Fire and ice. I burn for her and want to freeze her out. Something tells me she feels the same about me.

"I am sorry, Isla."

"I wish I knew how to believe that."

"Maybe in time. After we become friends," I say. After we learn these new versions of us and build a new foundation to build on.

"I don't need you as a friend, Wylder."

Need? Probably not. Want? Well, that's a different story. She forgets how well I know her. Isla is as tortured by me as I am by her. While her eyes pierce me, her lips part slightly and her chest heaves with extra effort.

"No? Maybe you want something more then," I goad her.

"Ah, you want to fuck, Cillian," she asks, pushing back and making my blood move to my lap. "We could do that. I'm sure it would be fun. But it will never be more."

Fun? Fucking her again would be soul shattering. Just then, a knock sounds at her door. She rolls her eyes and gets up to answer.

"Why is everyone so early today?"

"Hello to you too, babe," a deep, amused voice says. I can't see the intruder from where I sit, so I stand to move closer. "You okay?"

"Cillian is here."

"Fuck. Do you need to reschedule?"

"No. Come on in, you'll just have to wait while I get ready," Isla tells him, stepping aside to open the door wider.

"We can stay in. You know I don't mind," the man says at the same time I see who it is.

Tyson Murphy, star forward for Vancouver. He played for Coach before he moved up to the NHL. He was a hotshot even then. Made enough noise for us all to take more than passing notice the year he became eligible.

"Can you give us a minute," she asks him. He raises his chin and presses a kiss to her forehead.

"Wylder," he greets me on the way to Isla's bedroom.

"Murph." I attempt the same casual acknowledgment as he has. This is awkward as all fuck, to say the least. He's not surprised by me at all, not like I am by him being here. As soon as he's out of sight, I charge at Isla, backing her up against the wall. "Tyson Murphy is your date?"

Her defiance shows with her raised chin, a sinister smile playing on her lips.

"Unlike some, I don't go slumming. I looked for better after you. Or did you think my vagina has been a haunted house collecting nothing but cobwebs and the ghosts of my past?"

I burst with laughter; her snark compares to no other woman I've ever known. Her smirk gives way to a full smile, and she starts laughing, too. Another trait I remember, she succumbs to emotional contagion easily. She's the girl who needs to laugh when she hears a baby giggle, and she cries at videos of puppies giving sad eyes.

Maybe I've been going about this all wrong. Battling her is a gut reaction, but I know better ways to get under her defenses. She hasn't changed that much.

"No, that's not what I thought. Though I didn't expect you to be in a relationship with one of the biggest up and comers in all of hockey."

"It's not a relationship. I don't do relationships with professional hockey players." Just like that, her humor vanishes.

"Good, you shouldn't," I agree, turning the dig at me back around. "They can't be trusted."

It's a lie, and she knows it. Of all professional sprots, hockey is probably the most family oriented. So many of the players are husbands, and fathers who take their roles seriously. We don't have the same 'player' stigma as some of the other leagues. Yeah, every team has its share of puck bunnies or whatever the hell you want to call the more exuberant female fans that make their presence known. It's almost exclusively the young single players that partake in their company. Most of the women don't even try to fuck the married guys. Or, at least, that's what I've witnessed.

And I don't know any married player that gets his dick wet by random strangers in every city we visit. It's not part of our game.

"Don't I know that all too well." That hurt is back in her voice. It's the last damn time I want to hear it.

"You do, Cole. Again, I'm sorry. I'll keep saying it until you know you can trust it and me. All I'm asking is for a chance to be the man I'm supposed to be to our daughter, okay?" She doesn't answer. I imagine all the thoughts swirling in her head. It's fine, because I'd rather her confused and contemplative than pissed off. That's the new game, keeping Isla on her toes. Tracing my palm firmly up the column of her neck, I still it just beneath her upturned chin. "Okay?"

Her hard swallow presses against my hand, but she still doesn't verbalize her answer. I see the answer in her eyes though, she wants to give me this chance. She's fighting that desire, and that's okay.

I steal a quick, but deep kiss to her lips.

"I'm leaving Monday for Boston. The owners of the house I'm buying here are letting me rent it until the sale closes. I'm going back to get the movers going and drive my car back. I'll be gone for about a week. Tomorrow night, I'll stop by to say goodbye to Sadie."

"Okay," she says, dazed from that kiss.

"Have a great date, Isla," I say before leaving, wanting her to have a nice time but knowing I'll be on her mind the rest of the night.

The following day, Isla is in a fantastic mood. The kind of mood you're in after you've had an amazing fuck. It sours my already bad mood. I was up all night racking my brain and scouring my memory for the truth in this whole sordid mess, and I'm exhausted from it. But what really does me in is Sadie telling me all about the brunch she had with Mommy and Ty.

"I ate booberry pancakes that were this big," she says excitedly, spreading her hands out bigger than her head.

"Those are one of my favorites," I tell her, trying to keep the conversation on us and not Murphy.

"Ty loves them too."

Of course, he does.

"Did you have coffee to drink with your pancakes?"

"No." She laughs. "That's for old peoples. Ty brought me a new puck. Do you want to see?"

"Sure," I agree, begrudgingly. Isla notices my discomfort, and surprisingly, looks a little sympathetic as Sadie pulls out pucks from her nightstand one by one. There are a handful of commemorative ones from special games or nights. There is also an official game one signed by Tyson, and one from the season he won the Calder Trophy. I feign excitement. Sadie loves them, her pride in the collection evident by the big, crooked smile when she shows me each one. How am I supposed to feel about her having a puck with Murphy's face on it when I didn't even know she existed? Why does Tyson get to know I have a daughter, but I don't?

Bitterness is hard to swallow down so instead it manifests in that anger toward Isla that is becoming all too fucking familiar. None of this is my kids fault though, so I talk to her about everything she wants to talk about until her words start to slow, and her eyes start to droop.

"I have to leave in the morning to go back to Boston," I tell her.

"Why," she asks, her eyes popping back open.

"I need to get my cat and my car so I can bring them back here."

"You have a cat?"

"I do. I didn't like living by myself, so I got a cat to hang out with me."

"But it's been by itself now, cuz you're here."

"Yep, so I should go get her, huh?"

"I know that's right," she says slowly. "What's her name?"

"Saint," I whisper.

"Like Mommy."

I hum. "Go to sleep now, princess. I'll call you every night."

"Night, Daddy."

"Night, baby girl."

Isla stands outside the door; I grab her elbow and lead her down the hall.

"You named your cat after me?"

"You let another man play father to her?" I shoot back.

"She loves hockey and gets excited by knowing professional players."

"Like her dad?" I accuse.

"Listen," she says, getting bent out of shape quickly. "I told you. Whether you remember that or not, isn't my fault. Since that night, every decision I made was for Sadie. I couldn't afford to be weak or sad because she needed me. And it was *hard*, Cillian. Harder than you could ever fucking know. So, you don't get to come in here and be critical about the people, or the relationships, that kept me and Sadie healthy."

"What does that even mean, Isla? You've never been weak a day in your life."

"You haven't been around enough to say that. You missed a lot while you were fucking Trina." She struggles to get the words out. When she walks toward the bathroom, I let her go without a fight.

"What the fuck are you doing, Wylder," Willa asks, startling me. I didn't even see her hiding out in the kitchen.

"Fuck if I know, Willa. I'm not sure about anything anymore."

"Do you still love her?"

"Of course, I do. I never wanted to hurt her. This isn't all on me though, she's made mistakes, too."

"Sure, she has," Willa says, propping her chin in her hand as she leans on the counter to study me. "She also had a hard pregnancy and things didn't get easier after Sadie's birth. It's not a lie when she says it was harder than you can understand, and she still carries a lot of guilt."

"She should feel guilty for not telling me she gave birth to my daughter," I argue. "I'm not the only villain in this story."

"Maybe neither you nor Isla are the villains," she says as if I should know this already. "But someone let the villain into your relationship and that sure as fuck wasn't my sister. She tried, Cillian. And at nearly every step that twat, Trina, was standing in the way. But Isla wasn't the same woman after you broke up. She wasn't as strong. You want her to open up to you about everything you weren't here for? You're going to have to earn back some trust. She won't tell you anything if she doesn't feel safe."

Trina has been blowing up my phone since my plane landed in Boston. Each notification brings me closer to the idea that she has more to do with my current predicament than I know. I don't know what she could have possibly been sending Isla after our breakup, or why. I need to find out, though. And I will, but on my timeline, not hers.

When I ignore another incoming call, my mom sighs.

"She's relentless."

She knows everything I know, I laid it all out for her on the flight. She's never liked Trina much. On the flip side of that, she loved Isla from their first meeting. Like always, she's not hiding her opinion. While we talked about the little hints of information Isla and Willa have given me, Mom cried. There's some woman's intuition and motherly shit there that she understands more than I do.

It's harder and harder to hold on to my anger for Isla when I see the hurt in her eyes like I did last night. Hell, I even saw it in Willa's and my mother's. Isla's reactions tell me she hasn't been making decisions out of spite or to pay me back for being a complete asshole.

I'm scum. No matter what she has done, this all starts with me being a piece of shit.

"I know. I'll deal with it before I head back to Seattle."

"You need to tell Trina to stop sending things to Isla," she stresses.

"We don't even know if she's been doing that."

"Cillian, why would Isla lie about that?"

She wouldn't. Isla doesn't have a vengeful heart; she wouldn't make something up for the sole purpose of getting back at me for being a cheating idiot. Isla wouldn't, but I'm starting to think Trina would.

TRINA:

> Call me when you land. I want to see you as much as I can before you leave.

"She wouldn't."

"Right. Get to the bottom of it, fast. For the sake of my granddaughter, if not yourself."

ME:

> Already landed. Dropping Mom, then headed home. Meet me there?

Trina sits in her car that's parked in the guest parking spot assigned to my apartment when the car drops me off. This woman has been a constant in my life for years. I thought I knew everything there was to know about her. Now, I look at her and it's like I never knew her at all. She's spoon-fed me only what she's wanted, it's not like I've met her family or even friends of hers outside of circle of team staff.

Analyzing it, I realize there is a pattern to Trina's friendship. Anything I ever went through here in Boston, she had a story ready to go about how she could relate. That used to seem comforting, when instead it was probably all bullshit stories to create a connection that wasn't real.

It hits me that Isla probably feels the same way about me that I feel about Trina right now. My stomach knots with the truth of it. When you tell someone to trust you, to place their faith in you, you should mean it. You should live it. I didn't hold up my end with Isla. Apparently, Trina didn't hold her end up with me.

Whatever has happened, tonight, I get to the fucking rock bottom of it.

"Did you know she was pregnant?" As soon as she steps out of her car, I demand an answer.

"Isla? Or course not, how would I?"

"She says she called me and told me, and you were there."

"Isla has lied to you for years. Why would she start telling the truth now," Trina answers with an eye roll. Her jaw twitches though, and she shuffles her feet in an uncomfortable manner.

"I remember getting drunk with Tor that night, and I vaguely remember you showing up. But I didn't invite you into my bed for months after." I was so sure Isla would change her mind about cutting me out of her life. That if I just played my cards right, gave her the space she needed and didn't fuck around, I'd have the chance to win her back. Isla is stubborn as fuck and eventually the toll was too much, I had to accept that I'd lost her and if I wasn't careful, I was going to lose my career, too. Though I wasn't making advances on Trina, she was still coming around to listen to my woes.

"What night?"

"The night she broke up with me," I stress, not buying that she isn't following along.

"I don't know what you're talking about."

That's a lie. Not her first tonight, and as the conversation goes on, I realize it's not her last either.

"You were there that night, weren't you?"

"It's been years, Cillian. I think I stopped by, but how can you expect me to remember? It was your relationship that tanked, not mine."

"Did you get in bed with me?"

"It wouldn't have been the only night I had to help you into bed. You got out of hand more than a few times after Isla broke up with you," she says, shrugging.

"Why am I getting the impression you're full of shit right now, Trina?" My voice is dangerously low right now. She's walking on thin fucking ice right now.

"Because she's putting bullshit in your head," she whines.

We talk in circles for a few minutes before I decide it's a lost cause.

"Go home, Trina. We're fucking done."

"You don't mean that," she argues. "She's lying to you, not me!"

"Why would she lie, Trina? What would that gain her?" Fuck, this situation is infuriating. I'm over all the bullshit and wish I could move back time to avoid this bitch altogether.

"Because she wants you back!"

"She doesn't," I say with a laugh that sounds as crazy as all of Trina's excuses. "She hates me."

She can't hide her smile as it grows snidely over her tear-stained face.

"You're happy the mother of my child hates me?"

"No," she protests, despite the evident lie.

"Get the fuck out of here, Trina. Don't come back and stay the fuck out of my life."

11

ISLA

CILLIAN:

Will you look at this and tell me if it's okay for
Sadie's room, please?

The link I click on takes me to a children's furniture listing for a bed that has a tent built over it. It's adorable but excessive.

ME:

She'll love it, but she'll grow out of it in a few
years.

CILLIAN:

I'll buy her a new one when she does. But, like, it
looks safe, right?

He's been messaging me since he left a few days ago. They've all been about Sadie, and they've all been without any accusations or animosity. I promised him I would try to let him be the man he needs to be to our daughter, and I won't go back on that.

ME:

It's a safe bed.

His nervousness is cute. I hate admitting that because it's Cillian and I still hate him in so many ways. This also serves as a reminder that had he been around while I was pregnant, he would have experienced all of this at the same time I did. We would have navigated it together. The way it should have been. But now, if I give him an inch, it's only for Sadie. Not because of the way his bullshit sneak attack kisses make my body react.

Tyson called me out on it the other night. Accusing me of thinking of my other ex, instead of him. I couldn't even deny it. Ty is a good guy and understands my dilemma, even if he doesn't like it. It sure as hell didn't stop him from fucking my brains out, which was a nice tension reliever. Sex is a wonderful balm for my nerves, even if the effects are temporary. At least it led to a good night's sleep, which has been harder to come by since Cillian's return to my life.

CILLIAN:

Can I call you?

ME:

Why? You talked to Sadie before she went to bed.

CILLIAN:

Please, Cole.

Ugh.

ME:

Fine.

"Wylder," I say when I answer his call.

"Hi," he says with a softness I haven't heard from since that day at the office.

"Hi."

"Will you tell me about the day Sadie was born?"

"Cillian."

"Please, Isla," he interrupts. "There is so much I'm asking Sadie directly. I know her favorite color is orange on rainy days and green on sunny ones. She only likes cold meats because she doesn't like to think about animals getting cooked. Unless it's Hawaiian pizza, she makes an exception for that. Her favorite song, currently, is about a horse by Little Nas something or other. But she can't tell me about the parts of her life that she doesn't remember. I need you for that. I'm obsessed with our daughter, Isla. I want to know everything."

Before he left for Boston, he told her he would call her every night. I was sure he'd fail. He hasn't, though. In fact, he usually calls several times a day. Cillian even resorts to calling my mom when she's watching Sadie while I work. If he thinks of something he wants to know about her, he doesn't wait to find out.

It's hard to argue with him when he's making that kind of enthusiastic effort.

"It was a Sunday. The night before I dragged Willa out to dinner because I had a feeling it was going to be my last chance for a while, and I was weirdly craving crab legs. I woke up early the following morning and the contractions I'd been having felt different. Timing them proved they were coming about every twenty minutes."

"Did you go straight to the hospital?"

"No. I ate breakfast, even though they had told me not to do that. I didn't want to have an empty stomach though; in case it was a long delivery."

"What did you eat?"

I've told this story before, and nobody has ever asked this. They'll ask about the pain, the discomfort, or prompt me in some way to hurry the story along to more about Sadie. But never about the small details.

"Eggo waffles. Two of them."

"With peanut butter and maple syrup," he adds.

"Of course." I laugh. "Then I repacked my hospital bag. It had been sitting by the front door for so many months, I hardly remembered what was in it."

"What goes in a maternity hospital bag?"

"Clothes for her to come home in. Clothes for me to come home in, diapers, baby blankets. Any necessary comfort items for staying at the hospital, headphones, cell charger, things like that. Personal care items like hairbrushes and deodorant. Pads because you bleed so much."

"How much?"

"Why would you want to know that." I wrinkle my nose.

"I want to know everything."

"It's a lot, at first. Eventually it slows down, but it lasted for about eight weeks. And you have to take extra care when you get an episiotomy."

"A what?"

"The cut they make to, um... enlarge the hole enough for your baby's head to get through."

"Fucking hell, they do that?"

"Yeah, it's common. They numb you so you don't feel it, but I could hear them cutting me. Like, cutting through leather or something," I tell him, still shuddering at the memory. "Anyway, after I repacked, I woke Willa to take me to the hospital. Mom and Dad met us there. Sadie was still taking her time though and after a few hours of not enough progress, they broke my water. She came about two hours after that."

"Her delivery went okay?"

"Yeah, Cillian. She was great, healthy and loud. I was really weak and passed out every time I tried to get up, but that stopped after the first night. Dad almost passed out too when I delivered the afterbirth. We were quite the pair."

"The afterbirth?"

"They don't teach guys shit, do they," I tease. "The placenta. It pretty much just falls out onto the floor of the delivery room. Mom had C-sections with us, so Dad had never experienced it like that before. We still tease him about it."

"How long did you stay in the hospital?"

"They only let you stay one night unless you have a bunch of complications or whatever."

"You're fucking kidding me?"

"No."

"I know professional hockey players that have had less trauma to their bodies than producing a whole new human being who had longer hospital stays."

"Yeah, maybe. But that's the way it works," I dismiss. There is little I want to talk about less than the time after Sadie and I went home. I'm no longer depressed but I still have moments where I feel that guilt for not being strong enough to combat Post Partum Depression. Even though I know that isn't how it works. Since the day I decided I was going to stay pregnant I wanted to be the best mommy to my child. For a few months there, I wasn't.

Cillian hasn't earned that story from me yet.

"Do you have pictures from when you were pregnant?"

"Some," I hedge.

"Will you send me some?"

"No."

"Please? I won't say anything about how big you got," Cillian begs. That's the thing, though. I didn't ever get very big because I was always too stressed out. He repeats his plea, "Please."

"Hang on." Pulling up my photos, I find the right album and send a few, select ones through. Cillian doesn't say anything right away. I imagine him studying each one, seeing my gaunt cheekbones but swollen pot belly. Does he see the same things I see when I look at them? The pain, the sorrow, the pure anxiety written on my face because I didn't understand then that I wouldn't be raising this child by myself. Or does he only see Sadie growing and none of what surrounds her?

"Thank you," he eventually says without any judgment. "Tomorrow, the guys are having a going away party for me. I'll leave the following morning to drive back. Won't be stopping more than necessary so it shouldn't take too long."

"Okay. Drive carefully."

"I will." Silence descends again, conversations between us are always awkward like this. Neither of us knows exactly how to navigate the other anymore. What used to be so easy and natural is now jagged and hard to traverse.

"I'm sorry about your grandmother. I wish…" I wish I could have been there for her funeral. I wish I had known. I wish for too much but none of it should be said. Not to him, anyway.

"I know. Thank you," he says, giving me my out. "By the way, I named my cat after my favorite pussy."

Cillian hangs up before I have the chance to formulate a response.

"You're going to fall in love with him again," Willa says the following night. Kit's here and we're huddled in the living room, watching the latest episode of some teen romance show on Netflix.

"It takes more than one amicable conversation for me to fall in love. I haven't forgotten what he did," I protest. Admittedly, my body has. My mind and my heart remember so clearly the trauma of losing him to another.

What a stupid way to think about it. I didn't lose him. Losing him implies I was negligent or inattentive. And that just wasn't the case. Cillian wasn't a set of keys I misplaced, and I only needed to retrace my steps to uncover his location.

I always knew where he was. He was with her, the woman he chose to spend time with. The one he let into our lives and drop little tiny bombs to disrupt and dismantle what we'd built over the years. Funny that it only took months to destroy it all.

Or, you know, not funny at all.

"All I'm saying is the way to your heart is through your daughter."

"I know that's right," Kit says, laughing because she's using Sadie's current signature line. "But maybe, it's not a bad thing. Is it possible he's changed?"

"Stop with your bleeding heart, Kit," Willa teases. "Once a cheater, always a cheater."

"Statistically, that's not true. Studies say less than half cheat again, and somewhere between sixty and seventy-five percent of couples stay together after a cheating incident." Kit is a statistics major and this is her favorite game to play.

"Are those studies based on physical cheating only or do they include emotional cheating, too," I ask out of curiosity. Cillian did both with Trina. Except, it wasn't the physical cheating that bothered me most. It was how close their friendship grew, how much time they spent together.

How often he *wanted* to be with her. That felt like the biggest betrayal of all, because it was personal. It wasn't just biology.

"I'm not sure; I'd imagine just physical. But I can look it up if you want."

"Nah, just curious."

"Can we talk about other men now? Like, when is Zander going to fall in love with me," Willa asks. She's always had a little crush on him. Okay, big crush is more accurate. Zan isn't looking for a relationship right now though. And then there is the matter of Willa not having a dick. He likes vagina, but he loves dick.

"Are you in love with him? Or do you just want that *d*," Kit asks.

"Why can't it be both?"

"It can be," I tell her. "Just don't pin all your hopes and dreams on him. He's young, talented, and could end up anywhere."

"I'd follow that man anywhere," she singsongs. "His neck is bigger than my thigh. The things I want to do with his body, ugh!"

She's never been with a hockey player before. I'm almost scared for how obsessed she'd be with him if he decided to give in to her advances. Willa isn't a subject I've talked about with Zander, though I have noticed a few lingering glances her way. Whatever happens, or doesn't happen, between them isn't my business. Though, I do worry about them. Some of that worry might be projecting my own issues onto them, which isn't at all fair. Alexander Fane isn't Cillian Wylder, no matter how similar they might be.

"Is a big neck indicative of big other parts," Kit asks, then erupts in giggles.

"Will you two please quit imagining my best friend's penis? It's awkward as hell," I say, though I can't help laughing along with them both.

"You can't tell me you've never imagined his dick?"

My phone rings, and I hit answer before I can control my laughter enough to answer Kit or Cillian.

"She doesn't need to imagine it. Not when she's riding Ty's dick every time he's in town," Willa says, and I shoot her a wide-eyed smirk because I'm sure Cillian heard that through my phone.

"Hello?"

"Is this a bad time," he asks, grumpier than he's been the past few times I've answered. *Yep, he definitely heard Willa's comment.*

"No, but Sadie already passed out for the night."

He spoke to her earlier when he stopped for a quick bite somewhere in Ohio.

"Oh, okay. I'll try to call earlier in the evening tomorrow. It's such a boring-ass drive, I was trying to get as much distance in before I called it a night." He sounds off. Lonely maybe? He only left Boston this morning and last night he was with his former teammates. I can't imagine loneliness set in that quick.

"What's wrong?" Kit mouths the words 'why do you care' as soon as I ask Cillian the question. I stick my tongue out at her. She's not ready to give him any grace. I don't blame her, but I'm not her.

"I don't... It's not my business."

"What's not?"

"You and whatever you have going on with Murphy."

"You're right, it's not. I told you I have a healthy sex life. So why do you sound like a wounded fucking puppy over it?"

"You gonna be mean to me forever, Cole?"

"I don't know. You gonna deserve it forever?"

"I'm trying not to," he says, somber and maybe sincere. But what do I know about his sincerity? "I spoke with my lawyer today."

"Why?" My heart pumps blood so powerfully through me, it's nearly physically painful.

"What's happening," Willa asks, picking up on the distress she must have heard in that one small word.

"Not about custody, Isla," he rushes out. "Okay? It wasn't about that. I asked him to research how much child support I should have already paid and what I should be paying now."

"I don't need your money."

"It's not about need. Let me do the bare minimum here. Please?"

"Let me know what he comes up with and we'll discuss it then."

"That sounds like a stall tactic, but I'll agree to it. For now," he says, laughing. "I wanted to tell you that I talked to Trina the night I flew in to Boston."

"Good for you?" Phrasing it like a snipey question is purely a defensive move, but I'm only human here and I still hate the sound of her name on his lips.

"About what you said she's done," he says, his voice still a pitch higher with humor. "She didn't admit to doing anything."

"You're a bigger idiot than I thought if you believed she'd readily admit to being a harassing piece of human trash."

"Hey, hey! I didn't say I believed her," he argues. "I don't, for the fucking record. But I also don't know what *exactly* I was accusing her of. You never gave me details. Either way, I told her to leave you alone. I'm done with her. I promise, she's out of your life."

This should be good news, something that makes me happy. So why does my mind go back to all the times he told me there was nothing going on and she was just a friend?

Because he lied so much before… No matter how badly I want this to be true, I don't trust it. Or him. That phone call to Torsten and the video call later are all too clear. Time hasn't diminished the pain it caused me. My old, broken heart wants me to be an asshole and ask him if he stuck his dick in her one last time. Where will that get us though? Certainly not anywhere closer to being better parents to Sadie.

"Thank you," I say instead.

"You don't have to thank me, Isla. I would have done it a long time ago, if I knew she was harassing you."

"Cillian," I stop him. "Be real. You never protested anything she did before I broke up with you."

The silence stretches and I wonder if he's remembering all my pleas. All the time I tried to convince him that she was purposefully trying to get between us. My last trip to see him in Boston, we spent so much time arguing about her. He didn't see it the way I did, or he didn't want to admit that he did.

"There's always been so much I wish I could change or take back," he finally says. "I used to think that I wasn't all in the wrong. That what I learned that first year or two, and the man I became, wouldn't have happened any other way."

A silent tear trails down my cheek, and Willa wipes it away in worry. I blink at the care of my baby sister who has always been so strong for me when I've lacked it. She's the thing that holds me together when my foundation starts to crumble. It's not supposed to be her, this isn't her job, but she's yet to fail at it regardless.

"What does that mean?"

"That I didn't think we were ready for each other back then. There was too much growing up to do, or that's what I convinced myself of after you broke up with me. It made it easier to look at myself in the mirror every day thinking that you were better off without me until I could get my shit together. I was an idiot, Isla. Such a fucking idiot, and it's lost me years with Sadie. *With you*. I've missed you, you know? More than I can say. I'm not going to fuck this up again."

"Cillian—"

"I'm not the same guy you knew, Isla. I'm a man of my word. I'm telling you I'm not fucking this up again. You be ready for that. I'll see you in a couple of days." With that, he ends the call in his special way of leaving me in a tailspin, wondering what the hell just happened.

12

CILLIAN

It's late and I'm exhausted from the drive by the time I pull up to Isla's building. I've driven for thirty-six of the last forty-eight hours. Stupid? Yes. Necessary? Also, yes. Because something changed in the last two days but I'm blind as to what.

Isla was her typical self when I spoke to her the other night when I'd stopped off near Cleveland to get some sleep. Meaning she still had her guard up but was at least talking to me. When I called yesterday, she didn't spare me two words before passing me off to Sadie. The same thing happened today. She won't even respond to my text messages.

I've gone over everything I said to her, and none of it should have caused her to retreat to the 'pretend Cillian doesn't exist' stage.

It fucking pisses me off. An emotion I'm becoming all too familiar with these days.

So, I don't give a shit that it's after nine at night when I knock on her door. We're not playing whatever hide and seek bullshit game she's got going on. If there's a problem, we'll deal with head-on and right away. I've learned that lesson the hard fucking way.

When Trina and I got closer, I could have, no, *should have*, manned up and broke things off with Isla before the situation festered into what it became. Maybe then she wouldn't have felt as blindsided and completely cut me off. Maybe then she would have felt like she could have told me about the pregnancy.

Better yet, I shouldn't have fucked around with Trina in the first place. Heeding Isla's warnings about her would have been the smartest move, but I wasn't a smart guy. I was a lonely dumbass. We all agree there. That's not who I am anymore and I'm not losing another second with my family because of whatever is going on in Isla's head right now.

At first, Trina was just a friend. Something I didn't have in Boston. Coming from the closeness the Coles have, and all the support they gave me, it was hard to be there and alone. I clung to the attention Trina offered, thinking it came from a genuine place. She wanted to help me with the adjustments that you make as a professional player. Or so I thought. In the beginning, she would ask me about Isla regularly, making me think she wanted to get to know her, too. I didn't pick up on the subtle changes as time went by. What was supportive became something that I can recognize now as more manipulative.

What a hard pill that is to swallow, that I was taken by a woman with ulterior motives and my dick ate it up because my brain had shriveled up to nothing. That day in the gym, the one that I stupidly posted pictures of... it was the beginning of the end.

Trina had offered to meet me and take some photos and video while I trained. It seemed harmless. I didn't think about the fact that she could only make it late in the day when most everyone else would be gone from the team's training facility. I didn't even think it was odd that she showed up in barely-there workout gear, figuring she'd get a workout in, too.

In between taking shots of me, she would strategically use equipment in my line of sight. I recognize it now. Back then, I thought it was just an unfortunate coincidence for my young libido. She noticed when I started to get hard, because she kept looking and darting her eyes away. Which only made it worse for me to control myself.

I should have distanced myself then, like I told Isla I would. What a rookie fucking move. One that cost me way too much.

A few days later, she came by the apartment with dinner for Tor and me. She kissed me goodbye when she left that night. I gently pushed away and reminded her I had a girlfriend I loved. That didn't stop me from inviting her back. It didn't stop me from allowing her the opportunity to kiss me again. The second time I kissed her back, it was the greatest mistake of my life.

"Cillian?" I shake the regret away when Isla opens the door, looking confused. I drop Saint inside the door, and she immediately runs past Isla and further into the apartment.

"Hi." Damn, she's beautiful. Her messy waves are piled high atop her head, face freshly washed and glowing so I can see every small freckle that dots her fair skin. Isla is gorgeous no matter what, but this was always how I liked her best. Clean and bare; it was something not everyone got to see. Like it was a special, vulnerable part of her that she shared with only me. "I loved you so much. I'm so sorry I hurt you."

They aren't the words I planned yet I can't help but say them as I pull her close and wrap my arms around her.

"Cillian," she says again, this time muffled by my smothering. She tilts her head up to look at me, her face a rainbow of feelings. When I lean down to kiss her, Isla shakes her head. "No! You don't get to do that anymore."

"Why?"

"Because I'm not yours," she cries, her voice breaking a little right along with my heart. "You lie and I can't take that hurt again."

"I told you I've changed. I'm never going to lie to you again."

"You already have."

"What do you mean?" Isla pushes me away to go retrieve her cell phone. After a few swipes, she shoves the device into my hands. It's a message from an anonymous account on Instagram, and all it contains are pictures from the going away party the other night. All of which include me and Trina. "What is this?"

"Proof that I still can't trust anything you say."

"This isn't proof of anything except that we were at the same party together," I say. Of the three pictures, one is the most incriminating, only because Isla doesn't know the context of it. The other two are group photos that we both happen to be in.

"You said you were done with her before your last night in Boston. Clearly, that wasn't the case."

"I was, I am," I protest, holding up the phone so she can see the selfie that Trina took of us. "Look at me here, Isla. Really look at it. That isn't me enjoying myself. That's me at a party where I didn't control the guest list, where I played nice as to not make waves with the rest of the team. That look on my face? That's forced. Look at it, see it."

See me.

"Convenient." She scoffs.

"It's not convenient, it's the truth. I avoided her all night. This moment here? That's her rushing up to me, shoving the phone in front of us, and taking the picture. It would have been unnecessary to push her away and refuse in a room full of people."

"Like it would have been when she first started throwing herself at you?"

"No, not like that," I say, dropping her phone on the table and stepping closer to her. "It wouldn't have been a shit show back then, it would have been the right thing to do. I fucked that up. This time, I thought the best thing to do was to get rid of her with as few waves as possible. I never have to see her again; you never have to see her again. I didn't think riling her up would be the surest way to get her to leave us all alone."

"I don't know how to believe you," she says, sounding like a wounded animal.

"I know you don't. That's going to take time, but we'll get there."

"How do you know that?"

How do I know? Because I still love her, because she's the mother of my child, because I won't stop until we're on the same page. Because I'd give up my whole life to make life for her and Sadie better. Isla isn't ready to hear any of that yet, it would only make her more wary of me. Someday I'll have the chance to tell her and know she trusts it.

"I just do, Cole," I say with a casual shrug. Just then, Saint lets herself known with a loud mewling. "Shit, she's going to wake up Sadie."

"It's weird you have a cat," Isla says, following me as I pick up my furball and drop onto the couch with her on my lap.

"She's good company," I say, reaching for her hand and pulling her down next to me. "Isla, meet Saint."

"Your favorite pussy."

"No," I say, and she blushes a pretty shade of red. "Is this what's been happening all this time? Pictures from strange accounts?"

"Yes."

"When did they start?"

"My first birthday without..." she says, but stops abruptly and looks away toward the wall of windows. The world is as dark outside as the feeling in my soul.

"Me. The first birthday without me."

"Yes," she says, nodding. "It was a selfie too." She sounds scared, not sad or mad, but truly scared.

"Of her and me," I ask, wrapping my arm around her shoulders and snuggling closer to her.

"In bed." The two short words pierce my heart.

"The fuck?" I would have never let her take a picture of us in bed. "Do you still have it?"

"Probably, if I unblock all the accounts."

"How many accounts were there? Never mind, go get your phone. Let me see it all."

Isla does it without a word, which at least means she's not arguing with me. She plops back down, unlocks the screen, and hands it to me.

"Mostly, they came through Insta. Some on Facebook, but I deactivated that account a long time ago." Her focus shifts to my cat, who—like the traitor she is—moves off my lap to gain more attention from the one currently petting her head. "She's pretty."

I almost say not as pretty as you, except I'm instantly consumed by the long list of blocked accounts on Isla's account. There's at least fifty here as I scroll.

"Do these all have pictures of me?"

"No. Some were random dick pictures. I think those were from her, too. Maybe she wanted me to think they were you, but..."

"But you know my dick," I say absently.

"No, thank you," she snarks.

I screenshot every page of blocked accounts before I start the process of unblocking the first handful. "We'll block them again after I finish looking through them, okay?"

She hums but doesn't pay me much attention. Pulling up the first picture that was sent to her, my blood runs fucking cold as ice. Not only is the picture harassment for Isla, but it was a complete invasion of my privacy as I lay there in my bed, fast asleep. While Trina drapes herself artfully next to me and snaps an intimate picture. I'm naked as the day I was born, the corner of the sheet barely covering my junk while it also covers the important bits of Trina's body.

"Is this the first one you got?" I turn the phone to her. Isla quickly looks away, and I see her hand is tremoring while she smooths Saint's hair. "Isla?"

"I'm not looking at the picture that sent me into pre-term labor."

"What?" Now I'm shaking too. Not with fear, but with full-on rage. "Explain everything, Isla. No more fucking around. I need to know what I missed."

"After our breakup, I still intended to have a real conversation with you about my pregnancy. At least to let you know I was keeping the baby," she starts, her body slumping further in the cushions. "The first time I tried, I unblocked you from Instagram. I wanted to scroll through the time I'd miss while I worked out what to say to you. But your profile had so much of her in it. I had a breakdown. My therapist thinks I hadn't grieved the end of our relationship because I was so concerned about the pregnancy and seeing you and *her* together prompted it. Which then led to a panic attack. Not that I knew what it was then."

"Jesus, Isla. Is that when you started seeing a therapist?"

"No," she shakes her head, still not looking my way. "A couple of months went by and though I was still very emotional, I hadn't had any more episodes like that. Thankfully, because I thought I was having a heart attack or something. It was terrifying. But then on my birthday, I woke up to that picture. By the end of the day, I was having these sharp pains about every thirty minutes or so. Like someone was sticking a long needle up my hoo-ha and stabbing me with it. That was the night I spent in the hospital wondering if after everything, I was going to lose her too."

Too. She thought she was going to lose Sadie on top of losing me. All while I was off living my dream career and fucking around with whatever woman I felt like, whenever I felt like it.

I don't deserve to be forgiven.

"Fuck, I'm so sorry. I'm not even sure what to say. There's no way for me to make that right but know that I wish I could. If I could take away all the shit I caused, or was the reason for, I would," I say, pressing a kiss to the top of her head. She snuggles in the tiniest bit more, and Saint purrs in her lap.

The next few pictures I pull up are not as intimate. They do show the progression of mine and Trina's relationship though. She quickly became a bigger presence in my life, even if there was never a commitment there. I didn't want to be committed to her. Maybe my heart knew the truth my head couldn't see.

Trina cost me the woman I was always meant to be with.

"Okay, this one is plain insulting," I say when a picture of dick pops up on the screen. "No way would you have believed that was my cock." To this, she looks up. After a brief glance, she starts shaking with silent laughter.

"Right? It's way too big to be you." She laughs harder now, still trying to keep it quiet. Saint pops her head up in protest.

"You're an asshole, Cole. That thing is borderline a micro compared to mine."

"In your dreams, Mr. Egomaniac." That's not the nickname I want. She used to call me Superstar. I miss it.

"You need a reminder, then. You've properly fucking forgot."

"Never going to happen, Wylder."

Don't fucking count on that.

I stay up until I'm finished viewing every one of the uncalled-for messages she's received. There are a handful more of me in bed, but not a single one am I awake in. You can't be sure of that when you look at them. Trina knew what she was doing, where to place the camera to keep my closed eyes just out of the frame. Or maybe she cropped them later, I don't know. What I do know is that I wouldn't have agreed to any of them.

By the time I finish and get everyone blocked again, I'm too tired to move. Not that I want to. So, I don't. Instead, I pull the blanket off the back of the couch, drape it over a sleeping Isla and close my eyes.

"Daddy," Sadie whispers, her tiny hand patting my cheek.

"Hmm?"

"Daddy? Can I pet the kitty?"

"What kitty," Isla says. She's draped atop me as I lie flat on my back. This couch is too damn small for me, let alone the both of us. We made it work, apparently, since neither of us woke up and moved off it in the middle of the night. Saint is curled up at my shoulder, licking the finger Sadie holds out for her.

"Sure, baby. She's a nice girl."

"She's sooo soft," Sadie coos at her.

"What's happening?" Isla says, groggily.

"Looks like you all had a slumber party," Willa pipes in, walking into the living room, holding a cup of coffee out to her sister.

"Oh god," Isla groans, scrambling to get off me. Her effort only dumps her onto the floor.

"Careful, Mommy. You'll scare the kitty."

"Yeah, careful, Mommy," I chime, covering my lap with the blanket.

"Oh, god," Isla repeats. After picking herself up off the floor, she grabs the mug from Willa and runs off down the hall.

"Awkward much?" Willa playfully glares at me. "How the hell did all this happen? And why is there a cat here?"

"I got in late." I sit up and steal the other mug Willa is holding. It's probably hers, but I need more than she does. "Came by to talk but fell asleep. Just as well, since my house doesn't have furniture yet."

"Where will Saint sleep then?" Sadie climbs up next to me, pulling Saint to her lap.

"I guess I'll have to go to the pet store today and get her a bed."

"Oh. Can I come?"

"Let me talk to your mom and then we'll see, okay?" I drop a kiss to the top of her head, drain the coffee, then go to find my embarrassed ex-girlfriend. She's in the bathroom, so I knock.

"Go away, Cillian."

"Let me in, Cole."

"Why," she demands, opening the door only a few inches.

"Step back so I can come in."

"Don't you have your own house to be at?" She sighs and steps back.

"That's what I want to talk about," I say, closing the door behind me. "But first, stop being embarrassed."

"How? I slept on top of your boner, and I don't even like you!"

"Who's the liar now?" I laugh. "You're mad at me, and I get it. You should be. But you like me enough."

"Enough for what?"

"To sleep on top of my boner," I tease her. "To co-parent with me. To go shopping for house shit with me and our daughter today?"

"What?"

"I have a ton of shit to get, and I don't even know what it all is. Sadie asked to go to the pet store with me, anyway. Let's make a day of it, you both can see the house I'm buying and then we'll drop Sadie off at your parents for her Saturday night."

Isla gives me a contemplative look, then turns to the sink. Grabbing her toothbrush, she starts her morning routine, completely ignoring me other than the glances she shoots me through the mirror. I don't know what game she's playing. But I do know she's forgotten I play games for a living.

I drag my shirt over my head slowly, purposely making a show of it. While I'm doing it, she gags on a mouthful of toothpaste.

"What the fuck are you doing?"

"We're getting ready. Then I'm spending the day with my daughter. You can come with or stay here and be grumpy. Either way, I'm showering." I pull my sweatpants down, along with my boxer briefs.

"Stop that!" She rushes to rinse out her mouth, only making a big mess because her sight isn't leaving me in the mirror. Not for a second.

"No." I reach into the shower and adjust the water. "You coming? Or do I take our daughter out all by myself for the very first time ever?"

"This is manipulation. You know that, right?" Her fists find her hips, taking a defiant stance. Her eyes fight to not drop below my waist, but they never leave my body.

"You started this game; I'm only playing for the cup, Isla."

13

ISLA

"Will you be at the Iceplex on Monday?"

"Yes. I won't be there every day, but some." Cillian has been peppering me with these questions all morning. The man is relentless in his attempt to keep me talking when that's about the last thing I want to be doing. I'm so mad at him, and for the first time in as long as I can remember, it has nothing to do with his cheating.

Instead, it's about his presumptuous ass staying the night and snuggling up with me. Plus, that stunt in the bathroom this morning.

Fuck, he looks good. It's unfair, absolutely and incredibly unfair. Tyson has an amazing body and even it doesn't quite compare to the cut muscles Cillian sports. Or that stupid vee thing at his hips. I don't know what it's called. Something like panty-dropper or panty-wetter, I'm sure. Because that's exactly what it does. Then there was his still hard dick just flapping all over the place.

Fucking unfair.

He's very good with Sadie. Not only is he attentive and loving to her, but he also seems to have a natural intuition to gentle parenting. There was a moment in the pet store when she saw gerbils and wanted one in the almost obsessive way she can sometimes fall into. I recognized that she was on that toddler edge where it's too easy for them to go from casual interest to full-on tantrum. Or, to complete shutdown, which is more common for Sadie. She's a quiet pouter more than the throw-a-fit type.

My instinct was to step in, but Cillian handled it with ease. Waving me off, he had a conversation with her about how much responsibility gerbils are, explaining all the tasks it takes to care for them. Then he compared them to Saint, who's rather self-sufficient and only requires a bit of food and a ton of cuddles.

Sadie agreed cats were way more fun and moved on. Cillian didn't grow up around children, making his ease with her unexpected. I hate that it pulls at my heartstrings, but it does, nonetheless. Of course, I want him to be a great father. I want everything good in the world for my daughter. Except his goodness to her makes me want to forgive him and my pride isn't ready for that.

We're on our way to his new house to drop off Saint and meet with the furniture company who is delivering a load of items he's purchased, including Sadie's tent bed. Then he wants to go to Target for 'kitchen shit' as he put it.

"Sadie Baby?"

"Yeah," she answers him with a goofy grin from the backseat.

"Do you know how to swim?"

"Yes! Pops says I'm so strong."

"That's good," Cillian says with a nod.

"Does the house have a pool?" It's not a common thing here in Seattle except with more upscale homes. It's weird to think of Cillian living in a McMansion though. He has money now, sure. It just doesn't fit the guy I used to know, and I haven't wrapped my head around who he is now.

He's still the boy I fell in love with and the young man that broke my fucking heart.

"Not exactly."

"What does that mean?" He doesn't answer, and after a couple more turns, I understand. "You bought a floating house?"

"Yeah," he says, chagrined. "In my defense, I did it before I knew I had… her. Anyway, the previous owners had children, so I think it's childproofed or whatever."

The Eastlake neighborhood is well known for its quaint floating homes. Lake Union is lined with them, but this side of the lake has a higher concentration of them.

"I'm sure it's fine."

"If it's not, I'll make it better."

He parks in the communal lot, and we unload as much as we can carry. Sadie carries Saint as if her life depends on it. Luckily, the cat doesn't seem to mind the stranglehold. The path down the dock is even more charming than you'd expect and every home we pass is colorful and playful. Sadie points out all the bright flowers to Saint who I don't think can see anything but Sadie's armpit.

Cillian's house is on the end and one of the bigger homes on the row. Two stories, modern, and with a roof deck. It may not be the most practical thing, but it's lovely and has a great view of the rest of the lake.

"This is it," he says, typing a code in. The door opens with a chime.

"Do I have a bedroom?"

"Yeah, you wanna see it?"

"Yes, please," Sadie answers him excitedly.

"Drop that stuff wherever," he says to me before hauling Sadie up a set of stairs.

I don't follow, instead I set up the litter box and water dish for Saint. Once that's done, I take a stroll around the lower level. There is so much natural light pouring through the abundance of windows, I imagine the space full of deep cushioned furniture and houseplants hanging everywhere. They still haven't come back down after I've seen the entire first floor, so I go in search of them upstairs.

They're out on a small deck off the primary bedroom, where Sadie is pointing out a boat that is sailing by in the distance. It's a private spot, one that can't be seen by the surrounding homes. A great spot for morning coffee or evening wine.

I'm jealous of whatever future woman may get to spend her time here.

With him.

Fuck.

Immediately I retreat downstairs and keep busy unpackaging the rest of the items he purchased at the pet store. Today, so far, has been comfortable with him. Last night was too, if how well I slept has anything to say about it. Even after the conversation we had, there wasn't any panic or lingering depressive thoughts that kept me up or had me in fitful sleep.

The furniture arrives, and I take Cillian's place on the deck hanging out with Sadie while we make up stories of mystical creatures that lurk in the depths of Lake Union.

"If I live here, I can make friends with one of the mermaids. She'll have purple hair that sparkles, and her tail is blue."

"That sounds pretty. Will she have a name," I ask, ignoring the pang at the idea of her living here. She has all the faith in the world when it comes to her father. There hasn't been a moment's hesitation from her; she accepts that he's here now and always will be. I wish I had her confidence.

"Edna," she says with distinct confidence.

"That's a good name."

"I know that's right."

"Of course, you do. Does Edna have an underwater friend?"

"Umm, I think she has a turtle named Bob."

"Who has a turtle named Bob?" Cillian steps outside.

"The purple-haired lake mermaid named Edna," I tell him, and he grins. It's genuine and familiar, making me feel very unstable.

"Makes sense," he says. "You guys ready to go?"

"I'm always ready," Sadie says with a happy sigh.

"Good, because we need some sheets for your bed," Cillian tells her, picking her up he blows a raspberry on her neck. She giggles; it's infectious and I'm happy for her. For them. Yet no less confused by my own reaction to him.

Target is a situation I don't think Cillian was ready for. He vastly underestimated Sadie's love for the store, and she dragged him to every corner of it to show him all the things she thought he needed. I stood back with unveiled amusement.

He's more exhausted than she is by the time we load two shopping carts worth of home goods and toys into his SUV. Cillian's kitchen is going to look more like Barbie's dreamhouse than a bachelor pad, but he doesn't seem worried about it as he lets Sadie pick out all his small appliances and various dishes and utensils.

It's probably overcompensation and it's ridiculous, but her joy at him deferring to her makes me smile. She passes out before we're out of the parking lot.

"To your parents' house?"

"Yeah, I'll text Mom that I'm bringing her a bit earlier."

"Do they live in the same place?"

"Yes. Mom will die in that house; she loves it so much."

"She put a lot of work into it," he muses.

"She took the wall out between the bedrooms Willa and I had. It's one giant suite for her crafting that's nearly as big as our entire condo."

"Marney always did love her crafts, so I guess that isn't a surprise. But I'll miss your old room, we had some good memories there."

It's where we lost our virginity together. It's where he told me he loved me for the first time. It's where he made his first promises to me. Ones he would later break.

But before he was drafted, we were happy. He used to surprise me with random romantic gestures. Money wasn't abundant for him, so he'd sometimes pack a picnic for us to go eat at a park. Several times, we ended up soaked because he never checked the forecast. I didn't mind that though, I'd have run through thunderstorms naked to spend time with him.

Then there were the little notes. When we lived together, if he had to leave before I was awake, there was always a note on his pillow waiting for me. He never missed a day of saying goodbye, and he loved me without waking me up to do it.

I saved each note until after I had Sadie, when one night I was so sad, thanks to my postpartum depression that I pulled them out, read them one by one, then threw them all away.

The streets we drive are all familiar yet look different today. Something has changed; like the world has shifted on its axis without anyone noticing and now everything is only slightly askew. The lines are all blurred but the colors are more vibrant. I'm lost, floating out into deep water without an anchor or the knowledge that someone is ashore waiting to pull me back in. Sadie has been my tether and me hers. Does that change somehow with Cillian in the mix?

I'm an awful, selfish person to think that. Nothing much makes sense just now except that my intrusive thoughts are worrying. At least I'm not too far gone to recognize it.

By the time we get to the house, I'm on the verge of crying. Cillian hasn't tried to pursue a conversation with me. I leave him to get Sadie out of the car as I grab her overnight bag and rush inside. Straight into my mother's waiting arms.

"What's wrong," she asks, cupping my cheeks and pulling my face up to hers.

"I need to talk," I whisper to her.

"Hi, Grams," Sadie calls, sleepily behind me. "Where's Curly? I need to tell him about my new friend, Saint."

"He's in the backyard with Pops, why don't you take your dad out there?"

"Okay, come on, Daddy."

Cillian nods at my mother and follows his daughter.

"Tell me everything," Mom says once they're out of earshot.

I detail the last few days for her.

"You didn't used to put this much pressure on yourself, sweetheart."

"What do you mean?"

"I mean," she starts, swiping a piece of hair off my cheek that's stuck there from the few tears I allowed to fall. "That when you were younger, you were always so confident in your decisions. Whether you knew it was right, or you knew that even if it was wrong you could fix it, you never wavered. You'd dive in with surety. Even when it came to Cillian. You didn't tiptoe into dating him; you said yes to that first dinner at Dick's Drive-in and came home calling him your boyfriend."

"Look where that got me."

"I know where it got you, Isla. It got you your first love, your first heartbreak, and your first child. How do you think that balances out?"

I've never regretted my relationship with Cillian, because it brought me Sadie. However, I've never asked myself what my mother just asked me. Hating what Cillian did to us has been my go-to. How much I got out of it was never a conversation I had with myself. Maybe because then I'd have to analyze that same thing for Cillian.

Which would make me force myself to face what I was denying him.

"It's tipped in my favor, isn't it?"

"Is it?"

"I've had Sadie. He didn't get me or her."

"You didn't get him either."

"She's worth more than the both of us combined," I say.

"Spoken like a true mother," she says, taking my hand. "If you block out all your fears, and you quit listening to the voices telling you what you ought to do, can you say what it is you really want to happen?"

Mom can fancy up the question all she wants but the truth is that she's asking me if I want him back. Do I? Could I ever trust him enough to take him back? I don't know that answer. I don't even know why he chose her to begin with. There are still so many unanswered questions.

"Rubbing a golden lamp so I can make a wish to turn back time isn't the right answer, is it?"

"If only life was that easy." She laughs. "What would change if you had that power?"

"I'd have had different conversations with him. Made more effort. That first month or so, I took for granted that we were good. That *he* was good," I tell her. "He wasn't, and neither was I. Or, I wouldn't have cut him off so thoroughly, I would have been relentless about having a conversation with him regarding my pregnancy."

"If you had done all of those things, what do you think would be different now?"

"When did you become my therapist," I tease.

"When you showed up in my driveway with him following behind you and sadness in your eyes. Or maybe at birth," she says with a smile. "Can you answer?"

"If we'd handled his move differently, maybe he wouldn't have gotten close to her. Maybe he wouldn't have cheated."

"And had he not cheated?"

Maybe we'd still be together.

That's what she expects me to say. If I say that, the next logical question would be what's stopping us from trying again. We're both in the same place, our worlds impossibly connected. So, what's stopping us?

"I want him to earn a second chance," I finally admit. "I also have no clue how he possibly could."

"At least you're being honest with yourself about it, Isla. Maybe give it some time, it's all happening so fast." Yet it feels like it's been happening for my whole life. "I'm proud of you for knowing you needed to talk about it."

"No more internalizing my pain. I need to let it out like I let out my temper."

Mom laughs at the running joke that's been a regular for me since I was in therapy.

"You never did hold that in, that's for sure. Though, it's calmed down a lot since Sadie."

"Yeah, well, pregnancy changes you. You could have warned me, you know? My *feet* grew right along with my hips and ass. So many great shoes were wasted. Not to mention how my hair suddenly became susceptible to humidity."

"In my defense, I didn't know that was something that could happen," she argues. "It's different for everyone, I suppose."

"You going to take that shithead out of here so we can enjoy some time with our granddaughter?" Dad walks in, his chest puffed up like it gets when he's upset about something.

"Everything okay?"

"No. He's here," he answers.

"I'll have him take me home," I say. "You know you have to coach him, right?"

"Doesn't mean I have to like him."

"Be nice," Mom scolds.

"I was. I didn't punch him."

"Look at us both making progress." I laugh and hug them, then go say goodbye to Sadie before dragging Cillian out to his car. He waves goodbye to my parents; Mom is the only one who waves back.

"Your dad hates me," he says a few minutes into the drive.

"He's protective, you know that."

"I get it. I'm sure I'll be the same. Maybe we'll get lucky, and Sadie will be asexual."

"She's already told me she's going to marry Ryan Nugent-Hopkins, so don't count on it."

"Oh, fuck no," Cillian protests. "Why are you letting her watch Oilers games?"

"She loves hockey, dude." I laugh at the disgusted look on his face.

"Dinner," he offers hesitantly. I shake my head. "Listen, Isla, I don't know what I did wrong today. I tried not to fuck up. But if I did something to upset you, can you tell me, so I don't do it again?"

How do I explain that he didn't do anything but exist here in my space without sounding like an asshole? It's not where the conversation should start anyway. We should start at the start.

"What was it about her?"

We're stuck in some traffic, either from an accident or maybe there's an event at the arena which we'll be passing. Either way, I'm stuck in this vehicle with him for even longer so we may as well make use of the time. No better time than the present to ask the question I always wanted to know the answer to and equally never wanted to.

"It wasn't her. Not exactly, anyway. She's not more attractive than you, she doesn't make me laugh like you," he says, sounding as if he's talking more to himself than he is to me. "It was more that she knew the right things to say at just the right time. Trina inserted herself in the role of my everyday supporter, and I was so dependent on that from you, I let her."

"Her support wasn't the problem."

"No. But her support morphed into what became the problem. She was experienced. Both sexually and in her subtle manipulation. I can see it for what it was now. But then? I only saw a knowledgeable, successful woman throwing herself at me by telling me all the things I could be and do. Trina didn't make me work for anything; she laid it all out in front of me before I even thought about wanting it."

"Is that what I did wrong? I made you work for it." Anger works its way in to mask how painful this is to hear him say.

"Fuck, Isla, you didn't do anything wrong. And yeah, you made me work for you but only ever in ways that made me better. You challenged me to improve myself. I never felt good enough for you. Or for the coach's daughter. Or for the NHL Hall of Famer's daughter. I always felt like I had something to prove to you. It wasn't you who made me feel that way though, after I earned that first date you never asked me to prove myself to you again. Until I was drafted, and I failed spectacularly."

"You're saying it was as easy as her showing up with brownies on game day or some shit?"

I meant so little to him that anyone who showed him support could have him forget the commitment he made to me. That may not be what he's saying exactly, but that's all I'm hearing.

"No," he says and sighs. "Nothing was easy, except her. Damn it, Isla. I hate this, I don't want to have to say this to you and I sure as hell don't want to admit that I was the cliché shithead teenager who threw everything away for easy companionship. I hated myself for it then, and I do even more now."

The traffic breaks and the last few minutes of the drive speed by at the same pace as my racing heart. I don't acknowledge what he's said until he's pulled up in front of my building and the silence in this car has become all too deafening.

"I would never have agreed that you weren't good enough to date me, the NHL Hall of Famer's daughter. In fact, I would have called you ridiculous for thinking that. But I understand now what it's like to not feel good enough, or worthy enough for the person you love. You showed me what it meant, and Trina made sure to twist the knife over the years you were together," I tell him, though that costs me every ounce of strength I have in me. "I'm sorry if I ever did anything to make you feel less than. Because it's the worst fucking feeling in the world."

14

CILLIAN

"Nice work today, Wylder." Nicky, the head strength and conditioning trainer, pats me on the shoulder.

"Thanks to you," I call back as I make my way to the locker room. Nicholai Popov is a beast of a trainer. In his early fifties, he's been in the business my whole life. He works us hard, but he knows what he's doing so we all listen to every suggestion he makes. He's thoroughly kicked my ass this week in the weight room, but it's felt good. I've missed the hard work and ice time.

The routine of practice and training the past couple of weeks has kept me in check. If not for that and Sadie, I'd probably be spiraling over everything Isla had to say the day I moved into my new house. She doesn't know, but I heard some of what she and Marney were talking about. I went in to see if she was ready to leave, since I was getting nothing but side-eyes from Coach. Isla said she wanted me to earn a second chance.

Her forgiveness is something I want, as much as I want to forgive her. That thorn still pricks my side, regardless of how far we've come since I've been back. We've been getting along well enough, and she's now starting to trust me to take Sadie on short outings without her. Some days, it's enough.

Other days, I want what we used to have with such a vengeance I can barely function through the need to haul her sassy ass back into my world. The desire to be back in her bed, in *her*, grows with every fucking passing day. Especially when she sends me looks as I'm hanging out with our daughter. I know it affects her, but I don't want that to be the reason she succumbs.

Seducing her would be easier than gaining her acceptance and forgiveness. I'm sure of it. But where would that lead? To fuck-buddy co-parents? We're not ready for more, there's too much to work out.

I don't see why I can't get the same benefits as Tyson fucking Murphy, though. Except, that's a lie. It's because I let a viper into our house and let her destroy everything, that's why.

This Trina situation has been weighing heavily on me. She not only fucked with Isla in the most unforgivable ways, but the more I put the pieces together, the more I see how she took advantage of my trust. I've spent so many nights racking my brain on how I let it all happen and coming to terms with how blind I was.

"You coming tonight, Wild?" Axel grabs my attention as I start to strip down for a shower.

"Where?"

"Vaughn's. Caroline is cooking dinner for anyone who wants to come."

"Who's Caroline?"

"His wife," Hugo chimes up.

"I didn't know Vaughn was married."

"Has been since he skated in the minors. They're private though," Axel says. That's not unusual, and most guys in the league are married young. Gavin Vaughn just didn't seem the type, I guess.

"My mom's in from Boston and we have a date with a toddler, so I'll have to miss it."

"Every date you've talked about in weeks has been daddy-daughter. You be sure to get some adult fun time in between," Axel teases.

"My dick is doing just fine and isn't your business." I snicker. If the team has a manwhore, it's Axel Wallin. In some ways, he reminds me of Torsten, a lot of fun but easily can get you in trouble. "I'm keeping focused on Sadie and hockey. Coach hates me enough as it is. I need to be in top shape."

"Women help keep me in shape."

"Easier to do when you don't catch their name because that way you don't catch their drama either," Hugo says with a grin.

"You should try it, Wild. It's the only way to live," Axel tells him before disappearing out of the locker room.

"Don't listen to him, kid. You do you, keep that head where it's at."

"Thanks, Bloomy." It cracks me up when he calls me kid. At twenty-four, I'm the second youngest on the roster but that won't last long. Hockey is a young man's sport and there is a whole team of younger guys on the farm team waiting to be called up. I was one of the lucky few to skip the minors. It's rare and I almost lost my spot in Boston a time or two.

Tonight is a big night. Mom's back in town and Isla has agreed to let Sadie stay the night with me for the first time. We're both nervous about it in different ways. Isla is nervous because she doesn't trust that I can handle anything that comes up. I can though, because my daughter is my priority and I'll do whatever it takes to keep her safe.

I even had an alarm installed so all doors and windows chime in the most annoying way possible. There's no way she can wander off without me knowing.

My worry is that Isla will find any kind of reason to not let me do this again. Maybe that's not fair, but I had to bend over backward to get permission to take her out to ice cream without Isla tagging along. Not that I mind Isla around, I don't. But it isn't realistic for her to be with us every minute of every day.

It also makes it harder to keep my heart from getting too entwined with the woman.

What I said to Wallin isn't exactly true. My dick is most certainly feeling neglected these days. My hand hasn't seen this much action since I left for Boston. Once again, it's because of Isla Cole. Every woman that catches my attention pales in comparison, and for some insane reason, I compare every single one to her. Nobody's smile is as bright, no body as curvy, no other flirty glance makes my heart pound.

She has the same effect on me as she always did. Now, it's two-fold and confusing as all hell. I know she's here at the Iceplex today; she's been entertaining a group from the biggest local youth hockey leagues. When I was skating earlier, she was on the other side of the glass surrounded by a group of teenage boys all looking at her like she hung the moon.

I remember feeling like that at their age. Fuck, I still feel like that now, when I'm not so enamored with my daughter that I hate how much time I've missed.

Finishing my shower and tossing all my shit in my gym bag, I go find the woman who dominates my thoughts. She's saying goodbye to the group of walking hormones as I approach.

"Holy shit, that's Wild," one of them says when I get close enough.

"Hey, guys," I greet them, then press a kiss on Isla's cheek to a round of oohs and ahhs from the boys.

"Gentlemen, this is Cillian Wylder," she says, laughing. "If you want some selfies with him, now is your chance. You have about ten minutes before your bus takes off."

I play along, because I remember the days of being starstruck by pros and I'm not that kind of asshole. When we're done, I trail her as she escorts them to the main entrance of the hockey facility.

"Thanks for doing that for them," she says.

"No worries, I don't mind that sort of thing."

"I didn't know, and I don't want to push anyone's boundaries. But you walked right into it."

"Any time you need something from me, just tell me. You know if it wasn't for people encouraging me in youth hockey, I wouldn't be here. I'm happy to give back," I remind her because she's acting like she doesn't know me at all.

I don't like it.

"Okay, thanks."

"Are you done for the day?"

"Thankfully," she says, nodding. "Boys are exhausting."

"I know that's right," I tease. "Can I meet you at your place to grab Sadie? Mom's excited to see her."

Isla shuts down quickly. Her smile fades, shoulders slump, and eyes become vacant. Her skin turns ghostly and her chest rises and falls rapidly.

"Isla?"

"I... um."

"Fuck, Isla. We had a plan, don't make me disappoint her." I don't want to be harsh with her fragile anxiety. This is new territory for me, however. And I sure as fuck don't want to let my daughter down.

"Do you think I want to do that?" She gains back a little color on her cheeks as her temper ignites. *Good.* Maybe that's the key, keep her mad and she forgets about whatever else she's feeling.

"No, I don't think that's what you want. So, what's the problem?"

"I'm fucking scared," she whisper-shouts at me.

"How do we get past this?"

"I don't know," she says. She sounds defeated, like she's battling something I can't see, and she's losing.

"What if you come?" This might be a horrible idea, but Sadie's been wanting to sleep in her new room so badly. Besides, maybe this is a step in the right direction for us. We've been getting along fine but there's always that edge of... something lingering below the ease we pretend to have.

"What?"

"Come with her," I say. "You stay over, too. Try and let me handle everything that comes up without interfering, so you can see that I can do it. That I can keep her safe." It's a good idea. Even if having Isla sleep in my house turns me on in ways that it shouldn't.

I've made love to her a hundred times. That's not what we'd have now, though. It would be something more like hate sex and that thought has me fighting a stiffy.

"That seems... excessive."

"Why?"

"Because it makes me feel stupid and childish, and like, I can't let go."

"If it will make you less stressed out about her spending time with me, then who cares if it seems stupid or silly?"

"I don't like not having my shit together."

"You never have," I say. "We're forever family because of our girl.

That means I'm going to do what you need, too. If this is what that is, then let's do it and not make a big deal out of it. Okay?"

Look at me being all grown up and shit.

She mulls it over, nibbling the inside of her lip.

"Just say okay, Cole. It's not a big deal unless you make it one."

"Okay," she blurts out. "I'm sorry, I'm just nervous. But, okay."

"Don't worry about it. Go pack up a bag, grab our daughter and head over." She nods and rushes out the door.

"I hope you know what you're doing." The familiar deep voice comes from a short distance behind me.

"Only time will tell, I guess, Coach. I'm not going to do anything to hurt my daughter," I say, turning around.

"What about mine?"

"I don't want to hurt her, either."

"You sure about that?" Coach glares at me, daring me to lie to him. He'll know if I do, I was never able to hide anything from him.

"Some days, it's difficult to not be angry with her. Sadie is amazing and I've missed so much. All her firsts; steps, words, her birthday... I should have experienced those with her. I should have been there when she was born," I say, honestly choking up a bit on the words. "So, yeah, some days are fucking hard. But at the end of it all, I still have a lot of love for Isla. I'm trying to work through everything, same as she is."

"I probably never told you, but I missed Isla's birth. She came two weeks early and I was in Montreal. Marney gave birth sometime in the second period. I hated everything about it and held on to that guilt for a long time. Marney, of course, wasn't fussed about it at all. This career can be hard on families."

"No, you never told me that." Coach is the most devoted father I've ever seen, not that I've had a ton of experience there. But plenty of the guys on my last team had families. I bet it broke his heart to not be there.

"I still don't trust you or even like you," he says after a long pause of studying me. "But I can respect that you're trying to figure it out with her and not against her. It tells me you know Sadie comes first. Don't prove me wrong, kid."

Per Sadie's request, we had a charcuterie plate for dinner. Because dead animals are fine, just so long as they aren't *cooked* dead animals, she reminded me. I won't even pretend to understand toddler logic. She ate mostly cheese and fruit, anyway. Only picking at the various pieces of meat.

A few times she asked Isla for permission for certain things, and every time Isla said that when she's at Daddy's house, she needs to ask me for permission. Sadie's going with it, but I can't help but wonder how confusing this all is for her, too. Overall, I think she likes it here. She finds every excuse she can to spend time in her bedroom, which tells me it's past time she quit sharing one with her mom.

When Mom takes Sadie with her to wash up the dishes, I use the opportunity to talk to Isla.

"My attorney finally got back to me today."

"Okay," Isla says with a shrug.

"He came up with fifteen hundred a month for back child support. I think it's a little low, so I was going to write you a check for a hundred grand. If that's okay?"

"That's too much, Cill," she says. My heart skips a beat at the shortened name she hasn't really called me in forever. "I don't have a mortgage or a car payment. It's too much."

"Well, go buy a new car or get a mortgage with it."

She rolls her eyes at me. Isla has never wanted to depend on or be a burden to anyone. If I stop and think about it, I know she would have protested more about my relationship with Trina if not for that personality trait of hers. Had she been in Boston with me and witnessed the things Trina did or said to me, Isla would have dragged her off by the hair and put her in her place. But because of the distance and knowing how I was struggling with adjusting, she probably internalized a lot about how she felt.

Feeling both guilty and jilted simultaneously is a damned trip.

"I'll put it away for Sadie, for college or whatever," she finally says, and I laugh.

"You will fucking not. I'll be handling that shit. That's my job, just like your dad did for you and Willa."

"Cillian."

"That's not up for discussion. You do need to think about getting a place where she has her own room, though. You see how giddy she is over it?"

"I noticed, she's pretty cute about it," she says with the smile she always gets when Sadie's doing something especially cute. Which is everything, always, but I may be biased. "I'll move it up on the timeline. I should have done it a long time ago, but…"

"But you don't like help from your dad and you're just now starting to make money."

"There's more than that," she says, worrying her lip.

"What else?"

"Mommy," Sadie squeals as she runs back in from the kitchen, jumping into Isla's lap. "Can you read me one story and then you leave my new bedroom and Daddy can come in my new bedroom and read me another story?"

"I think we can make that happen," she answers, tickling Sadie's side and making her laugh that infectious girly giggle that I fall a little more in love with each time I hear it.

It's hard to understand how there are parents in the world that aren't ridiculously infatuated with their children. Maybe Sadie Baby is smarter, cuter, and funnier than most kids. Maybe I'm besotted. And now, maybe I sound like one of those stuffy men in the period movies Isla was always watching. Does she still watch them? I do, when I want to remind myself of her. When I want to wallow in what I had and let slip away.

That's a secret I'll never admit. My teammates would never let me live it down that while they're relaxing with Call of Duty, I'm watching shit like The Bridgerton's with a bowl of popcorn sprinkled with Cajun seasoning. Just like I imagined she'd be doing.

Often, I thought she might be doing things that reminded her of me. Isla was always a bit of gamer, so sometimes it was that. But maybe she'd go watch her dad's team practice and impart some wisdom to them. She might compare their form or their slapshots to mine. Her being so chummy with that Fane kid makes me think I wasn't that far off. Isla always was most comfortable sitting at a rink.

"What was her first word," I ask her when I come back downstairs

ALISON RHYMES

from reading Sadie to sleep, my mom now long gone. Isla is curled up on the end of my oversized sofa, watching some reality show.

"Poop."

"You're joking," I say, laughing.

"Nope. As much as I wanted it to be mama, or something along those lines, it was poop."

"She's got more hockey blood in her than hopeless romantic blood."

"Are you calling me a hopeless romantic," she asks with a curled lip, as if the thought is too disgusting to entertain.

"A little bit. Your mom is one, for sure."

"True," she agrees. "Your spare room doesn't have a bed."

Yeah... I meant to tell her that.

"You can have my bed. I'll sleep down here." I plop down on the couch, lying down with my head on her lap. She tenses. It sends a thrill through me, liking that I still affect her. "It's plenty comfortable."

"Is it clean?"

"Jesus, Cole. I wouldn't do that to you. Besides, the only women that have been here are my mother and you."

"That doesn't mean you haven't dirtied them up yourself," she says. From my vantage point, I can see she's trying to hide her smirk.

"Oh, that's happened plenty, but I put fresh sheets on before you got here." Her smile disappears and her cheeks turn rosy. "You want to help me out with that tonight, Cole?"

Before she has a chance to turn tail and run, I roll over, wrapping my arms around her. It only takes a few maneuvers to get her under me. She doesn't fight any of it, though her eyes narrow on me with curiosity.

"What the fuck are you doing, Wylder?"

"What the fuck do you want me to be doing, Isla?"

"You think I want you to fuck me?"

"I think you wouldn't mind if I made you come," I say, pressing a kiss to the underside of her chin, making her neck stretch. I like the extra access and trail kisses down it while I pull her shirt collar. "I miss the sounds."

"What sounds?"

"The sounds you make when I taste you and touch you. The sound you make when you break apart for me." I make it down to the top of her breast before she goes rigid again.

"You weren't here to hear me when I truly broke apart for you."

Fuck.

"No, I wasn't. I should have never let that happen, anyway." I brace myself up on my forearms so I can see her face, read it as I say the next part. "If you want to do that now, break down again and tell me everything you needed to say to me, then you can. I'll listen. I'll take it. It's my burden to carry."

Isla's eyes glisten with the water that starts to pool, the hurt I caused swimming in them.

"That's not the memory I'm craving to relive right now."

"What is?"

"I want to remember what it feels like to have you inside me. One last time."

15

ISLA

Did I just say that?
 Fuck, I did. I'm not going to let myself feel bad about it. Others can judge me, but I sure as hell won't be doing that myself.

It's true, anyway. I've always missed the intimate connection I had with Cillian. No matter how I've tried, it isn't something that I've been able to replicate. Not even with Ty. And now, with that body he has no problem showing off, I crave to know what it would be like with him.

One last time.

"You sure that's a good idea?"

"It's a horrible idea, Wylder. But I've gotten good at no-strings-attached fucking. I imagine you have too."

"There haven't been strings since you."

Bullshit.

"If you're going to tell me lies, do it with your body, not your words."

"You think I'm lying," he asks, and I nod. "Fine. Get your ass upstairs and strip."

He doesn't spare me a second glance when he climbs off me and heads up the stairs. I trail at a slower pace, building up every one of my walls and barriers. By the time I step through his bedroom door, the cage around my heart is securely locked.

This is nothing but sex. Hate sex, at that. Two bodies working out stress, finding release with each other, or a little retribution maybe. People do this all the time without any mess. Animals, too. That's all this is, I'm a lioness waiting to get railed by the leader of her pride. Or some other kind of nonsense... It won't be the first time I fucked a hot guy simply because he looks good. Why should this be any different? Besides maybe our pent up animosity will only make it better.

Cillian is pulling his shirt over his head as I walk in. His blonde hair, still a little long due to the off-season, falls over his forehead. Instinctively, I reach out to brush it away. He shivers under the brief touch.

"Have you gotten any better at following instructions?"

"I guess you'll have to find that out for yourself," I answer after a laugh. I've always been obstinate, but I don't mind being bossed around a little in the bedroom these days.

"I told you to strip."

Raising a brow at him, I slide the side zipper of my sundress down and let it all fall off me. It's hard, standing in front of a man whose chiseled form is what men dream to have and women dream to have over them. All while my body is showing a different sort of life. I don't hide it though, and he takes everything that my bandeau and tiny panties show.

Cillian takes his time with his perusal. Small infernos ignite on my skin as his eyes dart all over my skin. When he pauses at the belly that's not quite flat, I pull it in.

"Don't." He drops to his knees, placing his hands on my hips. "Don't hide where she grew. Where she lived while you nourished every part of her."

How am I supposed to survive words like that?

"I bet I don't look like the women you usually fuck." We both realize my defense mechanism.

"None have been nearly as beautiful."

"I told you I don't want to hear your lies."

He stands back up and turns me toward the full-length mirror leaning against the wall behind me. Towering behind me, his arms wrap around me. One strong arm snakes up between my breasts to firmly grip my throat. The other, a stark contrast as it gently caresses my lower abdomen.

"Look at you." The words softly breeze at my ear. "I've never seen you so beautiful. Though I can imagine how damned gorgeous you were when your belly was swollen with Sadie. I hate you for not letting me share that. I also love you in fathomless amounts for gifting her to this world. She's everything, but she's everything because this body protected her until she was strong enough to come into her own. Don't ever fucking hide that from me again."

I have no response to that. It's possibly the best thing anyone has ever said to me. Yet, I'm not ready to admit that to him.

The hand on my belly lowers, his fingers sliding under the thin lace barrier. Cillian still wears his jeans; the rough denim skates along my lower back at the same time a finger parts me and teeth nip at my earlobe.

"I hated you for moving on," I say, gasping when his hand tightens the barest amount. "I hated you for leaving me behind."

"I never moved on," he tells me, deep and angry. "I didn't mean to leave you behind. You should have been with me, so I could keep you wet like this all the time."

"You never asked me to go." Trying to focus on my anger is futile with his magic touch.

"I regretted it every day after I left," he says, thrusting two fingers inside me. "Fuck, you feel good. Yeah, Isla, suck my fingers in."

Oh God.

Dirty talk was never in Cillian's arsenal before. Before our separation, before Trina, before the countless women. What other new tricks has he learned?

"You're going to come on my fingers first. I won't fuck you until you do. Okay?" My knees turn to jelly when he pushes his palm onto my clit. "Answer Isla, I need to know you're here with me. Understand?"

"Yes," I gasp. "I'm going to come on your fingers first. Then you're going to fuck me into oblivion because you fucking owe me that much."

His hand loosens its chokehold as he chuckles, humor lighting his eyes in the mirror.

"And more, Isla. But it's the least I can do." His fingers change rhythm. The track of whatever internal mix tape he's hearing flips. In seconds, I'm edging. So close, so fucking close. "Nothing feels as good sliding against my fingers as you. Come for me so my cock can feel this, too."

He bites my collarbone, then he licks slowly up the column of my neck. I have to grip either side of the mirror to keep myself upright.

"Look at yourself as you fall apart for me, Isla. Watch how magnificent you are." He clamps onto my earlobe again, and I shatter. My body convulses with small ripples as he continues to hold me in place, his hard dick pressing into my ass with small pulses. Cillian giving me direct eye contact through the mirror only makes me come harder. It's more intimate when he's watching me, watching him get me off.

"Fuck," I groan when the waves subside some. He doesn't stop rubbing all the right spots until my body stops all movement besides my heaving chest. While still holding my eyes with his, he takes his fingers out of me and brings them to his mouth. Painting his lips first, he finally closes his eyes when he sucks them clean.

"Damn it, I've missed you," he says ever so quietly. "Now get naked."

He doesn't have to ask me twice. Not after that orgasm, anyway. My sex life is perfectly healthy for a woman my age and in my position. Though, admittedly, I don't let go easily with anyone but Tyson, who I only see a few times a year now. Even with him, it's never felt like this.

My body remembers Cill, it's comfortable with him touching me. Like a sexual muscle memory, he's where I learned everything.

"You first," I tease him since he's still wearing his jeans. He winks and pushes his jeans off, kicking them to the side. There's nothing beneath them. Just him, hard and ready. My sight doesn't stay there though. As impressive as it is, his whole body is breathtaking. As I suspected, Cillian is in the best form of his life. Angles and ridges, defined muscles atop defined muscles.

My mouth waters with the desire to be skin-to-skin with such a specimen. I reach around to unhook my bra, then shimmy out of my panties too. My flesh might not appear as perfect as his, but he's made me feel like it's equally worthy of worship. So, I stand brave and tall, letting him take me in the way I did him.

"Come here, Isla," he commands me. Before I can make it the full few feet to where he's perched at the end of the bed, he grabs my arm and pulls me closer. His mouth goes to my breast, sucking my nipple in without any warning. A gasp escapes me.

"Condom."

"Yeah, of course," he says, almost as if I've stunned him. Whether by my demand or the timing of it, who knows. "I am clean. For reference."

"So am I. And I'm on birth control. Not that it did me any good before, so I still demand condoms."

"That's good," he says while pulling open a drawer on his nightstand. "You should. You don't want any little Murphys running around."

I think he's trying for a joke, but it comes across snide and full of jealousy. It both pisses me off and turns me on.

"Tyson has been good to me, don't give him shit," I say, as he slides the condom over his impressive dick. "But it's cute that you think he's the only one I fuck."

"Don't make me lose my erection," he mumbles.

"Aw, don't lie, Cillian. The thought of me getting railed by some random in a darkened club hallway doesn't turn you off."

"You'll fucking pay for that."

"Gladly," I reply, propping my elbows on the bed as I bend over. Pushing up on my toes, I raise my ass in the air and wiggle it a bit. We're not doing this face-to-face. There was more than enough intimacy in that mirror a few minutes ago; I'll have no more of that.

Instead of driving into me as I expect him to, he lines me up and pulls me back on to him by my hips.

"Fuck," we say in unison. I drop my forehead to the soft sheet, hoping it can cool some of the flush I'm getting from Cillian being inside of me. Again. He must be feeling something similar too, because he holds there, unmoving, save for a thumb gently rubbing circles at the side of my ass.

"Maybe you're rusty, but this is the part where you fuck me senseless," I taunt.

"You just feel…"

"No." This doesn't feel sentimental or nostalgic. It's not like coming home after you've been away too long. "I feel like the woman that hid your baby from you for years." His grip tightens and he finally starts to move, pulling out slowly and slamming back in harder.

"I hate you." Truth or lie? I don't know.

"Fuck me like that then," I say, because it doesn't matter if he's being honest with me or with himself. This isn't a recoupling; we're not healing old wounds. Maybe we're causing new ones. Or this is the goodbye our bodies were denied. Whatever it is, it feels amazing, him sliding out and forcing himself back a little further each time. A little harder each time.

He trails a hand down my thigh, pulling my leg up on to the bed at the knee and adjusting his stance. It drives him even deeper, and I collapse down on my head and shoulders, muffling my moans in the bedding.

"Your randoms never felt like this, did they? Murphy can't fuck you the way I can."

"Keep telling yourself that, baby."

Slap!

The blow lands loudly on my butt cheek but isn't overly hard. It's the reaction I want, nonetheless.

"I don't need to convince myself; your body is doing that for me. I feel your greedy cunt grasping me for dear life each time I try to leave it." He palms my right breast, squeezing as he leans over my body bringing his mouth to my ear. "Your nipples are hard enough to cut glass. Every muscle in your body shakes with need, Isla. For me. For this cock inside you. You're fucking lucky I'm giving you the opportunity to have it again."

His ego makes me laugh; which earns me another swat.

"You're the lucky one here, Wylder. Me, in your bed, that's the prize."

Cillian's hands tangle with both of mine. He stretches them up above our heads, bringing the weight of him down on me as he slows the pace of his hips to a slow roll. It pushes my clit into the edge of the mattress, adding more sensation to my already electrified body.

"I know. For as much as I want to hate you with everything I have, the same way you do me..." With an even pace, he pushes the tempo of his hips. A little faster, then a little faster, then a little more. "It's always been you who haunts me. You're my every dream and every goddamned nightmare. Get there, Isla. Finish with me inside you so I can cover your secrets with my cum."

I'm not sure what he means by that, but his vicious dirty talk turns me inside out. I grind harder against the mattress and push against him, following the lead his body takes. Within minutes, I'm biting the sheets to keep from screaming out in pleasure. I don't want to give him that satisfaction, nor do I want to wake up Sadie and the closest neighbors.

"Try all you want, Isla. You can't hide how good that was from me," he says, pulling out before I've even finished shaking. Easily, he rolls me over and climbs up my body, pinning my shoulders between his knees. He pulls the condom off and tosses it aside as if it's offensive. "Stick that lying tongue out, honey. I'm going to wash your mouth out."

Holy hell.

I watch with rapt fervor as he strokes himself, placing the head of his cock to the tip of my tongue. He steadies my face with his other hand, his thumb hooking to the corner of my mouth.

"Mmm," he moans. "Just like that. Don't you fucking swallow until I tell you."

The first hit covers my tongue. I blink in surprise but don't close or swallow. The next one lands on my top lip, dripping down into my waiting mouth. After a few more, instinct takes over, but he holds me open with his thumb, angling me so at least I won't choke on it.

"Now. Rinse it around and swallow it down, baby," he says after his last groaning release. Narrowing my eyes at him, I push some of his cum out, letting it drip down. Cillian swipes it with his fingers and pushes it between my lips. "All of it, Isla. You know you've missed it."

I have. I hate us both for that, but he's not wrong. Missing what we had, or what I thought we had, has become like nature for me. It was easy with him and me. I could be myself, comfortable and vulnerable in ways I'd never been before or since.

Cillian rolls off me, sitting beside my splayed body. With difficulty, I peer up at him, allowing eye contact as I try to read his reaction.

"They're bigger now," he says, weighing a breast in his hand.

"I think they're supposed to shrink back up with breastfeeding, but Sadie wouldn't latch."

"Is that normal?"

"It's not uncommon. Especially when the mother has postpartum depression." Just like that, I lay it out. The last big secret I've withheld from him.

"What was that like," he asks, lying on his side next to me.

"It was awful. One moment, I was numb to everything, the next I'd be nearly manic. It was a struggle to eat or sleep, I'd just stare at Sadie as she slept and wonder what was wrong with me. Or how much she was going to hate me. I failed most of my classes that semester, which only added to my depression. I was failing at everything all at once. When the emotions I was supposed to be having started to wake up, I was overwhelmed with guilt that I'd spent so much time not bonding with her. So that was a whole other kind of torture."

"I wish you had told me. I'd have done whatever I could."

"You finding out terrified me by then," I confess. "I was convinced it would send you and Trina to my doorstep demanding I hand over my baby because you could care for her better." A tear leaks out and I let it, I won't hide my pain anymore. I'm strong enough to fight him on whatever he might bring my way.

"You thought I would do that?" He sounds horrified and accusatory.

"Logic didn't play a lot into my thoughts right then. It took a few months and a great therapist before I started to pull out of it."

"I'm so sorry," he says, wrapping an arm over me and pulling me close.

"For what, exactly?" I roll my back toward him, pulling my knees up to my chest.

"All of it. For the huge mistakes I made when I left. For not being the man you needed, one you could trust to tell everything to. I haven't been that even since coming back. I'm working on it though." His hand finds my hip again.

Trust is a rare find. Hard to come by, easy to lose. So impossibly difficult to regain. Cillian can fill the hole he made in my heart with all the pretty words he wants, but with no foundation to hold them together, they sift right back out.

So where do we go? What's our next step?

"I know this is your bed, and we're in your room. But get out, Cillian. This was the equivalent of a bootie call, nothing more."

16

CILLIAN

The first game of the season always feels like a birthday or Christmas as a kid. All excitement and anticipation. Someday, I imagine that will fade, but it hasn't yet. The world of professional hockey hasn't jaded me, I still love it as much as I did the first time I laced up my skates.

My only qualms about tonight's game are that it's away and it's in Vancouver. Which means I don't have my best gal, Sadie, with me and I'll be playing against the guy whose company Isla prefers.

Sadie gave me a stuffed octopus to pack with me, a reminder of her because she thought I'd be lonely on our one-night out-of-towner. The Blade's home opener is only a couple of days away and we're all excited for it. The breaking in of a new team at a new arena, plus the first game I'll get to play with my daughter in attendance. I want that more than I can say. If you'd have asked me a few years back if I thought fatherhood was in my near future, I'd have laughed. But now, I know I was born for it.

I was meant to be Sadie's daddy, and one day, I want more. A brood of Wylder children with my dirty blonde hair and Isla's curls.

The thought comes unbidden. Like always, the future I see for myself includes her. Even though she unceremoniously tossed me out of my own bed and hasn't been receptive to any of my antics to get her back in it. We're still walking that line between hate and love. Or at least I am. Most days she's still solidly in the hate category. Which, yeah, okay fine. I'm perfectly willing to hate fuck her all she wants.

Isla Cole gagging on and spitting out my cum was the sexiest damned thing I've ever seen.

I only need to figure out how to convince her to let me do it again.

"Grand gesture," Hugo reminds me. "I keep telling you, that's what the birds like. Now get your head right, Wild, or Coach will lob it off."

"I'm good." We march through the tunnel to an array of boos and cheers. Being this close to home has made our team's natural rivals, but also garners a lot of our own fans in the stands. The feigned rivalry only fuels us players, though. After we take our spots, the lights dim and the music changes while their team takes the ice for introduction.

Murphy is a crowd favorite; the applause near deafening. The asshole skates by looking directly at me.

It's going to be that kind of night.

Even during the singing of the country's national anthem, the asshole mad dogs me. I'm not a chippy player. Usually. But this fucker has me white knuckled.

"Ty treats me good."

Fuck that. If he treated Isla so good, they'd be more than two people who only hook up when they happen to be in the same city together. They would be a couple. But they aren't because Isla isn't meant for Murphy, and that shitbag is never going to be stepdaddy to my kid.

Am I rational about it? No. Do I give a fuck? Also, no.

Hugo gives me a light shove before he heads off to protect our net.

"Get that puck in the net for me, Wild."

"Will do, Bloomy!"

Six and half minutes later, I haven't fulfilled my promise to our goaltender. Neither have any of our other guys. Though, Vancouver hasn't scored either. We're beating them with shots on the net; their goalie must be getting tired. But he's damn good.

My line hops the board to get back on the ice while Wallin has the puck behind our own net. Seeing me open, he passes it off to me and in no time at all Murphy is there, tangling up with me for control.

"You be sure to tell my girls I said hi, Wylder."

"Find your own fucking family," I say, shoving him off against the boards with my shoulder and swatting the puck to Vaughn as Murphy laughs.

I skate clear, Vaughn passes it back, and I one-time it at Vancouver's net. It's a lucky shot, ricocheting off the bar and bouncing in behind Lindholm, their goalie, before he can swat it away. Lucky shots count though and not only have I scored the first point of the game, but also the first point for the Blades' franchise.

Suck on that, Murphy.

My guys crowd me in quick celebration, but I make sure to point down the ice to Hugo, so he knows that was for him.

The period ends without any more scoring. Coach stands at the door of the locker room as we file in.

"Anything I need to know?"

"He's goading me, but I'm keeping it clean, Coach." Hopefully, I can keep that up. We'll see.

Coach only raises a brow, following me in. He knows it all, which means he knows how easily this can all turn to shit.

That's exactly what happens in the third period. They're down by two. With over eight minutes left, there is plenty of time but they're still struggling to get shots on net. Our forecheck is on point, as is our passing. Making it difficult for them to gain control for very long. They're itching for a fight, a surefire way to get the fans in the seats behind them.

"You were nothing but a life lesson for her, Wylder," Murphy says, checking me as soon as I get my stick on the puck.

"Yeah, whose bed is she in, asshole?" I slam him into the boards, both of us tussling for the puck as it rattles around our skates.

"She teaching you all the things she learned from me?"

This motherfucker.

"You fucking wish."

"You're right, best pussy I've ever had," he says. I send a silent apology to my team and to Coach... and then I throw a forearm to the side of his head. Gloves are dropped, chaos ensues, and I get him down on the ice with a couple good punches in before I'm pulled off him.

"You okay, Wild," Wallin asks as he skates with me to the box.

"Yeah, but seriously fuck that guy." He grins wide before retreating to our bench, where Coach stands stoic and staring right at me.

Okay, so I fucked up. Murphy hit back and ended up with his own penalty so at least we're still even on the ice. Two minutes never feel longer than when they're penalty minutes and you watch from behind the glass, unable to help your team in any way. It's more nerve racking when the puck is mostly at your own net for those one hundred twenty seconds. Such is life in the game of hockey though.

With nothing else to do, I catch my breath. And try to remember that Isla isn't mine and she sure as fuck isn't Murphy's and I'm not going to let that chucklefuck back into my head.

When my time is up, I skate back out into the mix. Ignoring everything but the puck and my team. Polski, a winger for Vancouver, makes a bad pass and I'm able to recover the puck. Shooting to Wallin who's in front of the net and sails right in the five hole for another goal.

Suck on that one, too, Murphy.

"Now, is there anything I need to know," Coach asks later that night when he finds me with a plate of nachos at the hotel bar with Hugo and Oliver.

"He said something crude about Isla, I couldn't let that slide." I'm not fucking apologizing for it. Since the day I met her, I would throw down for her.

"Fair enough," he says after a minute of silent contemplation. His small smile says he's pleased, not angry.

"That man still scares the shit out of me," Oliver says.

"Just don't lie to him. He appreciates honesty and hard work, you'll be fine. If you don't date one of his daughters, anyway."

"Or have a kid with one," Hugo adds.

"Doesn't seem like he hates you, especially after tonight," Oliver says with a shrug. "He just doesn't talk to you as much as the rest of us."

"I've been relegated to assistant coach's problem. Which is fine," I confess. "Schwartz is a good guy." I'm interrupted by my phone. I sent Isla a text after the game to ask how much Sadie was able to watch before she fell asleep, but she never answered. Hoping it's her, I pull it out of my pocket, only to be disappointed.

TRINA:

Great game, babe!

"I need to make a call," I tell the guys. Dropping some cash on the table, I rise to leave. "See you in the morning."

As soon as I'm in my hotel room, I hit her contact.

"Hey, Cillian," she says as if we didn't have a talk not so long ago.

"I told you not to text me anymore, Trina."

"Come on, Cill. I was only congratulating you," she says, her signature pout coming through loud and clear.

"You don't get to do that anymore."

"I told you I didn't do anything. Why are you believing the woman who hid your daughter from you? She's such a liar!"

"She showed me everything you sent her. I saw it all, Trina. You have no idea what that shit did to her and to my daughter!"

Trina starts crying. Countless apologies included in-between. Flopping back on the bed, I stare up at the stark white ceiling. How did I ever find anything appealing about this woman? She sounds like a shrill child, and I feel like a complete idiot.

I want a clean slate. A do-over. If I could call mulligan and start over, I would.

"Why, Trina? Why send her anything? And how the fuck did you even know her birthday or anniversary date?"

"I…" She pauses.

"Don't try and think up a lie now, you're fucked either way. Tell me the truth."

"You never loved me," she finally says.

"I never claimed to," I shoot back.

"Yeah, but I wanted you to. I wanted what you gave her. What you wrote about her, I wanted those words to be for me."

What I wrote?

"Are you fucking kidding me? You read my letters?"

Isla may have cut me out of her life, but I couldn't do that same thing. Every time I wanted to share something with her, I wrote her a letter. None were ever sent, but I still wrote them and stored them in a skate box in the back corner of my closet.

Trina had no reason to know they even existed.

"How much of my privacy did you violate, exactly? It wasn't enough that you took pictures of me while I slept, you went through my shit, too?"

"I'm sorry," she cries.

"Fuck off, there is no apology big enough for the shit you've pulled."

"You don't mean that. We've been friends for years!"

"I sure as fuck do mean it. This is over, Trina. Whatever messed up fantasy you have going on in your head, it stops now. I want no part of it. And you were never my friend, were you? Not really, because the shit you've pulled is not what friends do. They don't take advantage, they don't interfere, they don't lie and manipulate. I've spent weeks trying to piece together everything you've done and why. But what it really comes down to is that I want it to be over. Stay the fuck out of my life. Don't make me tell you again."

I end the call. There's a heavy weight on my chest, pinning me to this spot with nothing but the blank white above me and my racing thoughts. Rubbing at it doesn't ease the ache. This is the pain of guilt and regret that only time dulls, but I've lost so much to it already.

"You scored, Daddy!" Sadie bounds down the dock to me when I step out to meet her and Isla. She's staying the night with me again, only the second time Isla's let us do this without her. Pigtails bounce at her temples in little ringlets, her face alight with pride.

"Did you see it?"

"Yes! It was so cool!" She jumps into my arms and wraps her tiny ones around my neck.

"You're so cool," I tell her, then blow a raspberry on her neck before setting her down to run inside.

"I thought the neighbors would call the cops at how much she was screaming in excitement. She hasn't stopped talking about it," Isla says, her face a little sour even if the words aren't.

"What's wrong?"

"What the fuck was that stunt with Ty?"

"He provoked that," I say, incredulously.

"I was watching the game." She rolls her eyes at me. "Tyson was playing clean; you were playing personal."

"Fucking right, I was, Isla. I take it very personal when he taunts me with crude suggestions about you and calls you and Sadie 'his girls'. That is extremely personal," I hiss, trying not to gain Sadie's attention inside. "You know what? I'm done being the bad guy in your life, Isla. All this time I thought I was only missing you, but now I know I was missing out on so much more. I could have had that bright smile and cheerful excitement from her. And yeah, that's my fault. But I was cheated, too."

"Cillian."

"Stop. I'm not doing this today. Wait here," I tell her and dip back inside to grab the letter I left by my doorstep. "This is for you. Let me know what you decide. Sadie Baby, come say goodbye to Mommy."

It's her play to call now.

17

ISLA

"What's in it?" Zander asks me after he bowls yet another strike.

"That's what I want to know," Willa says. "But she didn't open it."

"We can sit with you while you do?" Kit adds. She grabs her ball and lines up, only for it to roll in the gutter like most have before. She's awful at bowling unless she's drunk, yet she's the one that always suggests we come here.

Willa's the best of us all, but if Zan is with us, she lets him win. No matter how many times I try to convince her to stop it, she always makes sure he gets a few points more than her.

"She's got it with her," Willa tells Zan. "Now is as good a time as ever."

"What if it's bad? Legal shit or something? He was kind of ominous when he gave it to me," I say, admitting the fear that's kept me from breaking the seal on the envelope all day. I flipped it in my hands over and over. My three papercuts proof that I nearly got the courage a few times.

"What if it's not? Either way, you need to know," Kit says.

"Tell you what? If Willa wins, I'll open the envelope here and read it to you all." I send a wink her way, and she glares in return.

"You're a bitch," she whispers while moving to grab her ball.

"Love you, too, Sissy Poo," I tell her, laughing. She sticks her tongue out at me, then bowls a strike. Willa made it look so effortless that Zan narrows his gaze on her.

"I always suspected she was better than me," he tells me after our last frame. We've moved to a table in the restaurant and are waiting for Willa and Kit, who made a trip to the bathrooms. Likely so Willa can complain about me goading her into giving up the façade. I place an order with our server, adding mozzarella sticks, her favorite comfort food. She won't stay mad at me with those on the table.

"Maybe she thinks your swollen ego can't handle losing to a pretty little girl."

"Shut up, I don't have a big ego. Do I?" He laughs but looks mortified.

"No, baby. It's a normal sized NHL hopeful, male ego."

"What does that mean?"

"You've got to have a certain amount of cockiness to make it in this game, Zan. Some have more than others. Yours is just the right amount."

"That's good, I guess," he says, but doesn't look convinced.

"All right, time to open that fucking envelope," Willa announces, taking a seat at the table.

"Fine." Grabbing it from the side pocket, I gently open the seal. I'm stalling, of course, but I don't need another paper cut either. Inside is a handwritten letter on paper, imprinted with a Vancouver hotel logo. At least that means it's not legal documents. As promised, I read it aloud.

Isla,

There are no words heavy enough to carry the weight of how sorry I am for the turn our lives took because of me. You were so much of my world, and I took you for granted. I took the unconditional support you offered me for granted. I missed that every day.

I missed you. Every. Single. Day.

There were times I told myself it was for the best. That we both needed to learn to be adults, independent of each other. Maybe that's true in some sense, but I'm pretty sure it was just my wounded pride trying to convince me I hadn't let the best thing to ever happen to me slide out of my grasp.

And for what? Casual sex with women I didn't care about. Women that never compared to you. Women who pretended to be something they weren't.

You never did that. You were never anything but honest with me, brutally at times.

Until you weren't.

And now here we are. You, hating me. Me, wanting to hate you. I hate what you did, even if I'm starting to understand why. But at the end of the day...

I love you more than my anger and your hate combined.

Do you remember the notes I used to leave you? No matter where I was, or you were, I always wanted to talk to you. There weren't enough hours in the day for me to get enough of you. That didn't stop when you quit me. Every day I thought of something I wanted to share with you before anyone else. I have a box full of letters and notes that I wrote to you over the years. Naively, I thought they were safe from prying eyes; kept secretly and securely until the day they'd find their way to you.

I'm only starting to scratch the surface of how my actions became a landslide that derailed your life, your peace, your health, and your happiness. None of it should have ever happened. There are so many things that require my apologies, I'll keep saying it every time I find a new one.

I'm sorry.

My family comes first. That wasn't always the case, but it is now and with each day to come. Neither of us is completely innocent. So, I'm asking for a clean slate or at the least a way forward.

The letters are yours, if ever you want them.

I'm yours, if you ever decide you want me again. Even if it's just another angry fuck. Whatever you need from me, Isla, I'll provide it. I'm not the same boy I was, my priorities are straight.

Always yours,

Cillian

"Well, shit," Kit says when I finish. "That was romantic."

"When did you fuck him," Willa asks.

"I wonder what the other letters say." This comes from Zander, echoing my same thoughts.

"Isla?" Willa pushes.

"That first sleepover with Sadie," I answer Willa.

"Fuck you, for not telling me."

"It's not any of our business," Zander says.

"No, it isn't. You've been through a lot with me," I tell her. "I didn't want you to worry."

"I told you you'd fall back in love with him."

"It was just sex," I say.

"Right, you just tripped and fell into his bed with your body but not your heart or head," Willa says with a side eye.

"Hot sex?"

"Fuck, Kit, you have no idea."

"I would if you'd give me details."

"No, thank you," Zander and Willa say in unison.

"Damn buzzkills," Kit cries.

It's not until later that night, lying in my bed while I stare at Sadie's empty one, that his letter hits me. The two times I reread it while alone helped.

Cillian Wylder wants me back.

There's an indescribable buzz at the arena for not only the home opening game, but the first home game of the franchise in a brand-new arena. It's electric. So much so that it almost feels tangible. Like I could stick a finger in the air and get a little zap.

Everyone's all smiles, even with the eleventh hour troubleshooting and minor mishaps that inevitably happen the first game.

The boys from the youth league are here with me for a small pre-game exhibition on the ice. None of them can hold their excited fidgeting at bay, or their chatter.

"We'll be the first team to skate on this ice," one of them says. It's not entirely true, as the Blades have been on the ice plenty of times getting used to the new facility. But I get what he means and his fellow players all nod with the same enthusiasm.

It's contagious, this feeling of breaking new ground. I'm happy I get to be down here with them, behind the scenes. Not that it won't be equally fun in the stands with Sadie, Willa, and my mom.

But I don't get to go sit with the players' families until my work is done.

Which means getting these boys on the ice for a few minutes, then to their own seats.

"Have a good time out there fellas," Hugo calls as he passes us by in the tunnel.

"Holy shit, that was Hugo Blum."

"Legend," another boy says.

Their level of starstruck never gets old.

"He's almost as good as your dad was, Miss Cole."

"You think so, Andrew?"

"Yeah," he says, nodding like a bobblehead. "It must have been pretty cool growing up with your dad."

"It was," I agree. "But if you think he's strict with his players, you should have seen him with his daughters and homework."

"Oh, man." Andrew laughs. "I didn't think about that part. He's not really that scary though, is he?"

I raise an eyebrow at him and leave it at that. Dad loves that he has a reputation of being a hard ass when he's not at all. He's just quiet and stoic until he has reason not to be. It comes off as cold, but it's because he's paying attention.

"You're up, guys," I tell the group as the arena hosts begin to announce them. "Go show them what you've got."

"You're really good with them," Katherine tells me after the boys leave and we watch from the opposite side of the glass as they run through some shooting drills for the crowd.

"Kids like them have basically been my whole life." I shrug. My job won't always consist of hanging out with kids, but I wouldn't mind if it did. Boys are easy, I understand them. Men... not so much.

"I was the product of all girls' Catholic private schools. Boys still freak me out," Katherine says.

"Boys are simple. If you figured girls out, you're way more advanced than any boy you'll ever meet."

"I guess there's some truth to that," she says with a laugh.

Conversation picks up in the tunnel behind us. Turning around, I see my dad.

"Hey."

"Hey, sweetheart. They about done?"

"Yep." Dad offered to come out and say hello to my boys as they come off the ice. He doesn't really have the time to spare, but youth hockey has always been an important part of his life, so he made an exception. "I'll keep it quick."

"No worries."

With a little difficulty, I do keep it quick. The boys fan it up like a bunch of teenage girls at a Taylor Swift concert. Dad eats that shit up, even if I'm the only one who can tell.

"Thanks, old man," I tease him when everyone else clears out.

"Anything for you. Headed up to the stands?"

"Yep. Good luck," I say, giving him a hug. "Tell Cill... never mind. Old habits, I guess."

"Let's talk about that sometime soon, kiddo. Now go, it's almost time."

I hurry up to where the wives and girlfriends are sitting. Mom and Erin have saved a seat for me. As soon as I take it, Sadie clamors onto my lap.

"He's number six, Mommy."

"I know, baby." I press a kiss to the top of her head, then turn to give greetings to the few fellow family members I've already met.

"Hi Isla, I'm Caroline Vaughn." Very little surprises me, but Gavin Vaughn's wife does. In the small sea of significant others, she stands out. But not how you'd expect. Most NHL wives are on the polished side. Not like you'd see in the NFL, or NBA, or anything, but they all have made-up faces and freshly done nails. Caroline looks more like she just stepped out of a garden where she grows her own marijuana and might forget to brush her hair before she leaves the house in a pair of paint splattered overalls. I like her instantly.

"Hi, it's nice to meet you."

"Likewise."

"How are you adjusting to the move? Quite a bit different than Florida, I imagine," I say to strike a conversation.

"Oh, definitely, but it feels more like home here. I grew up in small town upstate New York. Florida wasn't my jam."

"Well, welcome home."

"Thank you. This is your daughter?"

"This is Sadie."

"Hi, Sadie. It's nice to meet you," Caroline says.

"Hi! Does your daddy play for the Blades too?"

"No, sweetie," Caroline answers, laughing. She's probably close to ten years older than me, Vaughn being one of the more senior players on the team. "My husband does."

"Which one is he?"

"Gavin Vaughn, number twenty-seven."

"What numbers are those?" She looks at my mother as she asks, because she gets to teach her numbers and letters. For some reason, she trusts her more than me. It's always been an amusement for my family how Sadie assigns silent roles. Willa is who she expects to watch all the animated movies with, Pops is everything sports and animals. Grandma is the educator. I'm the food expert and the designated butt wiper.

It is what it is.

"That's a two and then a seven."

"Okay, I'll look for him!"

"You let me know if you see him," Caroline tells her, obviously amused.

"Do you have kids," I ask.

"One, she's sixteen and currently doesn't find her father's life that enchanting. Tori is still feeling the sting of moving cross country and leaving a boyfriend behind."

"Ahh, that would be tough at that age."

"At any age, really," Erin adds.

Isn't that the brutal truth?

Sadie overflows when the game starts. Whenever Cillian is on the ice, she yells when she sees him. She's even more animated when he has the puck. Her little arms stretching over her head as she watches with anticipation. She screams as loud as any adult here when our team scores. I hope she never loses her enthusiasm for the sport or her dad.

It's my fault she hasn't experienced this before. The realization hits me like a train, pulverizing every lie I've told to convince myself that what I was doing was the right thing.

Neither of us is completely innocent.

Am I any less a villain than he is? What other special connection have I denied my daughter?

Cillian doesn't score, but ends up with an assist, something equally as good through Sadie's exhausted eyes. He managed the entire game with no penalties, too. I send him a text on our way to the family room to wait for him and my dad.

ME:

She's dead on her feet, might be asleep by the time you get out.

CILL:

I'll hurry.

Yeah, right.

I've yet to meet a hockey player that has a quick post-game routine. No such thing exists, I'm convinced. While he's one of the first bunch out, it still takes forever. Sadie collapsed in my arms, near comatose, but her eyes aren't fully shut just yet.

"There's your daddy, baby." Her head pops up a few inches.

"Good job, Daddy."

"Thanks, Sadie Baby," Cillian says, picking her up from my arms and cradling her in his. I think she falls asleep before her head even hits his shoulder. "Thanks for waiting for me before taking off."

"Oh, it's fine. I think we're all used to waiting around for hockey players," Mom tells him, and Erin agrees.

"I'll carry her out to your car," Cillian tells his mom who is having Sadie over for a Nana night.

Following behind him, I try not to feel the things I'm feeling as he snuggles into her wild curls. He's made it clear he doesn't see her as often as he wants. That's not because I'm unaccommodating or anything. It's just schedules that don't always align. Normally, it isn't something to feel guilty about. It's not as if I see her as often as I'm accustomed to either. Except tonight I do feel bad, like it's all my fault.

Clearly, Cillian has made her a priority. There's still a voice inside reminding me that he didn't do the same for me.

He carefully buckles her into the car seat, and we both say goodbye to our daughter and his mother. Then it's just the two of us in the middle of the dark parking lot. People come outside and drive off around us while we stare at each other.

Cillian waits for me to take the first step, he wants me to do it.

He's drawn the line, not knowing if I'll step over it or not.

"Good night, Isla," he says after a hefty, disappointed sigh.

"Wait." I reach out to grab his arm, feeling the flex of nervousness under my fingers. So much has changed for and about us, but not this. Not how we still affect one another. Maybe that's what we should focus on instead of our anger and our hurt. What brought us together in the first place? How did our fucked-up fairytale start? "Want to grab a bag of Dick's and talk about the game?"

"This was nice," Cillian says later. After we've finished our greasy late-night dinner on the upper deck of his house. The gas outdoor fireplace is lit but I'm still wrapped in a blanket to ward off the rapidly cooling weather. The chill is worth the view of the moon reflecting off the lake water.

Feels like old times.

"It was," I say instead.

"You haven't deposited the check yet."

"I never wanted your money, Cill." The check sits at the bottom of my underwear drawer, waiting for me to find the right place to stash it away for Sadie's future use. But I haven't made it a priority or anything. Because I make enough for us to live on, and Cillian has been providing for her in every way he can think of. They go on small shopping sprees regularly. Mostly, he provides for her the way it counts most, by doting on her with love and affection.

"What *do* you want, Isla?" He cups my cheek, turning my head to face him.

"I don't know how to answer that," I admit. "What I wanted was for you to adore me the way I adored you. The same way you did before the draft. What I wanted was the silly dream of young love that lasts until death. I was so confident, you know? In us, and in you. Looking back, I hate that I didn't walk away when I first saw what was happening. I was just *so sure* you'd do the right thing and tell me if it was going too far." I'm not mad tonight. Maybe it's taken me this long to move on to another stage of grief, or maybe I'm done mourning the us that used to be. "What happened shook me so thoroughly, it was like I was walking on earthquakes for weeks. What I want, Cill, is to be sure of something again."

"If only it was as easy as me saying you can be," he says sadly, pulling me under his arm so I can lean back on his chest. It adds another layer of warmth and a comfort I haven't gotten from him in so long. "What happened... what I did, I never intended it. I left for Boston as sure in us as you were. There's no excuse for what I did. Maybe I can explain, though. Everyone around me was feeding a side of my ego I'd never known. Not just Trina, but especially her. You always called me Superstar and for a hot minute, I was just that. The press, the fans; they loved me. Every step of the way she was in my ear, offering help and advice. Eventually, she started offering other things that fed my libido along with my ego. This older, experienced woman wanted me. And even though I didn't want her back in the same way I wanted you, the things she offered became harder and harder to resist. And I started to rely on her always being around in the same supportive role you had always been in."

"Did you only kiss her? I mean, while we were still together, before that night on the video call." It's something I've always wanted and been terrified to know.

"Yes. The first time she gave me a kiss goodbye. It surprised me, but I stopped her immediately, reminding her that I had you. In hindsight, I should have made a bigger deal about that, been clearer. I promised you I would set boundaries with her and then failed at my first chance. The second time was... more. Knowing what I know now, I can see she took advantage of the situation. Torsten had a handful of people over, which wasn't abnormal for him. We played some video games, watched movies, and sometimes drank more than we should. I'd gotten sleepy but hadn't gone off to bed yet, Trina snuggled up and waited until I was almost lights out. That time, it took me longer to stop because my head was foggy with sleep, and I half dreamed it was you. I opened my eyes to her and told her I couldn't do that. But again, it didn't stop me from hanging around with her."

"What do you mean by knowing what you know now?"

18

CILLIAN

How am I supposed to admit that I wasn't smart enough to avoid a trap like Trina? Or strong enough?

"At the time, I didn't see her actions as intentional. I didn't think she was purposefully trying to get between us. On my side, it was a friendship developing naturally and that, eventually, took step after step too far. Then you showed me what you'd been sent. I sat with that information and realized so much of my friendship with her wasn't what it seemed."

"You say friendship, but it was more than that, Cillian," Isla interrupts.

"Yes," I agree. "But also no. We were never a couple. Sometimes there were... uh, sexual benefits. I never loved her, I never wanted more from her. She knew that, because I never wavered on it. Sex with her was convenient, as much as that makes me an asshole, I made the parameters clear. What I didn't know was that she must have felt threatened by how much I still loved you, and because of that she was doing awful things. Like what she sent you, even taking those pictures of me is a huge violation of the trust I had with her. She also snuck around and read the letters I wrote you."

"What?" Isla bolts upright, that temper that I used to love so much lighting up inside her. There have been sparks of it here and there, especially when she hit me with that right hook. But largely, it's only been a simmer compared to how easily it boiled as a teenager. "She read my letters?"

"Yes. It's how she knew when to send you the bullshit she did. I never shared anything about you with her." The smile forms on my face without my control, as she jumps up in outrage.

"What the fuck is funny to you right now, Wylder?"

"Nothing, Cole."

"Then why are you smiling!"

"Why are you this outraged?"

"Because those are my goddamned letters, and I haven't even read them yet. How fucking *dare* she?" She paces, no longer needing the blanket. Her disdain is keeping her warm enough.

"Right? What an awful person."

"She's a fucking bitch. She better hope I never see her again. Not only because of the letters, but what kind of psychopath takes pictures of people while they're sleeping? Like, what the actual fuck? Not to mention the fact that she heard me tell you I was pregnant and then what? Conveniently fucking forgot."

"What exactly happened in that call? I don't remember talking to you."

"You answered saying you missed this, and I thought you meant video calling with me. But then you started saying how I'd never talk to you again and how you didn't want to see me because I'd look sad and that would make you feel bad," she says, pausing to swallow down some emotion. "Then Trina said something, and the phone turned so I could see her, see that she was giving you a hand job. I lost my shit, blurted out that I was pregnant, then the call ended. I didn't know if it was you or her that hung up, but I suppose we can piece that shit together now."

"I remember her showing up at some point that night, but I don't remember any of that."

"I'm sorry, Cillian, I didn't think you were that out of it. I fully believed you chose to be with her that night. If I had thought she was doing something you didn't want..."

"Stop, Isla. I think I would have known if something more happened. But I'm pretty sure the only thing she took advantage of was the situation. One that I let her be a part of, that's on me," I reassure both her and myself. A person in your life taking such advantage of you is a weighty thing to face. Trina had plenty of opportunity to pull stunts like that, and I'm only now realizing the gravity of it all and just how diabolical she is.

"Cillian, if you don't remember the conversation, then you didn't give her consent to be touching you like that."

"If I can't remember that conversation, I doubt she got very far." *Thank you, biology.*

"Don't blow it off, Cill. That's still assault," Isla says, tears in her eyes. "Do you think she slipped you something? I don't know how much you drank that night, but I never knew you to get out of control or blackout drunk."

"Fuck, Isla. I want to say she's not capable of that, but I really don't know anymore." Trina has a lot to answer for, and this is information I'll have to confront her on. She's not what I want to focus on right now, though. There isn't much that can be done about Trina tonight, but there is something I can do to help Isla and I get to where we need to be. "Do you want your letters?"

"Yes, they're mine, damnit. Even if they have her shitty smell all over them now."

"There's a Bauer box on the floor of my closet. Have at it," I tell her as I start to clean up the mess of our dinner. She doesn't spare me a glance while tromping her way inside.

A long history resides in that box. I give her enough time to explore it, but not enough to deep dive in. My anxiousness gets the better of me. I need to know how she's reacting. Does she believe the words she's reading were genuine when I wrote them? Does she see me offering them to her as my own form of manipulation? That's not what I mean them to be, not even a little. I only want Isla to come back to me if she comes willingly and of her own accord.

She sits cross-legged on the floor, the dim light from a single lamp barely illuminating the tear that drops from her eye to the paper in her hands.

"Isla," I say her name like it's a sigh of relief. A release of years of yearning. An admission of my guilt and regret. And a cry of hope. I'm done being angry at her; it serves no purpose. "Don't be sad."

"Do you ever wonder if there's an afterlife? That on some plane of existence we can't see, there are the ghosts of those that were. That the ones that died by their own hand live there in continuous torture over what they've done? I believe it's possible, because that's what life is like right now. You're gone and it's left a hole in my chest that festers and hurts every day, but the gun that caused it sits smoking in my clenched fist," she reads the words that I wrote too long ago.

"They aren't all that morose, I promise."

She drops that one and picks up another. *"I never told you this, afraid I'd scare you off when we're still so young. Ever since our first date, I've fantasized about a life with you and babies. I want what your parents have. Little girls, that look like you, hanging around the arena with me. Skating or just watching. Maybe there are boys, too. I don't know, I wouldn't care either way. The only major difference I see is that the parental roles would be reversed. You'd be the one to scare our kids' potential suitors with that attitude of yours. I'd be more like your mom, casually taking in their fear with amusement. The dream means more to me than the NHL, I see that now. I spent my whole life with one goal, the Stanley Cup. It doesn't hold the same shine anymore. Nothing looks the same with you gone."*

She fingers through a few more letters.

"There was a storm tonight. Thunder but no lightning. I sat outside on my porch and let the rain shower down on me. It wasn't cold, I hardly even felt the wetness. What I did feel was you. As if you sat there with me, holding my hand, and telling me we weren't completely lost. I remembered the time you made me watch Jane Eyre *with you and it felt like that. Like there was a string from my heart to yours. I don't know, but it felt like I was home for a few minutes."*

I sit down behind her, wrapping myself around her as she quiets. "What are you thinking about?"

"The whole time I assumed you didn't care. Or at least not as much as I did. There was this fixed vision of you happily living your life with her at your side. One where you never thought about me or what my life had become. It helped me convince myself that you wouldn't care that I had kept the pregnancy and had a baby. That even if you knew about Sadie, nothing would be different. That's not the truth though."

"No, it's nowhere near the truth," I say into the nest of waves above her ear. "The fact is, I've been obsessed with you every day since we met. If you would have told me you were pregnant, I would have done anything I could to make things work out differently."

Whatever that looks like, I don't know. I like to think I would have convinced her to transfer to some school in Boston, where we'd live in some house I bought, and I'd come home every day to her, our baby girl, and my cat. Her moving her entire world for me wasn't something I ever wanted for her, or for us. I can see now how stupid it was that I didn't try harder for that.

"Only I didn't have all the right conversations with you. Because I didn't want you to want me just because I was pregnant. And I was terrified that you and Trina would try to take her away. I was so, so angry and sad. Because of that, we both suffered in our own way. That part is all on me, isn't it? That's my crime to pay for."

"I'm not imparting a sentence on you."

"Because you want a clean slate?" She tilts her head up, which lets me see the change in her. This is the first time since I've been back that there isn't that gleam of hatred in her eyes.

"I do, but that's not why. I love you, Isla. It's as simple and as complicated as that."

"Is a fresh start even possible for us?"

"Anything is possible, Isla. For my part, I trust that you won't hide or run from me, again. I'm choosing to put my faith in that. You have to get to that same place on your own time, or not." Fuck, I hope she does. Living without her isn't something I want to do, but I will if it's what makes her happiest, if it's what is best for Sadie.

She blinks up at me and I imagine sparks lighting up in that brain of hers as she wonders how she can ever trust me again. If it was as easy as fucking that into her, I'd do it in a heartbeat. When she's soft like this, languid in my arms, I miss the easy times we had. I miss the connection that was there both in bed and out. I miss falling asleep with her in my arms and waking up with her sprawled over me.

"What makes this time different?"

Everything.

That's not what she needs to hear, though. Giving her an easy answer won't get either of us where we need to be. For me, that's with my family. Even if that doesn't mean Isla and I together, I need her to trust me as a father to our daughter, as a partner, and a support system.

"The obvious answer is Sadie, but she's not the only reason. I know what it's like to grow up without a father, and I've witnessed what it's like to have one who gives his support so generously. I'm never leaving her or being anything but the best dad to her I can be," I tell her, dropping my forehead to hers. "I've had you, and I've lost you. The pain of that loss, the misery of being without you... I never want to feel it again. But more than that, I never again want to cause you the pain I did. I hate myself for it, Isla. There's a sharpness in my chest whenever I think about it, and next to it, a need to be the man that you always deserved. I never want to watch a storm again and see your face in the clouds, your tears in the rain, or your thunder attempting to strike me down time and time again. I'm determined to be only a source of strength and support for you and Sadie."

Her expression softens some, then tension lessoning minutely. My heart wants to believe it means she's trying to take my words as truth. I don't hold out that hope, not yet.

"Trusting you is going to be a long road, Cillian. I can admit that whatever initially attracted me to you is still there, maybe it's a little faded from time, but it isn't gone. There's an easiness with you, I'm more comfortable in my own skin with you than I've ever been able to be with anyone else. Even Tyson."

"Fuck that guy," I hiss.

"What happened between you two," she asks me with a narrowed gaze.

"I don't want to repeat it," I tell her, rubbing my nose against her brow.

"If it's about me, I deserve to know."

God damnit, she's not wrong. We're sitting here discussing having a better, more upfront relationship moving forward and I'm here denying her the answer to one of the first questions she asks. Why do I even care if she gets upset with him anyway?

Because I don't want her to hurt.

"He said you were the best pussy he'd ever had and wanted to know if you were teaching me the things he taught you," I say softly.

"Of course, I'm the best pussy he's ever had," she agrees, but I hear the dismay she tries to hide. "Fuck that guy, though."

"You *did*," I say with a groan.

"Do you really want to have a conversation about our past sexual partners," she asks me, turning in my arms and raising up to her knees. "There are other things you could be doing with that mouth. Much more interesting things."

"What did you have in mind, Cole?" Instead of answering me, she digs her hand down the front of my sweatpants. Finding me bare beneath, her face alights with heat. Her forwardness is surprising, maybe even concerning, but I'm not capable of telling her to stop. I want to be inside her every time I see her.

"Kiss me." A demanding Isla is a wet dream. Matching my energy is something she always did, but going toe-to-toe with me in bed, not as much. She used to always let me take the lead there.

"Why me," I ask her the question she asked me when I was desperate for that first date.

"What?" She pulls back an inch, blinking through the lust that had started to skew her vision. Her fingers still fondle me as I rapidly harden.

"Why me? What is about me that has your hand down my pants, Isla?"

"Why not you?" There is perturbance and defiance written all over her face. She doesn't want to admit that she likes anything about me. I get it, but she's going to have to get over it quickly so we can get to the fucking she's asking for.

"Cole," I warn. She huffs in return.

"Fine, since we're being all honest and shit," she relents. "The way you are with Sadie is really fucking attractive, for one. Defending my honor, or whatever the fuck you boys were up to is also much sexier than I'd like to admit. But mostly…"

"Mostly what?"

"I missed you. How easy it was to be myself with you, how unjudged and supported. You didn't mind that I was different than most girls, or that I get obsessive about weird things. My temper never turned you off, in fact you were always so amused by it that I'd settle down quicker. I was at ease with you, until I wasn't at all anyway. You understood me and it wasn't awkward. I never felt that way with anyone else. Before or after you, no matter how hard I tried. Even after Tyson and I had dated for months, we were nowhere close to that type of comfort."

"You do not get to say another man's name while your hand is wrapped around my cock."

"Is there something more interesting I could be doing with my mouth, too?"

"Fuck, yes," I say with a grunt because she runs her thumb over the head of my dick, picking up the precum that her words encouraged. "You need that dick to shut you up?"

"Mmm," she purrs. "Or that mouth."

Her lips ghost along my own, a warm tongue darting out to taste my lower lip. I trap it between my teeth, halting all her movements except those talented fingers. She hums again, and I release her.

"Kiss me," I mimic her. "Kiss me sweetly, Isla."

"I don't want sweet."

"Too fucking bad. Kiss me sweetly and then I'll fuck you roughly." A gasp escapes her mouth, and the apples of her cheeks darken slightly. Dirty talk is new for her. Her kiss starts slow, tentative even, at the edge of my mouth and working inward, and soon, we're two tongues fighting for dominance over one another.

My hands roam over her body until I can't take anymore of her clothes. I dive beneath and feel her skin twitch at the excitement of my touch.

"Strip," I whisper over her jawline. "Right fucking now, Isla. I need that pussy on my mouth."

She wastes no time complying to my demand. Doing the same, our clothes quickly become nothing but a pile on the floor. This time, standing in front of me, is the same confident woman I used to know. She's not hiding what she thinks others will see as a flaw. She's showing me everything, and she's so beautiful I want to fall at her feet and beg her to lock me down forever. I'm never going to want anyone but her with those wild curls and that stubborn attitude.

Isla always saw her hair-trigger temper as a flaw, but to me, it was the hockey in her. It only made me love her more.

"Hands on the bed. I want that ass up high." She blinks a few times, clearing her haze before she assumes the position. The scent of her swallows me as I lower to a squat behind her. More than just about anything in this world, I want to bury my face in her. Instead, I take time to appreciate what's offered before me. Her legs are nothing short of amazing, toned and strong, as she perches on her toes. The ass that I used to hold tight with both hands is equally as big as I remember but also much firmer from muscle. "How often do you work out, Cole?"

"A couple of times a week, when there's time. Why?" Insecurity breaks through her high defenses.

"Just curious, since I'm staring at the most delicious ass I've ever seen."

"Well… shut the fuck up and eat that ass like a good boy, Wylder."

The laugh that bursts out of me makes her jump under my fingers, but I grip her tightly. Pulling her cheeks apart, I do as told. Starting as low as I can, I run my tongue slowly up her. Dipping into her wet pussy for a brief swirl, then further up to the place I've never explored much of. We were different people before, younger, far less experienced. I've fucked her cunt in every way imaginable and her mouth. But this ass? We hadn't gotten that far.

Isla raises further on her toes, her muscles tightening in response to my tongue rounding it. Pushing two fingers into her pussy, I collect the wetness there and transfer it upward. What a divine sight it is to watch her stretch open to accommodate my middle finger. Her soft, needy moan echoes my own.

"Are you still a virgin here?"

"No." The single word has no regret attached to it, but my reaction to it does. It should have been me there first. I should have had all her firsts; I hate that I didn't. Or that she doesn't have all mine either. While I don't ask, I assume Murphy is the one that took that from her. Next time we play Vancouver, it's going to be even harder to stay out of the box.

"Then I guess that means you can take whatever I give you," I bite out, pushing my finger farther in at a slow rhythm. My other hand plays with her pussy, as I steadily pick up speed in each place, her breath becomes shorter, faster. Isla wants to dive over the edge she's getting closer and closer to. Adding a second finger, I stretch her asshole, and she cries my name. "You want more? You want my cock in here?"

"God, yes."

"Too bad, you'll have to earn that. Until you do, I'm going to fuck the shit out of you with my fingers in your ass, just to remind you who it belongs too."

"You do that, Wylder. Maybe then you won't forget the woman you're supposed to be fucking."

My dick hardens but my heart softens. The war we've waged on each other's hearts has been no less brutal than had we been spitting toxic insults at each other every day for years.

I broke Isla thoroughly, and it stole precious time from me. Now, all I want is everything I can get. I plan for that to be a lot. Starting with her in my bed tonight; ending with her in my life for eternity.

"Never again. This is the only body I want wrapped around me, laid bare before me, and letting me come inside it. And I'm going to be doing that every chance I get, Cole."

"You're still talking," she taunts with a wiggle of her ass. Slapping my palm down on it, I push her cheek out to one side while pulling my fingers still inside her to the other side. Isla hisses at the tautness I create, and I reward her with another rimming of my tongue. Then a few plunges inside. I've fucked a couple women here before, but Isla's is the only ass I've ever cared to taste like it was my last meal. So, I keep at it, alternating between it and her cunt. Using fingers to edge her closer and closer, only to pull back only so I can hear her whimper in need. Her thighs start to shake, her arms stretching in front of her as she uses the bed to carry more of her weight. "Let me come, Cillian."

It's more of a plea than demand, and my heart triumphs some at that.

"Roll onto your back, I'll let you come the first time in my mouth. After that, I want it all over my dick."

"Ooh yes, sir," she says with a cheeky wink once she's face up. I grab her legs under her knees and pull them up to her chest, rounding her ass into the air. It's probably not the most comfortable position for her, but it will allow me see her face while I burry mine in her now very wet pussy.

"You going to take orders, Isla," I ask before taking one long lap of her.

"If they're good ones."

"Use your fingers on yourself while I fuck you. Let's see how quickly we can get you off." There isn't even a second of hesitation, she's so ready to finish the job I've been teasing her with. Stiffening my tongue as best I can, I dive in. If it's weird to remember how a woman tastes, then my new name is *Strange*. The years I've spent longing for this were not kind to me and her scent, her flavor, her beauty have all been seared to my memory.

Having her again should be a relief, a release of some of that pent up yearning. I fear it's the opposite. This isn't satiating my hunger for her, and Isla Cole is going to be impossible to let go of.

19

ISLA

I reach outer space from his talented mouth, my fingers doing little to help. Honestly, I could probably get off on just watching his perfect naked body with the blazing look he keeps giving me. It's heady to have a man who looks like Cillian Wylder focus all his attention on you. Knowing he wants me as much as I want him... it's something I haven't dreamed of in a very long time.

Everything between us feels different tonight. Like maybe we can start over as new people, more mature, and seasoned. Two people with their priorities firmly in place and with an even stronger bond.

But then again, what if we can't.

And there it is. That niggling doubt that's been there since Cillian came home. What if that never dies? Could I live with it? Which is the bigger sacrifice? A life filled with doubt and Cillian, or one without both?

He moans and it tethers me to the here and now. I lean up on my elbows as his head still moves between my thighs, though I've come down from my life-altering orgasm.

"Cill?" His head pops up, a wicked smile firmly in place. "What are you doing?"

"Getting as much of you as I can. I want this," he says, shoving several fingers inside me to collect evidence of what has just taken place. "All over me. Cover me in it, bathe me in it, Cole."

"You're strange," I say, and he laughs uproariously, as if it's funnier than I meant. I watch his muscles move as he grabs a condom from the nightstand. There's not an inch of fat on him, but a few of the scars he's collected over his career are visible. They don't hinder anything, instead adding a layer of artistry, or another chapter to the book of Cillian's life. It's what he meant about me and my own scars.

"I can't guarantee I won't be too rough," he tells me. "Let me know if anything is uncomfortable."

"Are you going to fuck me or wrestle me, Wylder?"

His grin widens as he sheaths himself in the condom. Easily, he lifts me further up the bed. Lifting my legs from under my knees, he presses them down toward my chest, opening me up for him as he scoots closer.

"I'm going to fuck you, Isla. Like I've dreamed of, and I'm not going to stop until neither of us can hold ourselves upright and I've spent every bit of myself all over you."

Jesus. His dirty talk does some kind of thing to me. The desire to feel him, skin to skin, inside and out is so overwhelming. He enters me and we both sigh. His moves slow at first but with a steady pace that picks up tempo beat by beat. I know he's holding back though, I'm not sure why after everything he's just said to me.

Except that's a lie. I know. I've always known him better than he knew himself. He's missing the connection we had, the security we once found in one another. Despite everything, I know with a soul deep knowledge, this isn't something he ever looked for with another woman. I'm not sure how I know, but I'm certain of it. This means more to him because I'm not some random hookup.

Since Cillian's return, it's as if all the broken pieces of me have been slowly fitting themselves back to their place of origin. This moment brings one more to its rightful place. Maybe not the last one, but one of them anyway. I'm not forgiving him for the things he did, but I'm no longer holding them against our future.

My hand finds his at my thigh, and I work my fingers in between his own, larger ones.

"Cillian?" His eyes flicker from my face to our entwined hands and back again. "I don't want to give up on you again."

My words aren't loud as they spill from my lips, but they're heavy with meaning and questions. If we truly start over, it starts here and now. Cillian stills, his free hand coming to cup the side of my head.

"I'll never give you another reason to." He speaks at the same volume, with the same depth of emotion.

"I'm scared, Cill. Not just for me this time." My heart could break a hundred times over and it wouldn't be as bad as if he broke Sadie's just once.

"I'd take all that fear away if I could," he says, his fingers curling in the hair above my ear. "This time will be different, I swear it."

Whether I should believe him or not, I don't know. But I do. The earnestness is there, written clearly over his facial features. Sucking in his bottom lip, he waits for my response, I brush my hand over his unshaven jaw, loving the tingle it sends through my fingertips. Resting them on his mouth, I match my breath to his.

"Then fuck me, Superstar. Fuck me like you have time to make up for. Fuck me until I'm ruined for anyone but you."

"Yes, ma'am," he says with a sly smile. My laughter dies as quickly as he pulls out and thrusts in with such force, I travel further up the bed. Both his hands entwine with mine, pulling them up above my head as his mouth falls to mine. "Pull your knees up, open up for me."

The new position lifts my hips slightly, which only allows him to drive in deeper with every forward roll of his own hips. He could be a dancer with the way he makes his body move. Dragging my heels over his powerful thighs, the feel of his muscles moving with such purpose heightens my arousal. I deepen our kiss, I can't get close enough, far enough inside. Arching my back, I press my breasts against his now sweaty chest as he continues his relentless pounding. He's bigger than he was, stronger, more... more... more.

Cillian's mouth leaves mine only to trail kisses over my jaw then down my neck. Gently, he nibbles at my vein and I feel it straight in my core.

"You like that, Isla? You want it rough; you want me to bite you. Eat you. Fucking devour you." The words trail cool air over my heated skin, causing me to shiver with needy desire. "You're quivering. I can feel it on my cock."

He sits up on his knees and adjusts our position until my ass is cradled in between his thighs. Cillian grabs my hips and pulls me down his farther on to him with his next piston forward.

"Oh, fuck."

"Keep your arms up, your tits bounce so pretty like that," he tells me. "Most beautiful thing I've ever seen. I bet it will be even better when they're covered in my cum."

I stretch as far as I can all while he fucks me mercilessly, the bed groaning beneath us as it bounces on the wall. Thank fuck he doesn't share walls with neighbors, I'd never be able to look one in the face again.

"You keep talking about it, but I'm still waiting for it," I purr.

"You first," he says and his fingers find my clit. Like the first one, it takes little to set me off thoroughly and completely. Only a little swirl from his thumb as his dick slides in with determination.

"Fuck, Cillian," I cry out.

"You explode for me so easily," he says as I writhe through it. "Why are you pouting?"

"I want you to come for me as easily."

"Baby, I've been thinking about how the locker room smells to keep from blowing since I first got inside you." He laughs and I fight a smile of my own. "Take the condom off, Isla."

Fuck me.

My greedy hands find his hard length. Though I want the thin latex gone as quickly as possible, I take my time. Enjoying the feel of him as he watches me intently.

"Cover me in it, Cillian."

He moves to cradle my sides between his legs, it brings his cock to nestle in my cleavage. Cillian fills my sight; I can't help but run my fingers along the ridges of his abdomen or rest them on his own as he works his long erection with one hand. The other firmly grips one of my breasts, swirling the nub into a hard, sensitive peak. Turning my chin down, I stick my tongue out to taste the tip of him. Salty and delicious.

"Not in your mouth tonight, Isla. This time, I want your rosy nipple covered in it. I want to watch it drip and roll down." His voice shakes because he's close, so close. I taste him again with a pleased hum. "Fucking hell. Fuck, fuck."

The first burst lands on my chin, then he's aiming it exactly where he wanted it, warming my skin under it. My eyes don't leave his face, watching as he concentrates on his task as if it's the most important thing in the world. His chest, blushing with his exertion, slows its heaving after a minute and his eyes return to mine.

"It's about time, Wylder," I tease seductively. I trail a finger under some of his release and suck it into my mouth. Cillian watches with rapt attention, his body unmoving. So, I give him more of a show and begin massaging it into the skin of my breast and my belly. My fingers graze the sensitive skin under his cock as it rests against me, and now it's him quivering. But he still doesn't move, not until I'm done. Not until there's no evidence left except what is glistening on my skin or tantalizing my tongue.

Then he flops down next to me and rolls me atop him, securing me in his hold.

"Give me a few and we'll get to round two," he mumbles into my hair. "Won't take long."

"Overachiever," I say.

"Nah, I just can't get enough of you. Besides, I think the rest of your body needs the same attention you just gave your tits."

"You just like that I smell like you."

"Fuck yes, I do. And I want to smell like you. Bottle that shit up and I'll shower with it every day," he says, and I wrinkle my nose.

"Gross."

"Look at me," he demands. "It's not gross. I fucking love you. I am *in love* with you, Isla Cole. I want you with me all the time, however I can get it."

Tears sting with how overwhelmed his words make me. I haven't trusted him for so long, but I know he means what he says. He always meant it, that just wasn't enough.

"I..." Words won't form past my racing heart.

"Shh, you don't have to say anything. I'm not telling you because I need you to say it back. You should know it though; I should reinforce it like I should have always done. I'll tell you every day and even if you can never say it back, that will be okay."

Love is a commitment I'm not ready for. It doesn't matter if I feel it, professing it is a level I'm not on. Of course, I love him... again, or still. Not a day has gone by that I haven't cared about him or what happens to him, but that's different than actively being *in love*. It's different than putting the security of my heart back in his hands.

"How will it be okay?"

Cillian's hand pets the side of my head while he contemplates his answer. He doesn't look unsure, or as confused as I feel. If it was as easy as looking to him for all the answers, I'd believe he had them all stashed away in his mind. He's sure. I'm firing every nerve ending in my body with how uncertain I am.

"It will be okay, because I have faith in you, in me, and in us. We've always been meant to be, in one way or another. I've forgiven myself for not coming home to find you after I fucked everything up, I've forgiven you for not telling me about Sadie. I felt the hurt and I let it go. Because I'm not keeping room in my heart for anger, resentment, or regrets when it can be filled with love, laughter, and Sadie's infectious smiles. Even if you still have hate for me the day I die, I'll know that from this day forward I've loved you to my fullest. And that I've been the best father to our daughter. So, that's how I know it will be okay."

"I don't hate you," I whisper.

"Then we're already okay, aren't we?" He presses a kiss to the crown of my head, the steady beat of his heart against my ear. Cillian makes it all sound so simple. And maybe some of it is as easy as just deciding. But the thought of being back with Cillian turns my stomach into a tornado and I don't know if it's butterflies, knots, or both.

We fell asleep in that position, Cillian cradling me against his chest. A few hours later, I wake similarly, except my lips rest against the pulse at his neck and his dick presses hard along my thigh. Resting my chin on my folded hands, I watch him sleep for a few minutes, letting everything that's passed between us settle.

Therapy has taught me to sit with my emotions, to feel them, like Cillian said. Feel the hurt, then let it go. I want to let it all go. For myself and for my family. For my future that inevitably includes this man. Clearly how we move forward is up to me; he's been direct enough about that.

Cillian is in love with me. When I think about it, honestly, I'm still in love with all the parts of him that haven't changed. His passion for his career, the way he's easy to laugh even when he's angry about something, or at me. He still likes my fiery temper, and we still have fun together when we're not at each other's throat. Which happens less often by the day. That only leaves the parts that had me falling out of love with him.

Except, those parts aren't present. Not here and now. He's not the same person he was in the ways that count. Neither am I, yet he loves the me I am. The version of Isla Cole that's more vulnerable, emotionally weaker, doesn't always have her shit together, and is sometimes much too afraid of change.

It's partly why I have lived in the same place I have for so long. I think I always wanted him to show up on my doorstep. It's why I've refused to get a new car even when mine is on its last leg. New things feel daunting and out of control. Maybe that's why I question him as much as I do, because letting New Cillian into my heart means I no longer have control of what happens to it.

Is Cillian Wylder worth the risk of another broken heart?

Yes.

Am I ready to go all in with him? No. I am ready for the idea that we can make this work though. And that alone is a giant leap for me. For us.

Trailing my fingers down his chest, I revel in the way his skin reacts beneath my touch. Even in sleep, he's aroused by my touch, his cock twitches and it's enough to make me wet. Needy. Slowly, I slither down the bed until I'm on my hands and knees between his widespread thighs and my vision is filled with his strong, veiny dick. It's mouthwatering.

"Cillian," I call as I run my cheek up his length.

"Isla." His sleepy moan carries down to me with the involuntary tap his cock makes on my tongue. "What are you doing, love?"

"I've talked so much shit about you over the years, I think you need to wash my mouth out a few more times."

"Fuck, Isla," he says, his eyes wide open now. "You're a goddamned siren."

I hum along his erection.

"How awful has your badmouthing been?"

"So bad," I pout. "Filthy." I run my tongue around his sack and his hands come to grip either side of my head.

"Then I guess you owe me. Open." As soon as I do, he pushes in hard and holds it. The end of his dick tickles my gag reflex, but I adjust quick enough, relaxing as best I can. "Jesus, that's a pretty sight; you choking on my cock."

Cillian slides out so slowly before quickly pushing back in. He gains his pace quickly, still holding my head where he wants it. There isn't much for me to do except play my tongue over and around him, moan against him, and raise my ass as far in the air as I can because I know it enhances his view. His eyes don't close, they don't look away, even as tears from the intensity stream down my face. He encourages me to take more and more. Every word he utters to me is soaked in the same desire that's bleeding out of my every pore.

I know when he's close, when his body takes over and he loses that last thread of easy control he's had. His muscles bunch, tightening with the impending release, his words become breathier.

"God damn your mouth is talented, that tongue of yours... pure fucking magic." One hum of agreement and he's bursting down my throat. "Swallow it all, you little thief, take all of your punishment."

Oh, fucking gladly.

It isn't with ease, but I do keep up, swallowing it all and sucking him clean until he starts to soften in my mouth. I'd have stayed here longer but Cillian yanks me up his body, bringing us face-to-face.

"Best way to wake up, ever," he says, nuzzling his nose against mine.

"You did promise me another round before we passed out."

"Sorry, baby. You feel free to wake me up anytime you want to have a go around."

"It's that easy, huh?" I laugh.

"Mmm," he agrees. "My body feels like an insatiable teenager around you, I want it all the time."

"I want this," I blurt out before my brain has a chance to form a web and tangle all my words up.

"This," he repeats, his eyes bouncing between mine, looking for clarification. "Us?"

"To try. I can't say that I... I can't make promises. Not yet, but I want to try again. I want to see what we can be now."

Cradling the back of my skull, he pulls me in for a long, deep kiss. I feel his arousal waking up again between us.

"I'll never let you regret it, Isla."

20

ISLA

"Hello," I answer my phone, then promptly start coughing. My head feels like it's full of quicksand; both Sadie and I have caught some sort of cold or flu.

"You sound awful, Freckles."

"I feel awful."

"You should go back to bed. Why did you even answer my call? You haven't the past twenty-eight times I've tried."

"Maybe it's my fragile physical state, but I'm ready to hear you explain what you taunted Cillian with on the ice." I've avoided this for long enough and I need to stop doing that. Stop being the woman that sticks her head in the ground and get back to the badass bitch I used to be. The one that took no shit from anyone, especially men.

"Only wanted to know how serious he was about you. That's all."

"Tyson, that's not your job. Besides, that sounds like bullshit."

"I'm serious, Freckles," he says with a laugh. "He wasn't going to risk the bin if he didn't give a shit about you. You were more important than the game. No hard feelings."

"You hockey players are a fucked up bunch. You know that, right?"

"As well as you do. Yet here you are, back with one. You are back with him, yeah?"

"No. I mean… no?"

"Level with me here, Isla," he says without the same humor he held moments ago.

"I'm trying," I admit. "I'm trying to trust him again. We're trying to see if there is still something there."

Tyson is quiet for a few beats while I nervously await his opinion. Love never played into our scenario, but he has been a good friend and someone who I respect. I also know he won't blow smoke up my ass; he's never shied from being honest with me.

"That 'something' was always there, Isla. You never let it go."

"I'm sorry for how that may have made you feel, Ty. Hurting you, or anyone, wasn't ever something I wanted to do." My tear ducts, already sensitive from being sick, trigger. I'm going to be a clogged up, snotty mess by the end of this conversation.

"There's nothing to apologize for, you were always perfectly honest about your lack of availability. Even if you wouldn't admit the reasons to yourself," he says. "I'm happy you're getting a second chance."

"Because I'd never be able to move on without one?" I accuse. Maybe it's not fair of me, but it sounds like that is exactly what he's implying.

"Or because maybe you two really are meant to be," he admits. "Either way, I don't want to lose you as a friend. Okay? I'm always around, but I'll be respectful of your decisions and relationship."

"You don't think I'm wrong for trying again?"

"It's not my decision to make, Freckles. Right or wrong, you owe it to yourself to try anything that is going to make you and Sadie happy. I won't beat you up for that and I'll stop egging on Wylder unless he does something to deserve it."

Owing it to Sadie is something I've thought about, but I never wondered if I owed it to myself. I do owe it to myself, don't I? Exhausting all options that could lead to the happily ever after I've always wanted isn't a bad thing. That dream started with Cillian Wylder, it grew every day with my daughter, whether I wanted it to or not.

Some days I did; I'd fantasize about Cillian's return, him coming to find us and falling to his knees with guilt and regret. Other days, that fantasy was of me punching him in the face and kicking him in the balls. I imagine his have been much the same about me since returning to

Seattle. But he still wants to try again, because on the scale that holds our lives… the good has outweighed the bad.

"You're a good man, Tyson Murphy. Don't ever settle for a woman who doesn't see that. Okay?"

"I promise, Freckles."

"What's wrong," Cillian asks when I open the door to him later that day.

"Sorry, I fell asleep and forgot to message you. We're sick. I don't think it's a good idea for you to take Sadie tonight."

"Both of you?" He brushes the hair from my face, his eyes bouncing all over my face.

"Willa, too," I say with a nod. "But she's been dead to the world all day. I was up with Sadie all night. She's feeling better, but I'm exhausted."

"You're hot," he says, feeling my forehead. "Go sleep, I'll keep her entertained."

"You don't have to do that."

"Arguable," he says, easily. "Come on. Let's get you back to bed."

Cillian shuffles me back to the bedroom. Sadie has her nightstand lamp on and is flipping through a book, her eyes hooded.

"Daddy," she says with a shadow of a smile.

"Hey, Sadie Baby. How you feeling?"

"Okay. Mommy says I'm restless, but I think I just need to do some things."

"Why don't you come out to the living room with me? We'll find some things while Mommy takes a nap."

She holds her arms out, not rising on her own. With a big grin, he picks her up and snuggles her under his chin. Since the day he crossed our threshold and she recognized him from that nameless picture she's always had, her trust in him has never wavered. Instinctively she knows he'll take care of her. Instinctively, *I* know she's right.

Cillian's devotion to her isn't anything I question anymore. He loved her at first sight like I loved him at first date.

Drifting off to sleep, I wonder when he first fell in love with me.

I wake hours later, my headache finally gone, to find Cillian hovering over me.

"Hey, we made dinner. And there's a storm."

"A storm?"

"Your favorite kind," he says, his arms sliding under my shoulders and knees to lift me.

"I'm sick, not paralyzed."

"Fuck off and humor me for once, Cole," he says, laughing off my snark.

I relent as we round the hall corner to the living room. "What is this?"

"A fort!" Sadie is all smiles, even though her nose is raw and red and her voice hoarse from coughing.

Sheets are draped all around, creating a giant tent in the middle of the room with a wide opening facing the floor-to-ceiling windows that look out over the city. Fairy lights are strung artfully, giving the room a comfortable glow. Sadie must have shown him where we keep the holiday decorations.

Cillian squats to set me inside the makeshift tent. It's full of cushions, pillows, and blankets. They make a perfect, cozy little spot to nest. Sadie follows us in, curling up next to me and pulling a blanket over us both.

"Isn't it magical?"

"It is, baby," I say as a shard of lightening lights up the sky and the walls inside. *My favorite.* It's a rare storm for Seattle. We get rain and wind, but rarely do we get rumbling thunder and striking lightning. But when it does happen? Yeah, it's magical.

"I'll be right back," Cillian says.

"We made dinner and special medicine."

"Oh yeah?"

"Yep," Sadie says, popping her lips on the word, a clear sign she's not feeling too poorly. "Daddy says when he was my size, his mommy made him special medicines. So, he made us some, too. It's yummy, I didn't even have to hold my nose."

"Wow, it must be special," I say with feigned excitement.

"I know that's right," she says, petting my head like I do her when she's tired or ill. "Did you see that one?"

Another flash strobes around us.

"So cool," I say. Sadie nods, as excited as I am by it all.

A few minutes later, Cillian's head pops back in. He carries a tray laden with mugs. Some hold chicken noodle soup, the others must be this medicine Sadie talks about.

"Hot water with lemon and honey. Yours may have a dash of bourbon in it, too," he says with a wink.

"That sounds amazing right now, thank you." I press the mug to my face first, letting the heat radiate through my war-torn sinuses as Cillian settles into the pile of pillows on Sadie's other side.

Nothing about this is uncomfortable or awkward. Shouldn't it be? I've spent so long being mad at him, then sniping at him, and he me. Yet tonight we feel like any other couple just making the best of a shit situation.

We feel like a family.

The warmth of that only grows as he encourages Sadie to eat her soup. And how he helps her blow her nose. For a man that was never around babies and toddlers, he's aced the learning curve on it. He anticipates her needs and moods like a seasoned father. And the way he looks down at her with such concern and care is enough to melt the remaining ice around my heart.

I don't know what the future holds for us. Or if that dream of growing old together will ever solidify into reality. But I do know that these moments are worth the risk of loving him again.

21

ISLA

"You're back together?"

"No, it's not like that, Zan. Not exactly anyway. We're working on it, but not labeling it," I answer.

"Because you are too scared to commit."

"Why do you think it's me who won't commit?" I take another drink of my coffee as Sadie climbs the ladder up to the slide. The sun is shining, even if it's a little cold today. She doesn't mind that though, so long as she can get some energy out in the fresh air. The walk does me good too, since I won't have a chance to work out today.

"I see how he looks at you," he answers with a shrug. "He knows what he wants, and Cillian doesn't seem the type to shy away because of fear."

"But I do."

"You have reason to. I'm not judging. Nor am I judging you giving him a second chance, so long as you're sure and you're doing it for you, not for Sadie."

"It's for me, but I'm glad she'll benefit from it."

"Then don't let your fear stop you." Zan throws his arm around my shoulder and pulls me in for a hug. "You deserve to be happy."

Willa's reaction to a similar conversation wasn't quite the same. She's been by my side through my lowest lows and while she believes in me, she's cautious. But she, too, said she wasn't judging me and she's trying hard not to judge Cillian for his past indiscretions. It's not an easy situation for any of us.

One thing I'm sure of though, waking up in Cillian's bed with him making me breakfast downstairs felt like a dream come true. Much like him being there to take care of us when we were sick. It felt natural and right. I'm not ready to move in together or anything, Sadie doesn't need to see her mommy and daddy waking up in the same room when we've made no commitments. Not verbally, anyhow. I'm more cautious with her heart than I am mine, and that's saying something. But I'm not afraid of a future that has Cillian in it anymore.

"Have you talked to Tyson?"

"I did. Maybe he doesn't agree with my decision, but he understands it. Still, it wasn't the most fun conversation I've ever had."

"He's never struck me as anything but a good guy. Despite what he said to Cillian on the ice," Zan says.

"He is a good guy. I think that was just weird hockey dude posturing bullshit."

"We're good at that," he admits with a laugh. "They play in Boston in a couple of weeks." As if the date doesn't loom over me like a dark cloud, he reminds me anyway. The back of my mind sees it as our first real test of trust. I could go, nothing is stopping me from traveling with the team. Except for my own pride and need to not be a babysitter. If I'm going to trust him, I'm going to have to prove it just as much as he's going to have to prove he's trustworthy. We can't do that if we're constantly in one another's pocket. That's not a healthy relationship.

"We'll get through it," I say confidently.

"Mommy!" Sadie comes rushing toward us.

"Daughter," I say back.

"Does Daddy has all his teeths?"

"Of course, he does," I say with a giggle.

"I thought so," she huffs, her tiny fists finding her hips. "That boy said hockey players don't have teeths. I said he was a liar."

"Well, you're kind of both right. Your dad has all his teeth, but other players are missing some."

"Open your mouth," she tells Zan. He does, and she studies his gaping maw for a few moments. "I don't see any missing."

"That's because I have all mine, too."

"Axel is missing two, you can ask him next time you see him," I tell her.

"Two? Oh, my good gravy!" She runs back off to the swings, her hand to her forehead as if she can't possibly believe it.

"Your kid probably just jinxed me."

"Probably," I agree with another laugh.

"If I lose one, I'm sending Wylder the dental bill."

"You do that."

Days pass and we fall into a new routine. Work is busy. It's a part of professional hockey franchises I didn't have much insight into as a kid, but that's the goal. Learn as much about the business as I can. Who knows where it will take me? I'm not sure I care what I'm doing in the industry as long as I'm in it, as long as I'm a part of the game.

Cillian's finding his groove here, too. He's found a balance between training, working out, playing, and being a dad. He has his nights with Sadie, and I have mine. But we share more dinners together than not. And on the nights she stays with one of her grandmothers, Cillian and I share some adult sexy times.

He hasn't pressed me for more than that, and I'm thankful for it. Every day I grow closer to giving him my whole heart. It doesn't need to be rushed, however. Mom reminded me that we have our whole lives ahead of us and I'll know when the time is right.

Spending so much free time with Cillian has, however, taken a toll on my time with Zander. Tonight, he's hanging out with me and Sadie as we watch Cillian's game on television. It's the game against Boston, where I assume Trina is in attendance. As far as I know, she still works for the team. I haven't asked if that assumption is correct.

Cillian sees her for who she is now and the toll it's taken on him has been heavy. His guilt is evident enough, but it's the rest that worries me. A woman, someone he thought was a friend, took advantage of him in profoundly awful ways that helped change the course of his life. He's struggling to come to terms with that level of betrayal.

It's not the first away game Cillian's had since our conversation about trying again. Not by a long shot. He calls as often as he can. Which is more than necessary. He misses us when he's gone, but I know it's partly in effort to reassure me of any doubts I have. There hasn't been any though, not until this trip. Not until tonight, the first of a four-night trip.

CILLIAN:

I love you and I miss you. Tell Sadie the same for me.

The text comes only minutes before they take the ice.

"Daddy says he loves and misses you," I tell her as she tries to roll up the sleeves of her jersey, Wylder emblazoned on the back of it. It's much too big, but she loves it and wears it every time we watch the games on television.

"I hope he scores a goal for me." She says the same thing every time. He scores plenty, but of course not every game. Sadie's proud of him no matter what, but she goes nuts when he gets even an assist. Between that and yelling "Pops" every time the camera pans to my dad standing over the bench, she's a handful on game nights.

"Did you see that," Zander asks, his eyes trained on the television as the players line up for the anthem. Trina is standing just inside the rink, her camera to her face. Her Boston players are not her focus, though. She's taking shots of the Blades. When Cillian steps on the ice, he shows her his big, gloved palm and skates right past, while she visibly balks at something he says to her.

"Good boy," I say with a smile. It's years late, but I'm not holding it against him. Not anymore. This time we're fighting the battle named Trina together, as a team. No more secrets, no more lies, nothing hidden away in the shadows never to be spoken of.

Our daughter deserves better than who we've been. We all deserve better.

"You're warming up to him," Zander teases.

"A little," I agree with a shrug. It's true that we're getting closer since we've quit sniping at each other, at least. My Saturday nights are no longer spent with anyone but him. But that's the only commitment I've made. There still hasn't been a proclamation of love.

Regardless of what I feel.

"You don't have to hide it with me, remember?"

"I know. It's more that I'm hiding it from myself."

"Well, you don't need to do that either," he reminds me.

"Always holding me down," I say with a small laugh. "But what about you? You haven't been on a date in forever and a day."

"No, but I've been talking to someone."

"Ooh, do tell?" I sit up, excited.

"It's nothing. Yet anyway. He's in New Orleans but moving here soon."

"And?"

"And... he's a little bossy. I like it." Zander's grin is wide and bright.

"That's promising!"

"We'll see."

"Oh, good job, Daddy!" Sadie throws her arms up when Cillian wins the faceoff. He's been playing great this season. Like he should have always played. When he was with Boston, I never watched his games. I tried a few times when I was by myself and feeling lonely but seeing him on the ice only heightened my depressive emotions. But I'd see highlights. He never played horribly, though he certainly wasn't playing up to the potential I knew he had.

That's changed since coming back to Seattle. Cillian plays cleaner, skates faster, takes more shots, misses less passes.

I'd love to say it's partly because of me and Sadie. My ego isn't that big, though. In truth, I think it's helped separating himself from a toxic environment, even if he didn't see it as that.

Willa had a friend when she was younger. Penelope had a big personality and was always fun to be around. Yet she took being a snarky bitch to a near professional level. Though she never focused that on Willa or their small friend group, it affected Willa all the same. Having a cloud of negativity floating around you takes a toll on you and when Willa and her finally quit hanging around, she said it was like she'd shit a brick she didn't know was sitting in her stomach.

I imagine it's much the same for Cillian. Besides all of the details he's been realizing about the relationship they had, I think being removed from a presence like Trina is an automatic aura cleanser.

Not to say it wasn't stressful for him to come here and find he had a daughter. It's different though, and Sadie has made him a lighter and happier man. As for me, I don't know what I've made him. Likely only confused, the same as he's made me. Every day we make strides at clarity, every day we get closer to understanding each other.

Every day we get closer to forgiving ourselves.

"Watch, baby, they're about to score," I tell Sadie.

Wallin moves the puck down the ice, passes it off to Koch who is the youngest member of the team. He's fucking fast, too, and glides right past Boston's players to get a shot on net. It bounces off the bar, but Cillian is there and able to get a clean pass to Wallin who shoots it in for a goal.

"Yes," she squeals before turning to me. "How do you always know that?"

"I've watched a lot of hockey," I tell her with a goofy grin. I learned to read the game early on in life, thanks to my dad. Sadie will, too, if she doesn't eventually lose interest.

"You do that better than most hockey players I know," Zan says.

"That's because you guys are busy playing, you don't necessarily see everything I do."

"I guess. Or maybe you just have a hockey sixth sense or some shit."

It's not the first time he's said this. Like always, I laugh at him with a wink and avert my attention back to the game.

"Some day I want to have some six shit," Sadie says, throwing both Zander and I into fits of giggles we can't hold back. I don't even bother telling her it's a word she shouldn't say.

Willa gets home from school in the second period and joins us to finish the game. Sadie curls up on her lap, nearly asleep. She fights it hard on game nights and rarely makes to the end of one.

A for effort, kiddo.

"There's Pops," she says, sleepily when the camera shows the bench and my dad stoically standing over his guys.

"Looking as handsome as ever," Willa says, her canned response to what happens about a dozen times every game.

"I know that's right."

The Blades end up winning the game, even though Sadie isn't awake to witness it. After saying goodnight to Zander, I tuck her in bed and curl up with the Bauer box that I now keep under my own bed. I haven't read all the letters yet. There are a lot and some days I still don't want to hear what he had to say. Other days, days like today, I pull one out and let his words lull me to sleep.

Isla,

It's been three years since I've heard your voice. A little more since moving here to Boston. Yet it still doesn't feel like home. It never will, I'm sure of it.

Every day feels foggy. Like there's something I'm not seeing, or something I've forgotten. Whatever it is, I know it's important. But no matter how I rack my brain, I can't figure out what it is.

I'm left with a belief it must be you, Isla.

You're what is missing, what I'm supposed to find.

So why can't I bring myself to do that? Why haven't I taken any one of the million opportunities I've had to come find you?

Shame for what I've done. Fear of the idea that you'd slam the door in my face.

It's the knowledge that I can't get past either of those things that makes me not nearly a good enough man for you. I hope to be one day. I wish I could tell you that, explain to you that I am trying to grow the fuck up.

I'll get there. And when I do, I won't give up on being a person that you can count on. Whatever that looks like, however you allow me in your life. I know what I want, but my wants are what got us into this mess to begin with. If I ever have the chance again, I'll listen to you the way I should have at the start. I won't come to you unless I have the confidence to be what you need.

That's been missing, hasn't it? It's something you always had in spades, and maybe I relied on you for it. Fuck, Isla. Why did you ever love me? The more I think about it the less reason I find.

I'm learning though, and evolving. I promise. And not for you, or not only. For me. Next time I see you, I'll be different.

But I'll still love you.

Cill

It wasn't me he was missing. It was Sadie. It was my pregnancy he'd forgotten. He's right about one thing though, he is different.

No matter how hard I tried fighting it, it hasn't stopped me from still loving him, too.

22

CILLIAN

"**G**ood game, tonight, Wild," Torsten says as he takes a seat in the all-night diner we used to haunt after games when I still lived in Boston.

"Sorry we kicked your asses," I tease back.

"Fuck you, one goal does not constitute an ass whooping."

"You guys almost had us, but I won't be admitting that to anyone else." The server comes by for our orders, which is always the same. Double bacon cheeseburger for him, spaghetti and meatballs for me. It's not the greatest food, but it's the carb load we're looking for after a game.

"How's Seattle treating you?"

"Good, I missed more than I knew."

"And Isla?"

"Fuck man, there's a lot to unpack there."

"That's why I'm here, bro. We aren't teammates anymore, but we're still friends," he says. "You seriously have a kid?"

"Yeah," I say, smiling as I pull up a picture of Sadie on my phone. She's laughing maniacally while she holds Saint, who licks her chin. "Sadie is amazing."

"Cute," he muses. "How'd that go down?"

"She tried to tell me. The night she called you? That was to tell me she was pregnant," I tell him, and his face falls.

"Fuck, Cillian. That's… I'm sorry."

"Not your fault," I say, dismissing that line of conversation. "She video called later that night. I don't remember it, but Isla told me she was pregnant when I was naked in bed with Trina."

"The hell? You didn't fuck around with Trina until way later, I thought."

"I didn't. Listen man, Trina is not what she seems. She went through my shit; read letters I had written to Isla. She took pictures of us in bed while I slept and sent that shit to Isla. For years, she's been fucking with her, I had no idea."

"She's been obsessed with you since she first met you," he says, then takes a big drink of his vodka soda. "But that's next level stalker type shit."

"Some of it's borderline assault, man," I say. "I don't really care what she's done to me, but she caused Isla so much distress that she had scary complications while she was pregnant. I've seen a few pictures and she looked sickly, like she hadn't been eating or sleeping. Seeing that shit, knowing it was because I was a fuck up? Worst feeling of my life."

Falling back in my chair, I rub a hand over my face. Besides my mom, this isn't something I've discussed with anyone else. The guys on the team are great, but I don't know any of them that well yet. Not well enough to confess my greatest mistake, anyway. Not well enough to set my pride aside and admit all the things I should have seen but didn't.

"Jesus. Has she been in contact since you moved back?"

"Some. I've told her we're done, completely cut her off. Didn't stop her tonight."

"What happened tonight?"

"She was taking shots of our guys taking the ice, which is weird. She's Boston's photog, not Seattle's. Then she made some comment to me about meeting up at the hotel later. Like she wanted the other guys to hear it and think we had some predetermined date. I told her to fuck off."

"I'm sure that went over well." He laughs. "Seriously though, Wild, you should think about filing a complaint with the team, or maybe the league."

"Yeah, I thought about that. It might make shit worse though, you know? I was hoping she'd just take the fucking hint and stay the fuck out our lives."

"I get it. Either way, I've got your back. And I'll keep an eye on her from here. As much as I can, anyway. At least make sure she leaves any of the new pups alone."

"Thanks, Tor. I appreciate that."

"Anytime, man. I owe you at least that much," he says, but he doesn't. This was always my mess.

I'm feeling slightly better about the situation when I get to my hotel for the night. Knowing that someone here in Boston is in my corner, if I need it, helps somehow. The lock on the door flashes green with my keycard and I open it to flower petals spread all over the floor.

The hell?

Following the trail to the bed, I find Trina lying there. Naked as the day she was born.

"Fuck no," I say, turning around I walk right back out of the room. Shutting the door behind me, I hold the door handle with one hand while I dig my cell out of my pocket with the other. The first person I call answers on the second ring. "I need your help, it's an emergency. Room three-twenty-seven."

The second call is to 9-1-1.

Trina rants on the other side of the door but I don't respond until Coach Cole is standing in front of me, his narrowed gaze focused on me.

"Explain."

"I just got back from dinner with Tor, walked in my room to find her here. I walked right back out and called you, then the police."

Something crashes against the door behind me, making me wince. Coach takes a few steps away to make a quick call.

"Open it up," he tells me with a head nod after he ends the call and shoves the cellphone back in his pocket.

"Jesus," I shout, ducking to miss the glass that comes flying at my head. Coach catches it, his old goalie reflexes not missing a beat. Trina stands in the middle of the room, which she has thoroughly trashed over the past few minutes. She's still completely naked. Glancing around the floor, the first thing I see is one of my shirts. Grabbing it, seeing that she's tried to rip it to pieces but failed, I toss it at her. "Put some fucking clothes on, the police are on the way."

"You called the police?" She sounds incredulous, only adding to how unhinged she truly is.

"Fuck yes, I did. You broke into my fucking room, Trina."

"You want me here. You invited me here." The words are said to me, but she's directing them at Coach.

Oh, this bitch.

"I did no such thing. I've told you several times over to stay the fuck away from me and stay out of my life."

"Bullshit."

"Yeah, this is bullshit, Trina. You're fucking bullshit," I growl, taking a step toward her. The only thing holding me back from throttling her right now is Coach's hand on my shoulder. "You've been in my ear for years, fucking with my head. It's enough for me to hate you. But what you've done to Isla, *to my family*, is beyond unforgiveable! I could fucking kill you for that."

"You would have gone back to her," she says, her face turning away so she doesn't have to look me in the eye. "You always wanted to go back. All I wanted was a chance."

"You fucking knew, didn't you? You knew she was pregnant?" She doesn't have to answer, the truth is written all over her face. Since Isla explained what happened that night, I had a niggling belief that this was the truth of it all. If I hadn't already nailed Trina's coffin shut, this would have done it. Keeping that knowledge from me is too big of a betrayal. She's crying and trembling now, trying to untangle the shirt enough to get it over her head. "How could you keep that from me? I can't believe I ever let you in my life."

"She did that! Isla kept it from you. All I did was love you and I know you loved me, too."

"I never loved you. Never. And you'll never say her name again, do you fucking understand me? You erase my family from your memory."

Her eyes dart around the room, when she finds what she's looking for, she runs to it. It's her handbag, but it's not a cellphone or tissues or any other harmless thing she pulls out. It's a gun, and she points it right at me at the same time there is sound at the hotel room door. I register the noise, the police are here, but I can't move from the woman holding a gun in my direction.

Coach appears in front of me, shoving me behind him.

"Get the door, son," he says, as calm as ever. I don't know how he does it, keeps his cool in every situation. It takes a minute for the cloud of anxious confusion to clear and realize what he's said.

Get the door. Get to the door. Before she fucking shoots us both.

23

ISLA

"Dad," I whisper when answering the phone, not wanting to wake Sadie up. Checking the time, it's almost midnight here, hours later in Boston. "What's wrong?"

Panic kicks in instantly. My father would not be calling me from across the country and at this hour, for nothing.

"Everyone is okay, sweetheart. But Cillian and I are at the police station here in Boston."

"What," I whisper shout as I move to the living room. "Dad, why?"

"That woman, the photographer, was in his hotel room when he headed up for the night."

"Oh, my fucking god," I interrupt him. "What a psycho."

"That's not all, Isla. Cillian walked right back out, called me and the police. She pulled a gun on him."

"Dad," I cry. "Is he okay?"

"Yeah, he's rattled, kiddo. Understandably. She didn't get a shot off before the police arrived."

"Can I talk to him?" I don't know what I can say, but I want to hear his voice.

"No, he's giving his statement. Probably going to take some time. The team is going to have a lawyer here first thing tomorrow to help deal with it."

"You're supposed to be in Toronto tomorrow," I say, as if the game means anything right now. It doesn't, not in the grand scheme. But I'm shaking and can't make any sense of anything as I knock before entering Willa's room. She wakes when I crawl in bed with her, immediately picking up on my panicked state.

"What's wrong?"

"Fill Willa in, then try to get some sleep. I'll send any updates as I get them."

"Don't leave him, Daddy."

"I won't sweetheart," he promises then hangs up.

"Isla? What's going on?" Willa rushes in.

Tears clog my throat, long minutes pass before I can calm down enough to tell Willa the small amount of information I was given. My mind won't stop conjuring images of Trina holding a gun to Cillian. I could have lost him tonight. For good, this time. Before I'd even had a chance to tell him I love him.

I do. Despite everything we've been through, I do, and I want a second chance at what our life was supposed to be.

"I love him, Willa," I tell her after she's consoled me enough to where at least my shivering has subsided.

"I know you do."

"Am I wrong to?"

"Of course not. He's different, we all see it."

"What do you see," I ask her. My family and I haven't spoken much about it, not really. They've taken a back seat and let me and Cillian figure things out without their input. But I know the three of them have talked about it. But I'd like to know if what they've witnessed aligns with what I have.

"Before he left for Boston, it was like you were his sun and he orbited around you. Almost like he'd crumble to nothing if you weren't around. We all thought he was just that enamored with you. And he was, but he did fall apart without you. Honestly, you did without him too."

"You never told me you saw it that way."

"I don't know that you were ready to hear it before," she says, soothing my tear damp hair from my temple. "Besides, it's not like I saw it as it was happening. My third-party perspective came after your breakup. You're both different now, though. Neither of you relies on the other for anything. Maybe that frees you both up to be with each other out of choice and desire instead of necessity. Does that make sense?"

"I think so, but I'm not sure I have enough functioning brain cells to make sense of anything right now," I say, snuggling further down under the covers with her. "When did you get so smart?"

"It must be all this expensive ass higher education," she says with a light laugh. "Sleep, sissy. I'm sure Cillian will call you when he can."

I hope she's right, but I can't sleep without at least letting him know I'm here for him.

ME:

> Dad called. I hope you're okay. Please call me when you can, I don't care what time it is. 🩶

Ending it with a heart emoji is the best I can do. I won't tell him that I love him over text message, not for the first time since we discussed trying again.

He hasn't called by the time Sadie wakes us up in the morning.

"Did you have a sleepover without me," she asks with a pout.

"Not on purpose, kiddo. Mommy just fell asleep in here talking to me," Willa answers her.

"You look sad," Sadie says to me. "We can watch that movie with the fancy dresses and eat mint candies to cheer you up, if you wanna." She means Marie Antoinette, for some reason, Kirsten Dunst is my go-to when I feel shitty.

"That sounds like a really good plan, but I have to go to work and you're spending the day with your grandmother."

"Okay, but if you're still sad later, I know where Auntie Willa hid the candies."

"*Bitch,*" I silently mouth to my sister.

"Be happy I didn't throw them out all together," she says. "No word?"

"Not since Dad texted that they made their flight." That was an hour ago. I guess that means Cillian has done all he needs to do with the police. It's hard to believe that after the night he had, he's business as usual. Since he didn't call me, I have no way to know where his head is at. "I wish he'd have called."

"Give it a little time, I'm sure he's exhausted."

She's probably right. That doesn't make the next few hours any easier for me. The office is buzzing with the story, as it's already made it around. Sports radio has picked up the lead, too, but everyone has been quiet about the details, so they don't have much to tell except that police were called when a woman was found in an unnamed player's hotel room. Our legal team is on top of it and is doing their best to keep Cillian's name out of it for as long as they can. That won't last, of course, due to public records and whatnot. But at least it gives Cillian some time to rest before being hounded.

The team's flight landed a few hours ago. My test messages and call logs still show nothing from him.

ME:

Are you sure he's okay? Should I fly out there? I don't know what to do.

Instead of texting back, my dad calls me.

"You don't need to fly out. It was a rush to get all our things together before the flight, his phone ended up in cargo and died. We talked the whole flight and then I sent him to his room for a nap, he's dead on his feet. He knows I've been keeping you up to date. He'll call you when he wakes up."

"You're sure?"

"I'm sure, sweetheart."

"What did you talk about?"

"You, mostly."

"Is that good?"

"It's good, Isla."

"I'm getting on a flight."

"I expected nothing less. Let me know what time you land."

"I will. Thanks, Dad."

I have to rush to make my own flight, but just over seven hours later, I've cleared Canadian customs and am walking into the lobby of the hotel the Blades are staying at in Toronto.

Cillian must have tried to call while I was in flight because there was a text message waiting for me to land, asking me to call him. I haven't though, I just want to see him, to talk to him face to face. Put my hands on him and reassure myself that he's truly okay and that viper didn't hurt him.

Dad meets me in the lobby to hand me a keycard which is needed to gain access to the upper floors of the hotel.

"How was the flight?" He wraps his arms around me for a long hug.

"Too long, but fine."

"Legal called. They've hit her with a handful of charges and a hefty bail. She didn't obtain the gun legally and she had drugs in her purse. Some kind of sedative or something. We don't know what she had planned, but whatever it was, it wasn't good. They're filing protection orders for him, you, and Sadie."

"Jesus," I curse. The gun is still a shock, but I've resigned myself to the belief that she is diabolical enough to drug Cillian. "Do you think she'd come after us?"

"No way to know, but we're not taking that chance. Every precaution will be taken, and you'll follow all the rules. Understand?"

"Of course," I agree. "What room?"

"Four-oh-two." He presses a kiss to the top of my head.

"Thanks for looking out for him," I say, giving him another hug.

"I protect what's mine, Isla. You know that," he says as if it's a given. Which it is, except I know in this case he isn't counting Cillian as only one of his players. He's counting him as family.

Getting to his door feels like it takes hours when it's only been minutes. Every nerve in me is frayed and fragile, nothing seems right. Until he opens the door to my soft knock.

"Isla," he breathes out with such relief. My eyes roam every inch of him, taking in the dark circles under his eyes, the tightness in his neck, his fingers that flex like they don't know what to do with themselves. It all matters, and at the same time, none of it does. Because for the first time in so, so long, I see clearly.

Everything this man has put me through floods me, it rushes through my veins with fiery speed and then leaves me altogether. There's nothing left but the good times, the laughter, the promises I know he can keep, and the life we can create together.

Except alongside all of that… the other thing I can see with crystal vision is all the pain I've put him through, too. My stomach roils with guilt.

"You're here," he says, pulling me to his chest. "I thought you were mad at me."

"Why?"

"You didn't answer or call me back."

"I was on a plane," I mumble into his chest as he lifts me from my feet and carries me into his room. "I needed to see you."

"Why," he mimics.

"Why?" I push at him until he sets me back on my feet. I feel tears prick the corners of my eyes. "You could have died. She could have killed you!"

"I'm right here," he says, gently, his hands reaching for me again. "I'm safe. Coach made…"

"Dad what?" He doesn't finish his sentence, his eyes closing as he fights back whatever feeling is taking over him.

"He made sure I was safe. When she pulled the gun, your dad pushed himself in between us." Cillian can barely get his own words out. My dad is the only one he's ever known. Though I know it's been hard for him to play for Dad without his personal approval, Cillian hasn't ever complained. Regardless of how much it must have killed him inside.

His actions don't surprise me, it's the kind of man he is, and he'd do this for just about anyone. That doesn't take away from what Cillian is feeling though. I can't imagine witnessing someone ready to put their life at risk for you.

"He never stopped loving you and he protects what's his," I repeat my dad's words to him.

"I wish I could say I've always done the same."

"Cillian," I start to argue, but he doesn't let me.

"I didn't, Isla. You were mine; Sadie was mine when she was nothing more than a nugget inside you, and I didn't protect you. I held open the door for danger to walk right through," he says, his fingers clenching in the fabric of my coat. He holds me at arm's length but doesn't let me go either.

"You were a kid; you didn't know what you were dealing with. We're still kids, practically."

"I can't afford to be that, Isla. Not anymore." He lets go of me, turning away. "What means more than sorry? How do I express how much I regret everything I've done?"

"You already have." Closing the distance, I wrap my arms around his waist and rest my head on his back. His muscles bunch with tension and the anger he's directing at himself. "I believe you, Cill. I forgive you for it. I don't forgive her, I never will. But I forgive you."

"I should have fought for you. I should have been on the first flight to Seattle, fallen at your feet, and begged for forgiveness. That's my biggest regret," he says, still not hearing what I'm saying to him.

"Yes, you should have. But I should have fought for you, too," I say, letting my own anger tinge my words. "I always knew there was a chance, *a good chance* that you didn't hear me tell you I was pregnant. Would things be different now if I'd have called you the next day? Or the day I had my first ultrasound? Or the day Sadie was born?"

"Yes," he says, finally turning in my arms to look at me again. "It would have changed everything."

"Then how can you ever forgive me?"

The expression he wears tells me he never expected me to ask him this. That's my fault, because I've spent so much time since he's been back telling him that he's to blame. Or that they are. But never me. What a load of bullshit. We're all at fault in our own ways.

"You had your reasons," Cillian says with more conviction than I feel.

"What? My ego, my pride?"

"Your self-preservation, Isla. The health of you and Sadie. That's more important than anything else."

Tilting my head, I study him with a knowing smile as I wait for him to catch up. The tightness in him slowly subsides, his shoulders fall, and chest slows.

"You're good for my health, Cillian. You're good for Sadie. If you can forgive me, and I can forgive you, surely, we can forgive ourselves."

They always say two wrongs don't make a right. What if that's not entirely true? Maybe I wouldn't have been able to forgive Cillian so fully if I hadn't caused him pain, too. There's no way to know, of course. Life dealt us a difficult situation and neither of us handled it well. But faced with the consequences of our actions, we could rail against them or accept them and make the best of it. *Make better of it.*

Kingdoms have been built on rubble. So why can't we do the same? Pick up all the broken pieces and forge them into a new shape, something stronger and impenetrable. Something nobody can break through and something we can't tear down ourselves.

"Are you saying you forgive me?"

"With everything in me, I forgive *us*," I answer without question. "I love you. I could have lost you yesterday before I had the courage to tell you that. We just got you back and I almost lost you again."

"You love me?" It's more an astonishing gasp than question, making my smile grow wider.

"I love you."

His lips seal over mine, the kiss hungry and heated. I hope he always kisses me this way. With this level of need and passion. Winding my arms around his neck, I let him pick me up and carry me to the bed. Our mouths never part during the process, not until he's splayed on his back and I'm hovering above him.

"I love you too, Isla."

"But do you forgive us?" It's the most important thing I need to hear right now. I know he loves me; he's shown me that. What I need to know is that the past is behind us for good. No more looking back, only forward.

"If I forgive you, do I still get to wash your mouth out with cum?"

"Oh my god." I laugh, placing my hand over his lips. "Is that all you care about?"

"You know it's the least of what I care about," he mumbles through my fingers, his eyes deadly serious.

"I do," I tell him. Then I kiss him, initiating intimacy with him so he knows I'm all in. My hands pull at the hem of his t-shirt, moving it up to expose more skin for me to rain kisses upon. "I know you, Cillian. I know your heart and your mind. Now I want to get to know your body."

"You know that, too."

"Let's pretend I don't."

"I don't have condoms," he admits. "I don't travel with them. Since you."

Straddled over his waist, I sit straight up.

"When was the last time you were with another woman?"

"Probably a couple of months before I was drafted to the Blades. I don't exactly keep a diary of my one-night stands," he says, wincing.

"Who was it?" I don't want him to say Trina, but I'll accept it if that's who it was. I'll accept it as his past and we'll move on to our future.

"Her name was Jennifer. I met her at a charity thing for the team," he says. "Yours was Tyson?"

"Yes," I say, nodding. "Just after you came back. There hasn't been another time since. You're always safe?"

"Always. You?"

"Always."

"It's your call, Isla," he says, his hands finding the softness of my belly where his thumbs rub small circles. "If... it would be different. If there was another surprise, it would be different."

"I trust you."

"I won't let you regret that," he promises, and I smile.

"I *trust* you."

"Then get naked," he says, yanking to get my shirt up over my head. We're a tangle of limbs as we undress each other in a rush. But with quick work, he's leaning his bare back against the headboard as I straddle his lap. "Down, Isla. Slide down on me. Slowly, I want to feel every inch."

Cillian's hands cup my ass to aid me while I go as slow as I possibly can which is really hard once I feel his raw tip slide in.

"Fuck." I exhale hard, dropping my forehead to his. "How does it feel so... much?"

"Good you mean?"

"I said what I said," I tell him, laughing. But, yeah, good. Amazing. "I'd forgotten what it felt like."

"I didn't. The feeling of being inside you is branded on my soul, I think."

"Well, can I drop all the way on to your soul right now? Because this is fucking torture, Cillian," I whine because he's still holding me too far up. I need more.

He lowers me down as he thrusts up, both of us gasping at once.

"Ride me, Isla. Find a rhythm and I'll match it, but don't look away." His eyes bore into mine as he assaults my face with sweet kisses.

I remember all the times we had like this before. Before we fell apart, before we let egos and pettiness get in the way. Back when it was just him and me and the delusion that our life would always be so easy.

They say there isn't light without dark, or relief without pain. I don't know how much I believe in that. But I do know that what we've been through has made us both stronger. And because of that we're able to love deeper, more fully. Or maybe that's all bullshit and I really am just a hopeless romantic at heart. Only time will tell, and I want to spend as much of it with this man as I can.

"I love you."

"Say it again, Isla," he demands, pushing harder into me. His fingers play at the other hole he seems to have a newfound fascination with.

"I love you."

Again, he kisses me. Hard, needy, he finishes it with a gentle bite and tug on my bottom lip.

"Come, and I'll follow." I do, more explosive than I could have imagined or anticipated. Like promised, he shatters with me, and all our separate little pieces coming into a new, unbreakable us.

EPILOGUE

Four years. Less if she can manage some good behavior. It's been nearly a year since Trina stole into Cillian's hotel room with a gun, drugs, and who knows what going through her mind. Four years is the sentence the judge just dropped on her. We'll have however much time she's in prison to further build our lives without any interference from her. After that, who knows? One thing is certain though, we'll be handling it together, as a family.

She wrote us both apologies. Neither of us read them, knowing they were written to gain favor with the courts. Maybe she said something genuine in them. Or, maybe they were filled with more bullshit and manipulative tactics. Either way, we'll never know. We lit a fire, burned them, and toasted marshmallows for s'mores.

There were many more details revealed during the process of prosecuting Trina. As I suspected, she'd given Cillian sedatives before. The revelation wasn't easy on either of us. No matter what we do to try and relieve the guilt we both feel, it's not easy to let it go. I hadn't been speaking to my therapist with much regularity before Cillian came back to Seattle. But it was apparent that I needed to. Cillian wasn't only supportive, but active. We've had many sessions with her and the both of us.

It's helped tremendously. Neither of us wears our past like a cape of doom around our necks anymore.

"Ooh, pinch it," Sadie yells from her perch on my lap, causing my mom to laugh.

"She's starting to sound like you," she says. We've been watching even more hockey since Cillian's return and my job requirements. With all the adults in her life connected to the sport in one way or another, she's started to pick up on the rules, the plays, and all the silly things we say when we're watching games. She doesn't let her age get in the way of her obsession.

"They're gonna score, Mommy! Watch, watch!" Sure enough, Cill fakes a slapshot, instead passing it perfectly to Wallin at the other side of the net who angles it to fly perfectly behind the Vegas goalie. After a few games losing streak, this overtime win is exactly what our team needed.

"*Just* like you," my mother reiterates as the crowd goes wild. It never gets old. Or, it hasn't yet and I hope it never does. Every win is as exciting as the last. We may never again live up to the spectacular inaugural season that ended with a Stanley Cup, but nothing says that trophy won't be in our future again. And this team plays for it with everything they have.

"Make sure Daddy gets my letter," Sadie says to me after the fans are all gone and she's about to head home with Erin for the night.

"I will, baby. But you know he always looks for it," I tell her. Cillian hasn't stopped writing me little notes here and there. Now, it's something he and Sadie do for each other, too. He likes that it's more personal than a text message from her saying goodnight while he's still sequestered away in the locker room doing whatever the hell those guys do in there for so long. Sadie loves it when he leaves her a note and she goes to great lengths trying to write him ones in return. It usually means I have to write down what she wants to say so she can attempt to trace it, but I don't mind. Most days I find the relationship between my daughter and her father is too fucking adorable to put into words.

It's another hour before Cillian finally manages to pop his head into the family room. His smile widens when he sees me sitting with Caroline off in a quiet corner. I say my goodbyes to her and a few others around and meet him in the middle of the room, straining my neck up to look him in the face.

"Nice game, Superstar."

"Thanks," he says, his dimple showing. "Want to grab a bag of Dick's to celebrate the win?"

"I could eat some Dick's," I answer, making him and a few of the wives around us laugh.

"You're trouble," he says, wrapping his arm around me and guiding me out to his SUV. Like so many game nights, we end up in the same spot. Outside on the deck off the primary bedroom, cuddled under a blanket with the outdoor fireplace on. Cillian never lets me get cold and I like to watch the lights play over the lake when the water is just a soft ripple. He says it's my new storm watching. Maybe there's some truth to that.

Maybe I'm done with stormy weather, or maybe I've just found my calm to balance it all out.

Sadie and I moved in with Cillian not too long after that fateful night in Boston, but not too soon either. We started with some sleepovers to ease Sadie into the idea. Well, that's what we told ourselves anyway. She was ready from the day he moved that bed into her room. But when you've made years of mistakes, you get a little gun shy. Perhaps we're overthinking everything now, but I imagine that will fade along with unseen scars we left on each other.

"Ready for bed," he says as he nuzzles my temple.

"Mmhmm," I say, though I dread leaving our cozy nest, too.

"You go, I'll clean up and grab Sadie's letter." She leaves it in the same spot, safely tucked under the pillow on her bed.

"Okay," I say, quickly jumping up. The cold air tingles my skin, but Cillian warms it back up with a light swat to my ass. After game sex is on my agenda. It's my favorite kind of sex, because he uses all that pent up adrenaline that still lingers in his veins, never failing to work me into the same sort of frenzy before we both collapse with exhaustion.

I beeline it into the bathroom for my nightly routine. An array of my beauty products has taken over a good portion of the vanity. Once, I suggested maybe he'd want a bigger place now that Sadie and I are here, too. Cillian shut that down quickly, he prefers us all being atop each other and said that my stuff everywhere only makes it feel more like home. I get it, because I feel the same. Home is walking through the front door and it immediately smells like him. Even if that smell is stinky hockey man.

Sadie's been skating more. She's always enjoyed it, but now she wants a stick and a puck whenever she's on the ice. I have a feeling I'm going to have a stinky hockey girl smell in my future, as well.

"You found it?" Cillian is sitting on the end of the bed when I come out of the bathroom, our daughter's crayon scrawled note in his hand.

"Same place as always," he answers with a big grin that says he's up to something.

"What did she mean by just do it?" She was adamant that the letter ended with the words just do it daddy. I asked her what she wanted him to do and all I got as an answer was her little laughter.

"She wants me to give you a letter tonight."

"You write me letters all the time."

"This one has something else that goes along with it," he says. "Check under your pillow."

"What are you two up to now?" It's typical of Sadie to form special connections with each adult in her life, she's always done that. But the relationship between her and Cillian is next level. They're constantly putting their heads together and making up some sort of game or making special plans that usually end with a surprise for me or any one of our family members.

Cillian answers with nothing more than a raised eyebrow. Lifting my pillow, I freeze at what I find. An ivory envelope with both my name in Cillian's handwriting, and Mommy in Sadie's. Next to it sits a pretty round ring box.

"Cillian."

"Open the envelope first."

Isla,

That first day I met you, I fell in love with the girl who rolled her eyes at a boy who would go onto be a league leading goal scorer three years running. That love only grew when you asked me why I wanted to date you at sixteen. You never saw yourself for what you are.

You've always called me Superstar, but in my life the star has always been you. My true North, my guiding light. The one thing that's always been true.

You don't lie, you don't sugarcoat. You're supportive without conditions.

Next to Sadie, you're the best thing in my life. And she shines brighter than the sun because she came from you.

We talked about me asking you to marry me. I said I was pretty sure you'd say yes. She said, 'I know that's right'. Then she told me I had to ask you in a letter and hide it under your pillow.

So here it is.

Please, Isla, will you marry me?

Cillian

Under his words, Sadie wrote a few of her own.

Mommy,

Can we all be Wild now?

Sadie

"No pressure," he says, as he presses his chest to my back and wraps his arms around my waist. All I can do is laugh and stare at the ring box through tear curtained eyes. "Do you want to see it? Sadie Baby picked it out."

"Oh, god," I say, both of us laughing now. "I can only imagine."

"You don't have to imagine it, just open it."

"Did you really let her pick it out," I ask, picking up the smooth box and running my finger along the seam.

"Completely. I gave zero input."

"You're brave, Wylder."

"So are you."

Inside the box I find a soft gold band lined with tiny sparkling stones, with a singular pink princess cut diamond taking prominence. It's simple, like me, and Sadie's favorite color.

"It's kind of fucking perfect," I say quietly, turning in Cillian's arms so I can see his face. "You sure you want to do this forever thing with me?"

"I want eternity with you, Isla. This life and the next, and all the ones after that. We'll always find each other."

"Then, yes. To this life and all the rest."

SADIE

MANY YEARS LATER

My father scored the goal that won his team the Stanley Cup the year he came back to Seattle. The year he won back my mother's heart. It was the seventh game of the series against New York. They were tied at the end of the third period, 2-2. I rewatch the game at least once a year, so I know with great detail how Koch made a perfect pass for my dad to one time into the net just forty-seven seconds into sudden death overtime.

He's been my hero for as long as I can remember, but that night he became Seattle's hero, too. Luckily, I'm good at sharing him. Mostly because he's never shown me anything but love and adoration. He's a little obsessed with his children. It goes both ways.

Their love story is one they've told often enough for me to know it by heart. The first time I was old enough to understand it, I was angry at them both. It's hard to understand how two people so perfect for each other caused themselves so much misery. And they really are perfect together. They balance one another, each with qualities that smooth the other's rough edges.

My anger didn't last, of course, because they're nauseating in love with each other now and that's the only way I really remember them being. The years without my dad are vague and blurry.

221

I remember Mom being sad a lot back then. She hasn't been that in a long time now, though. My siblings never witnessed that version of her. It's something I'm thankful for. Because my mother is a ray of fucking sunshine with a temper as hot as the sun if you fuck with her family, and that's all they ever need to know about her.

Mom's been wildly successful with her career, working her way up through the Blades franchise and is now their Assistant General Manager. That didn't happen until after Dad retired. They didn't want two demanding careers when they were trying to raise a family. Besides, it would have been some kind of conflict of interest since my dad never played a game for another team after he was drafted to Seattle.

Dad could have played longer; he was fit enough and young enough. At thirty-seven, he called it quits. I was about to graduate high school, Rowen had just had his twelfth birthday, Kelsey was ten, and Ellie was nearing eight.

When they were younger, my mom used to call my dad Superstar. That changed to Supersperm for obvious reasons. She loved having babies as much as he did, though.

She videoed when she told Dad she was pregnant with Rowen. After all the time they lost, they're sticklers about preserving memories now. That's another video I watch regularly. Dad cried like a baby. My big, strong, hockey player dad who never shies away from a fight on the ice, cried on his knees into my mom's tummy.

Cillian Wylder isn't scared to show his emotional or vulnerable side, but mostly he's all smiles and laughter. That's how our family rolls. Mom and Dad don't fight, even when she tries to, he shuts her down with a joke or a kiss. He calls it her hockey temper and we've all learned to appreciate that it's just who she is. Dad finds it attractive enough that he's usually the one to set it off, purposefully, of course.

Every day they show how much they love each other. Not always in obvious, flashy ways, though those happen too. Every time they part, they kiss. The same happens when they see each other again. No conversations end without the words I love you, that goes for us offspring, too. It's instilled in us all to not take love for granted. To be loyal, honest, and true.

Sometimes, we fail, but my parents are always there to walk us through our troubles.

They still hump like rabbits with no shame. I once heard Mom and Grams talk about hockey player stamina. I didn't understand then, but I have a hockey player of my own now, so I get it. I guess being with hockey players runs in the family, because Auntie Willa has one too.

But she'll have to tell her own story. And someday maybe I'll tell mine.

ACKNOWLEDGMENTS

As always, I want to thank Autumn with Wordsmith for continuously holding my hand. I trust you with my life, lady.

Z, fuck your smartass (but know that I couldn't do this without you).

My Beta Extraordinaires' –
    Annie, Nicole, Mylene, Chanpreet, and Amy – your honesty is my lifeblood.

And Jeff... thank you for answering all my numerous questions as I continue to learn more about the craziness that happens on ice with a stick and a puck.

MORE FROM AUTHOR ALISON RHYMES

Subscribe to Alison's Newsletter for Early News and Bonus Scenes

Broken Play

They have ties that bind.

June grew up in the shadow of her brother and his best friend, Drew McKenna. She stood back while Drew dated his way through high school and college, watching and waiting. Waiting for him to realize he loved her as much as she loved him.

When he did, it was the happiest she'd ever been. Until she found him with another woman only five years after their marriage.

Leaving her husband was a simple decision, but there was no easy way to cut him out of her family.

When June receives a fresh start to her career, she also finds what could be a new lease on love. Reality hits Drew with a vengeance.

He wants her back.

She wants to make him suffer.

Brutal Play

Mistress.

Whore.

Lorelai has been called every name in the book. Except for the ones she's always dreamed of.

My love.

Mine.

Noah Anders is the only man to have ever owned her heart. But it's her soul he wants.

Theirs is a battle of wills, tempers, ego, friendship, and loyalty.

He wants retribution.

She just wants to survive.

Bitter Play

Reed Turner has loved his sister's best friend, Leighton, for damn near a decade. He's given her space to grow in her career and her life. Now he's ready to claim the woman he's always believed was his. It's too bad another man in her life keeps getting in the way.

Leighton Ward has never been in love. Now, just as so many things are changing in her life, she finds two men vying for her heart. Both hold strong ties to her future and making the wrong decision comes with heavy consequences.

He knows what he wants.

She's as confused as ever.

Deconstructing Delilah

A modern-day retelling of Samson and Delilah...

As the son of a preacher, Pope Blackwell believed he learned the difference between good and evil early in life. After all, it was beaten into him regularly. Now as an adult, he's traded in his life of abuse for one where he holds all the power.

When a young woman strolls into his life full of more bravery than she should possess, he becomes consumed by her fire.

Delilah believed escaping her family's abusive ways would be the hardest challenge of her life. Then she met Pope Blackwell.

One sinner and one saint. A world of differences between them.

Faith. Experience. Age.

His obsession only grows as she challenges him until he's ready to topple any pillar that stands in her way, and she'll fight every demon to be by his side.